GRIM CITY

GRIM CITY

JOE L. HENSLEY

ST. MARTIN'S PRESS ■ NEW YORK

Library of Congress Cataloging-in-Publication Data

Hensley, Joe L.
    Grim City / Joe L. Hensley.
       p.   cm.
    ISBN 0-312-11429-X
    1. Mexican Americans—Kentucky—Fiction.   2. Trials
(Murder)—Kentucky—Fiction.   3. Lawyers—Kentucky—
Fiction.   I. Title.
PS3558.E55G75   1994
813'.54—dc20   94-28310
                                                                  CIP

First Edition: November 1994

10   9   8   7   6   5   4   3   2   1

For Evan, who showed me Alvin and his Witch

GRIM CITY

CHAPTER ONE

That afternoon, for what was the ninth time since I'd moved to Grimsley City, I received an anonymous letter. It came in a cheap white envelope like the others. The postmark was Lexington, Kentucky, the area's local postmark.

Inside there was a single page ripped from a slick magazine. In an ad a man lolled happily in a folding chair on a sunny beach. Bikini-clad lovelies attended him. The scene was beautiful.

One thing was wrong. The man's eyes were slashed out.

I put it in a drawer with the other eight.

Someone was watching.

MY NAME IS James Carlos Singer. The middle name is also the first name of my mother's father, now old and dying in south Texas. He was/is a Texican-Mexican. He'd been born and lived all his life north of the Rio Grande. Growing up, I lived in his rambling home in a fishing village not too far from Corpus Christi. In my small town there were enough Mexican-Americans to guarantee my being seated at most local restaurants. This growing up of mine was accomplished after my mother died in childbirth (bearing me) and after my father abandoned me with her family.

All of this happened long before I wound up practicing law in Grimsley City, Kentucky.

I became circuit court probation officer of Grimsley County in a different way. I didn't know the job was soon to be vacant and I never formally applied for it. I got the job because I could sing a little, was of the right political party, and owed local allegiance to no one.

Another reason I got the job was because I sought solace during the holiday season in Grimsley City's "lawyer bar," the Stardust. That was on a late Friday afternoon the week before Christmas.

1

Before that time I owned a year-plus old solo law practice going no place. I ran my legal business, mostly collection junk, from a walk-up office in a decaying building near the courthouse. I did my own typing. I drove a ten-year-old Mustang car left me by my father. I had one local acquaintance, "Silver," who'd helped sell me on the town, where I now realized I was that "dark, foreign-looking, new shyster."

I was shy of the world, careful and watchful. There were no women in my life because nothing much happened "down there" anymore and hadn't for a long time.

The letter, as always, frightened me. If I could have run, I'd have run. There was no place to run. If I'd been found here in Kentucky, I could be found anywhere I'd try to hide. I was a lawyer. If I wanted to practice my trade in another state, then I'd have to move there, live somewhere while I passed the bar and satisfied the residency requirements. By that time any searcher would find me again.

I could quit being a lawyer, but I wasn't going to do that. Not now.

I'd had my usual slow workweek. I totaled it up on the Friday afternoon before Christmas.

I was semi-broke, but there was enough for a drink or two. Even if I were dead broke, the Stardust illegally let lawyers run tabs. So I went.

There was canned soup for the hotplate in the apartment and a full box of Zestas. I'd survive the weekend.

Maybe next week would be better.

Grimsley City, Kentucky, at times called by its almost fifteen thousand inhabitants "Grim City," was wealthy in downtown bars. There were bars that sought to attract the farm-tobacco crowds, others (costing more) that appealed to the horsey set and the university people; bars for factory workers and coal miners, and one that attempted to latch onto the downtown merchants.

I cut across courthouse square to what we lawyers knew was the best bar in town, our bar: the Stardust Bar and Grille.

I used the cross-walk, skirting the area where the farmers market operated daily in the warm seven months of the year. Around me, Grimsley City was a pretty, postcard town, a bustling county seat, a state university city. In the summer the *Delta Queen* docked and tourists from its decks wandered the city and the campus. Retirement people fell in love with Grimsley City and came to visit, to stay, and in many cases die and improve the legal economy with their estates.

I liked the town.

It was now December cold. A few November leaves still lay neglected on the ground. The frigid world smelled of the muddy Ohio River and downtown garbage. The grass was brown, and there was snow in shadowed areas.

My good eye ached and my left eye, the one that was not so good, stung from the cold. My Louisville ophthalmologist had told me that such feelings meant little and that I was now "aware" of my eyes and noticed things in them only because I'd had past troubles. He'd stated that my eyes were reasonably stable. Perhaps, to copper his bet, he'd added that such was no guarantee and to return in three months, sooner if need be. And so I worried about both myself and my business. I wanted to be the same as I'd once been. I wanted to be "normal." I wanted to be successful. But some days, like today, I felt like leaping out of the dark hole I'd dug, a hole just big enough to hold me and my slop jar of depression. So to the Stardust.

I nodded at the tall green figure of a bearded, dead governor whose statue and its entourage of multicolored pigeons guarded the courthouse yard. I outwalked two aggressive panhandlers seeking late-afternoon wine money. Four stripling boys played war in the metal seats of a battery of Second World War cannons. They trained the weapons upon me and the panhandlers and yelled "Fire!" without mercy.

River-town, small-town, southern America. Immune from many of the problems of the cities, but with other problems replacing them. Things moved slow in Grim City. Family and money were important. Black was better than it had been, but still not a hell of a lot better. I was to most residents a semi-black

3

Tex-Mex. Seeing my reflection shining in their eyes made me consider moving on. But I was born stubborn and I was now a lawyer with a degree from the U. of K.

Moving and trying to hide in another place was not for me.

I had no money and no family. I had a one-room office and a minor (government-purchased from a private insurer) disability pension that came monthly. Canned-soup money.

I made it inside the bar and out of cannon-panhandler danger.

Coveys of TGIF lawyers, a single user-friendly local doctor, and a brace of insurance adjusters sat about the plush Stardust. I looked for Dave "Silver" and saw him at the bar in deep conversation with a couple of politicians. He waved vaguely and then turned back to his companions.

I could smell spilled liquor, cooked meat, and fried onions. It was a warm, comfortable smell. It made me realize I didn't know whether I wanted scotch or a cheeseburger.

Christmas decorations hung from the lights, and a sign painted on the bar mirror advertised Tom and Jerries instead of the all-summer-present mint juleps.

A lady pianist played at the back of the great room at a piano bar. A few lawyers were seated there. One of the lawyers nodded distantly to me. A man stood in shadows next to the piano and sang bravely and loudly. The voice sounded familiar. I took a couple of steps further and saw it was the judge of the circuit court, Lionel Simon Daggert, called "Simple Simon" by his detractors.

The song finished. The lawyers near the piano clapped heartily. Piano lady waited for another request.

Daggert nodded at me. He was a bear of a man in his fifties. He had bright blue eyes set deep under arched, heavy eyebrows, a tiny line of mustache, and a good, wide mouth. He wore rumpled, well-tailored clothing: a dark, pinstriped suit, a white shirt, and a Countess Mara tie. He was old Kentucky family and looked it. Someone had facetiously told me that his great-great had shown Daniel Boone where both the bears and the *bars* were. I'd heard several of his haters say he drank too much and too often. I knew his wife had died shortly before I came to town and that there were no children.

4

In my few times in his courtroom he'd been friendly and kind to a new bumbler. I'd seen him be short with older lawyers.

I admired him.

He smiled an intoxicated smile. "I could damn well use some singing help here, old partner. Not one goddamn one of these big blue basketball-talking U. of K. clowns can sing."

I smiled back at him. I'd been in his big courtroom exactly three times. Most of my occasional legal work was done in the inferior courts on the floor below his courtroom, where I had sometimes (but not recently) been appointed to represent indigent defendants.

"I'm a poor tenor."

"At your age, Jim, you should believe you have the best tenor voice in the whole friggin' world."

I cocked my head, surprised that he knew me. He smiled again.

"Your last name's Singer, and I hear you came up here to Kentucky to escape out of either Texas or Hell. I try to know all my lawyers. I'm happy to see you on this Friday afternoon. I was about to call you." He looked at the lawyers who listened from their piano bar seats. "I could maybe use you for a job, Jim Singer. What's your politics?"

"I was born and raised hard in the same party as yours, Judge. I started passing out candidate cards at polling places when I was eleven."

"You owe anyone in the local hierarchy anything? I mean, is anyone pimping clients for you or promising a political job after the next election? Like maybe Dave Silver Estrada over there at the bar?"

"No. I know Silver some, though. We were in law school together."

Silver and the two politicians watched silently, their eyes disapproving of the scene. I thought Silver shook his head at me warningly, but I ignored it. His look when I'd entered had said, *Stay away*. Now I returned it.

The judge sipped solemnly from a brownish drink. He nodded at me and then at a hovering bartender. "I guess knowing him doesn't disqualify you. Bring this lad a drink, Eddo. Whatever he

5

wants. On me." He looked down at the piano lady and then back at me. "Come see me Monday after Christmas. Part-time job. Probation officer. My P.O.'s retiring. The pay's eating-and-drinking money for a careful man. You can still do limited practice. How old are you?"

"Thirty-one."

He looked down again at the piano lady. " 'Irish Eyes,' Miss Mary." He then kept her silent with a wave.

"You're old to be beginning a small-town law practice. Most of our boys come roaring back here from law school at about twenty-five, buy themselves either a pickup truck or a BMW, and wait for genteel cases that don't interfere too much with basketball season."

"I took some time out after I graduated undergrad at Grimsley U."

"Doing what?" he asked.

"Some of this and a bit of that. I worked for the government." I had done exactly that, but as to what the job had been, I'd signed a contract not to talk or write about it. Not Treasury, FBI, or CIA. Just a worker-watcher for a covert Washington group that now wanted me back, even if I possessed only one good eye. That group was something I thought on when I contemplated the possibilities of personal bankruptcy. Frank Ballinger, the man in charge, called me now and then, sent me letters (perhaps some with eye problems, mailed anonymously?), and, now and then, came visiting me.

"Washington government or Lexington government?"

"Washington."

He nodded again to the piano lady, who sat patiently, ready for song. "Okay, sweet Mary. Play songs for us."

Mary played her piano. We sang songs, with others joining in. I wasn't much at singing, but four years at Grimsley and three at U.K. law school had taught me most of the words, and I remembered them. A lawyer or two I knew slapped me on the back in approval. Silver and his two pals vanished.

Daggert nodded and smiled at me as we sang.

6

"I'd heard you worked federal," he said between songs. "And someone told me you used to jock at Grimsley."

"Soccer."

"Was soccer your undergrad major?" he asked, grinning superiorly. I'd found he was heavily into U.K. basketball, even if he did josh others about it.

"French." Soccer had been a fun athletic scholarship, a way out of south Texas. French had been an easy major. I already spoke Spanish like the native I almost was. Silver had some Spanish, while I was at home in the language. I was also fluent in Italian and Portuguese. I could make myself understood in several other languages. It was the knack that had originally made me of interest to the group I'd worked for.

"Family?"

"Not much. There's some relatives in Texas, mainly a ninety-one-year-old grandfather who's had a stroke and no longer recognizes anyone. There's aunts and uncles who live in his house. My father died here in your town a year-plus back. It was a hit-and-run."

"That would have been Allen Singer?"

"Yes. Did you know him?"

"I knew him a little." He looked me over critically, maybe having second thoughts about the job offer. "I remember that he got run over, that the police said he might have been drinking or maybe on drugs, and they never caught the driver who killed him."

"Not yet. I hope they're still looking."

"Is your health all right?"

"It's okay," I answered. *Better than my father's.*

"You look tired. I've noticed that in your face before." He inspected me in the overly friendly fashion a half-drunk will adopt upon meeting someone new. We were suddenly bosom buddies. "There's something about your eyes."

"My left eye got injured. People say it makes me look sleepy. The lid's slightly closed from tiny burn scars I never went back to

7

have repaired. I have peripheral vision out of it. The other eye's twenty-twenty.''

"You'll have to drive a car in the job. Do you have a current driver's license?''

"Yes sir.''

He nodded, perhaps satisfied. "Monday past Christmas.''

We sang us some more songs, mainly country western and college songs about Grimsley and the U.K. Blue, plus a few dirty ditties.

Good old boys.

When I got back to my efficiency and attempted sleep, I found it difficult.

The phone rang after midnight. It was Silver. He said: "Okay, I guess you got the job.''

"Sure. And I need one.''

He gave me a short laugh. "Look and listen. Your job may not last long. Keep in touch and keep the faith.''

"Sure. Why did he pick me?''

"He picked you because he can control you. He's into a murder case the whole town knows he doesn't like and which may do him political damage.''

"Why doesn't he like it?''

"Because of the pretty lady defendant, Jim.'' He laughed his good laugh. "You watch. But watch for yourself and not for Simple Simon.''

Before I went back to sleep, his warning rang a few more times in my ears.

It took a while to actually start the job. But two weeks later, on the Monday following New Year's, after Daggert's former P.O. headed out for Clearwater, Florida, I went to work as the new probation officer for the circuit court.

Soon after that I got involved neck deep in the ongoing Kentner murder case, which was the case Silver had warned me about.

I also found that becoming a probation officer was not as hard as a hop, skip, and jump to a blueblood-area distillery party or box seats to the Kentucky Derby. There was a twice-a-year test given to new appointees. I learned that most people, with preparation, passed the test. I also learned that in the years before I took the job, in an attempt to professionalize probation officers, the Kentucky legislature had passed statutes which said that all newly appointed P.O.'s had to have at least bachelor's degrees from an accredited college. The legislature had also agreed to pay higher P.O. salaries, but then had not honored the law by funding it. Salaries were still paid totally by the counties. Some judges, because of recalcitrant county funding boards, made the P.O. job part-time rather than seek more county money in years of already groaning budgets and disgruntled taxpayers. Grimsley Circuit had done that.

I moved into a small courthouse office adjacent to the circuit court offices after having agreed that I'd work five half-days a week, get paid umpteen thousand a year, plus have two weeks' vacation my first year, three weeks' thereafter. I also learned I got sick days. I became part of a group medical policy and a minor state retirement plan intended to hold county workers till coronary time. Very soon after employment I began receiving letters from unions intent on organizing me.

The former probation officer had been a man named Robert Coulson. He retired after a party I heard was memorable, but to which I wasn't invited.

I moved into the job cold.

I kept my one-room law office and put new office hours on the door. Also, on bank credit, I bought an answering machine for my private office.

A few days after I moved into my new courthouse job, they began picking jurors for the Kentner case in Daggert's ancient courtroom. In that dank, huge room even loud orators could lose their voices in the upper reaches of the high, dark ceiling. It was a room hot in summer and cold in winter. The grey ceiling ate both the light of the sun and the glow of the dangling fluorescents. The room was inhabited by squads of flies in summer. In winter the

9

flies were replaced by mice invading inward to escape the killing cold of northern Kentucky winters. The courtroom smelled of damp wood and decaying lawbooks. It was, if you believed local legends, inhabited by the mean spirits of two lawyers who'd hated, dueled, and died on the courthouse lawn in the early nineteenth century.

I had decided I'd work afternoons as a P.O. and spend mornings in my private office, but soon became aware it wouldn't work out exactly that way.

There were some legal things I couldn't do, lots I could. There were two other courts in the Grimsley County courthouse. Those two courts shared another P.O., a dour, male, retired teacher who appeared offended by me, perhaps because I'd purloined my job from someone he politically favored. I resolved to ask him nothing, after I learned he'd been master of ceremonies at Coulson's farewell party and had made "funny" racial remarks about me.

I could do civil cases in other courts, but no criminal cases in any court. I could settle estates, draw contracts and mortgages, possibly file divorces, and file and defend small claims. The limitations were vague. What I mainly couldn't do was involve myself in any case that might embarrass Daggert as high judge. I couldn't work both sides of the local legal street.

It seemed obvious to me also that I couldn't personally represent, in any case or any fashion, probationers who reported to me after being released from prison or who were placed on probation after pleas in any of the local courts.

The first afternoon of the trial, Judge Daggert left word for me to stay over until he called a halt to the day's court proceedings. I complied, using the extra time to continue to go through old files, trying to understand what had transpired. There were multitudes of juvenile files, cabinets stuffed with pre-sentence reports, hundreds of cards and files on individuals of all ages who'd sinned, been caught, and so become part of the P.O. papers. When I tired of files, I read the juvenile statutes line by line. I was soon confused. *The Kentucky law both giveth and taketh away.*

Near dark I heard prospective jurors shuffling homeward. I walked curiously out of my office and watched a lady deputy ushering the blond defendant down the back steps. The defendant's back was to me, so all I got was a glimpse.

Built cute. I usually didn't notice, because that part of me uneasily slept.

The court reporter came into my office. Her name was Anne Kelly Melville and she was regarded by all as a "nice lady." She was white-haired and long widowed. She had no children, so she adopted all new lawyers who came to Grimsley City. I was the newest right now, which made me her littlest boy. She was plump, soft-spoken, and friendly to all but the most tiresome.

"He wants to see you in his office, he does," she said nicely in an Americanized brogue. She was pretty. Her eyes were both kind and interested in me. She'd treated me as a first-class citizen the three times I'd been in Daggert's court. We'd shared minor risqué jokes and found common ground in an abiding, shared hatred of conniving lawbook salesmen.

She whispered: "It's going on six. Get him to take you to dinner. He's interested in you. Get a free meal and drink. Lord knows he can afford it and also use food. Try to make his one drink not be a dozen." She shook her head at such conduct, perhaps longing for her own past years. "Ever since his wife died he's been like an Englishman in Belfast. He got better for a while and then he got worse. People say nasty things behind his back and he overhears or senses what's being said. And he mourns. God how he mourns." She nodded. "Make him laugh a little if you can, but the look in your dark eyes tells me that you're not much of a heehawer either."

"I like to laugh, but sometimes life doesn't seem funny to me," I answered respectfully. I followed behind her. The judge sat behind his desk in chambers. He'd removed his robe and put on a bright sport coat. He didn't look bad except around the eyes, a place I always inspected. His eyes were dark-circled and disoriented, perhaps like mine. He glanced up confusedly when I entered his room and then apparently remembered he was to see me.

"You all settled in, partner?" he asked. He smiled mechanically.

"Some. I've been spending my half days looking over the former P.O.'s files and doing some statute reading."

"Remember there's a test. It's in March. Plus our probationers report in to your office monthly. If you do it the way Coulson did, that'll be mostly on Mondays."

"Yes sir. I'll try to be ready for both."

"Are you against a bit of social drinking and some dinner?" he asked slyly, knowing from the Stardust encounter that I'd take a drink.

"No, Your Honor."

He smiled. "Then we shall dine, if you'll join me, at the country club. We'll have a few drinks and some talk so as to get to know each other a bit better. I'll buy your dinner to celebrate having a probation officer."

"Thank you. I herewith accept your offer," I answered in legal terms, making him smile.

He put on his fine cashmere overcoat. I was carrying my drab wool. Anne Melville beamed at both of us as we exited the office. We took his car.

I was glad to be asked out for dinner. At my apartment there'd be V-8 juice, canned soup and crackers, and the bottom of a jar of delectable peanut butter. So far I'd gotten by on my own. I was determined to continue doing so. The long months spent in hospitals had made me despise being dependent on anyone. I found I was, here in Kentucky, still suspicious of any proffered help. And I was wary of the world around me, although I'd seen nothing other than in my mail to alarm me.

We had a nice evening. The club was old, aristocratic, and uncrowded. The walls bore framed photographs of horses, riverboats, golfers, and tennis players. The food was expensive and rich.

Daggert told me war stories about being a Marine officer in early Vietnam. I told him what I was allowed to tell about working for the government. *Not much.*

The waitresses and two bartenders, white and black, were attentive and kept his glass full before and after dinner. They seemed fond of him. I drank sparingly, and no one noticed me a lot.

He ate too little and drank too much, so I drove him home. I parked his car in a circular drive and opened the front door into a cavernous, ancient mansion. From my vantage point down the hall it looked as if his home was full of antiques, family portraits, and cold fireplaces. In one big room there was an entertainment center with a CD player. Bright-jacketed classical CDs strewed the table beside it.

I saw a portrait of his father, one of his mother, and a lovely one of his handsome, deceased wife. There were, as I'd been informed by many, no Daggert children.

I walked him to the sweeping, curved stairs. Once there he seemed recovered enough to stumble upward.

"Goo' night, partner," he called from the stairtop. "You want to know something?"

"Yes sir."

"One reason I hired you is that the word's around that you had a hand in a practical joke on our esteemed downstairs judge, Judge Rainbolt, something about him being nominated to the state supreme court."

I smiled to myself. "Not me," I said. *But Rainbolt no longer appointed me.*

"I've heard otherwise."

"It's untrue."

He was silent for a moment, perhaps disappointed. "Let yourself out."

I went out into the night. Someone had falsely telephoned Rainbolt, a pompous judicial ass, and told him he'd been nominated as a replacement state supreme court judge. He'd believed it, reported it to the Grimsley City *Trumpet.* He'd found out it was untrue only after the news was in print. He was still seeking the culprit. Lots were suspected. I was a favored suspect. I hadn't done it, but I'd openly liked the happening, and I knew who *had* done it.

I walked home. I'd meant to ask Daggert about my father, but that could wait.

Someone had viciously run a car back and forth over Pop in a parking area near the river. I'd arranged his spartan Grimsley City funeral. I'd asked the sheriff, Runner Riggs, about my father's death. I'd also asked the chief of police and Commonwealth's Attorney Lynn Corner about the state of the investigation. I'd been informed by all that it was "proceeding."

Maybe I'd not come to Grimsley City solely to investigate my father's death, but that was part of it. Grimsley City had been a place I *could* come to practice after I'd passed the Kentucky bar. I'd had to work some during law school, limiting study time, and no one had come to Lexington recruiting me for a job. So, Grim City.

Pop had left little behind. There were a few photos, a dab of furniture, some well-thumbed car books, and the Mustang.

We'd grown closer when I'd been in U.K. law school. By that time he'd partly forgiven me for my mother's death. And I, in turn, had forgiven him for absenting himself, except for short visits, after her death.

He was taller than I was and his features were thin and aristocratic. Some thought him handsome.

He was what he was and I was what I was.

Now he was dead.

"You look like her," he'd told me at times. "I wish . . ."

I knew what he wished and never put into words. He wanted her back. He saw her dark eyes in mine, and saw that I resembled her more than I did him.

I'd thought about burying him in south Texas next to her, but had decided against it. He'd loved my mother, but not Texas.

So long, Pop.

The court reporter would notice the judge's hangover in the morning. It's hard to stop someone from drinking too much. I believed that without my even knowing of it, Daggert had told the people at his club to keep his string of drinks coming.

And although I'd waited, expecting it, he hadn't mentioned the Kentner murder case.

14

CHAPTER TWO

That night the phone rang.

"Hello, Carlos," Frank Ballinger said. He perpetually called me Carlos. "How you, boy?"

"Okay. Ballinger, could you, sometime, just for the pure hell of it, call at a reasonable hour?"

He laughed. "I call late so as to get your full attention. I got some people working near where you are, watching some river runners. Sometime soon I'm going to shuck this office and stop by and see you again. You best be ready."

"You have people working around here?"

"A few."

"Why? And what are river runners?"

"They ain't nothing you need to bother about, boy. I'll tell you my secrets only if you come back to work. And that reminds me to tell you again that we need you bad. I can get you a contract you can't sensibly turn down."

"I can turn it down, Ballinger."

"You know some of your crazy Mex cousins been getting bad stuff out of Iraq, don't you?"

"No." I wondered if I could believe him. He was a consummate and continual liar.

"They have. Sometime, late or soon, them bastards are going to figure ways to use their goodies."

I waited. "What goodies?"

He ignored the question. "I'll see you sometime. You think hard about working for us again for a while. A year contract. Just one more goddamn year out of your life, Carlos. Big money. I know you're not doing much good there in Kentucky." He laughed. "You're just as bad as I am to them Kentuckies."

Ballinger was black.

"I've got a new job," I said.

"I already know about your new job. Probation officer."

15

I thought about asking him or telling him about the blind mail pictures, but I decided he'd answer me with lies.

THE NEXT MORNING, with a grey-looking Daggert riding the bench, I listened in on the Kentner murder trial for the first time. I sat in a chair above the spectator rail and trusted my answering machine to take care of possible private legal business. I did my best to forget Ballinger and his latest call. I admitted to myself that I was afraid to go back to work for him.

Outside the grimy windows, Grimsley City sat in cold, windy sunshine. Once I heard two towboats blowing horns on the nearby Ohio.

Inside, the prosecution and defense stayed busy picking jurors, voir dire.

I listened and examined the defendant. Her name was Shirley Kentner. She reminded me heartbreakingly of a girl I'd known in high school, a blond girl a year older than I was, and therefore unattainable. I'd experienced a hot crush on her, one that wouldn't go away, and managed to place myself in situations where eventually she knew who I was. But seniors seldom date, or even see, juniors, and Jan Tomlin had many boys panting after her. She was small, blond, and cunningly formed. She was a cheerleader and vice president of her class. In my senior year she'd gone away to the University of Texas, pledged Pi Phi, and married a football player before graduation.

Ten years out of high school I'd gone back to a combined reunion. She'd nodded at me distantly, still beautiful, but with three children and a fat, strong husband who sold insurance.

Shirley Kentner was taller—five and a half feet—and had wide blue eyes, sun hair, and a face with a good bit of aristocracy in it, unlike my old crush. Shirley was dressed in black, the dress meant to be formless, but nothing that covered her dangerous curves would ever be that way. She made my old Jan into a witch on a broom.

I shook my head and wiped my eyes. Shirley Kentner was lovely.

She was also accused of murder and conspiracy to murder.

She sat at counsel table with her lawyer, Henry Lee. I'd heard Lee was "good" from other lawyers of the local bar. He was late-fiftiesish, medium in size, and had a belly. His movements were quick and sure. So were his grey, penetrating eyes. They roamed the courtroom restlessly. His speech was swift and nasty. I decided that he was mostly mean after I'd listened to his frequent objections. He had a way of curling his upper lip when he lost arguments, the curl saying to ruling authority, "You're both asshole wrong and bullshit stupid."

I'd not encountered Lee in court combat. Most of my skirmishes had been with the younger members of the bar. Lee looked me over when I took a side chair, perhaps puzzling over who I was to occupy favored seating above the rail. He either figured it out or decided not to care, because he ignored me after his few early glances.

Shirley Kentner saw me also. I could see her watching me, and so I watched back. She seemed locked in despair and shock, but trying as hard as she could to act normal and natural.

I found that *State* v. *Kentner* was not a death penalty case. The prosecution was asking only for slow death: a long term of years in women's prison.

I paid attention to the voir dire and watched Shirley, on her side on looks alone. Her legs, what I could see of them, were slim and encased in dark nylon. In the black, balloon-like dress she was elegant, a late-night prom queen dressed for a funeral. Thinking about that reminded me of my own high school prom a dozen years in the past and of my south Texas loves who'd joyously hop into backseats with me, but not openly date me.

Henry Lee said to Judge Daggert, after some warm juror examination, "It's apparent this panel member has read widely about the case and formed an opinion, and that it would be impossible for the defense to change it."

Judge Daggert shook his head slowly. "You've been trying cases before me for eleven years, Mr. Lee. You know the standard for a challenge for cause, having seen it spelled out both here and having read it in cited appellate decisions. This juror must say he won't follow the law when I instruct him in what it is. He must say he can't remove what he's read or heard out of his mind. Finally, he must say that he has such a feeling of conviction about the case that it can't be changed by what he sees and hears here. After trying long and hard, you've not gotten him to admit anything even close.''

Henry Lee inclined his head grimly and let his lip curl. ''The law ought to be different, Your Honor. There's great need for it.'' He approached the bench and spoke soft words with Daggert. The prosecutor, Commonwealth's Attorney Corner, scurried close to listen. He was small and sported a medium-length mustache and a flashy tie. Lee and the judge smiled at each other, and Corner joined in the smiling ceremony. All were old trial acquaintances, but from rumors heard politically, not all were friends in this election year.

Lawyers who prosecute felonies in Kentucky are officially known as commonwealth's attorneys, but the public's title for them is just ''prosecutor,'' and that's how they're known except on the election ballot in the district they run in.

I watched the trial.

Moments later, after Lee had finished questioning all the jurors, he used a peremptory challenge to rid himself of the juror he found offensive, an aging town businessman with stubborn, scandalized eyes, gossipy answers, proudly sporting his bright Kiwanis pin.

And so it proceeded. When the prosecutor had the jury, he read them complicated preliminary instructions he claimed the judge would give and asked them if they could follow such instructions as the only true law. When Henry Lee got the jury back, he read them other instructions more favorable to the defense and asked them if they could follow those. The jury, game but confused, nodded and affirmed for both lawyers.

''You ladies and gentlemen all understand that Mrs. Kentner stands before you presumed to be innocent?'' thundered Lee, sounding as if his statement was the *all* of it.

Nods. Assurances. A couple of peeks from the back row, where two males sat next to each other, perhaps admiring Mrs. Kentner almost as much as I did, but doing a better job of disguising it.

I watched the voir dire strategies. Prosecutor Corner wanted young women on the jury, women who'd dislike Shirley Kentner because she was beautiful. Lee wanted young men. What they wound up with, after both challenges for cause and peremptory strikes, were mostly older men and women. Many of the prospective jurors on the panel were blue-collar workers or farmers, because a high percentage of the people in Grimsley County fell into those categories. A lot of possibles seemed to be people who'd been abused and wounded by life. I knew the breed. There were lots of abused people in south Texas.

I favored Lee's client, not just because of her looks, but also because I didn't like Lynn Corner. He'd been brusque with me the several times I'd inquired about my father.

"Leave criminal investigation to the police," he'd ordered. "Is your father's death the reason you set up practice here? If so, it's a damn poor reason." He'd shot his cuffs and admired his gold cufflinks.

"I came to Grimsley City to practice law. I'm inquiring in your office today because it looks to me like all police investigation has ended."

"The case remains open. Maybe your father had been drinking or taking drugs. This time he wandered into a tough river parking lot where some bad people hang out at night." He shook his head piously. "It can get wild and mean on the river after dark. Gang people converge down there. You can buy drugs and stolen goods. We patrol it heavily until midnight. About two or three in the morning someone struck your father with a motor vehicle, maybe on purpose. After your father was down, the driver then backed over his body a few times. The driver then plundered the body and fled. We've not found anyone who witnessed the crime."

"How about the car that hit him? Wouldn't it have damage? Is anyone looking for it?"

"It might and it might not. Your father may have been on the ground when he was struck."

19

"How about parts from the car that struck him? If he was hit hard, something might have broken off. A piece of a light, some plastic or metal."

"Sometimes the people who hang out there at night play chicken with each other, running from fence to fence. The police who investigated said there was car debris all over, some old junk, some new."

"What were the new things? What were the ones found close to his body?"

He shrugged. "I don't remember. The police continue to investigate. Go away. Ask elsewhere. Maybe Texas."

I'd left. But I'd stayed in Kentucky, and now Corner couldn't just brush me off; he would have to deal with me. I was now, just as he was, *establishment.*

I knew that Corner was a letter-of-the-law man. I believed that if two men had feloniously stolen loaves of bread, he'd ask the same penalty for each. He'd do this despite the fact that Man One stole his bread to feed his family and Man Two stole his so that he could hide crack cocaine inside the loaf and enter a grade school to furnish supplies to young adventurers.

Corner now smiled companionably at me in the hall, but my hostile feelings against him remained.

Mean ass. King of the local jungle. Take the commonwealth's offer or go to trial.

Despite the fact that I was now establishment, I disliked him.

Recently he'd sent me, or had the police department send me, copies of the police report on my father's death. The return address on the envelope was that of the local police, but I thought Corner was responsible for my getting the document.

I learned, from reading that report, that my father's body had been found at about four in the morning, that he'd been dead an hour or so when found, that his blood alcohol had been only .04— he had *not* been under the influence—that he'd died of multiple fractures and massive internal injuries, and that there were no skid marks left by the car that had struck him in the parking lot. Pop's billfold had vanished from the body. It was never found, and there was no money in his pockets. He'd been paid earlier that day. So whoever had killed him had also robbed his body. Or maybe, I thought, someone had come along after Pop was dead and taken what they could find from the body. A scavenger.

There'd been no tests for drugs, but Pop wasn't on anything that I knew about.

I further learned that the "newest" pieces of evidence found near the body were shards of a red lens from the rear lights of a recent Ford product. The police officer writing the report thought the pieces of red plastic had splintered off a rear brake light as the car was backed over my father.

Or maybe my father, still alive, had raised an arm to hold away the moving machine of death?

I kept a file on Pop in my office. I put the police report there along with the clippings on his death from the local newspaper, his autopsy report and death certificate, and the order of the court on his small estate.

On Wednesday, middle of the afternoon, prosecution and defense had a jury plus two alternates.

Daggert swore the jury by having them stand and raise their right hands while he read and had them repeat the oath in short phrases. He admonished them about reading or listening to anything concerning the case, or discussing it with anyone. Newspapers, television, and radio were forbidden to the jurors.

I assessed the jury. Of the twelve plus two, there were six farmers or farmer's wives, four blue-collars, two older university teachers, a high school teacher nearing retirement age, and an engineer in his early forties. Six men, six women on the jury, one alternate female, one male. Eleven whites, three blacks. Some smarts, some not-so-smarts. A fair enough mix.

Outside the windows of the courtroom a January wind blew ominously and sleet rattled against the glass. Daggert frowned out the window and told the jurors to return at ten the next morning. He watched them exit.

When he left the bench, I followed behind. He hung his robe on an office peg, then sat behind his huge desk and examined me.

"Pretty lady," I said tentatively.

"Yes, very pretty. I saw you watching her. What have you heard about the case?"

"Not a lot. Her husband was killed the same day or the day after I arrived in town. I wasn't reading the local newspaper at that time, but I did read about the murder in the Louisville *Courier Journal*. From what I remember, there was a hired man. He killed the husband and said, when he was caught, that the wife traded him sex to get him to do it."

"That's the state's claim. The murderer was in this country illegally. He pled out. In his guilty plea he said that Mrs. Kentner first bedded him, then talked him into killing her husband. She told him there was a lot of money in the house and that he could keep all he found as a bonus. He was supposed to go off on vacation and then slip back. That way he'd not be heavily suspected. So she went to play bridge and the aging, ill husband was tortured and killed. The killer was caught. He's now serving fifty years, the prosecution having made a deal with him for promised testimony against the wife. Our present defendant is not yet thirty. Her deceased hubby was in his sixties. He left two children, a boy and a girl, both older than this second wife."

I nodded.

He looked down at the stacks of papers which covered his desk. "It may or may not fall to you to do the pre-sentence in this case, so it would help if you'd keep close watch on the trial."

"Why would it not fall to me?"

He shrugged. "I might ask my old probation officer to come back and do it. He was in on the case when it all started."

"All right," I said. "Whatever you decide."

"And I may want to use you to do other things in the case."

"What things?"

"Find the answers to questions that bother me."

"How about the police?"

He shook his head. "The case is finished as far as all area police are concerned. Once Shirley Kentner was indicted, they quit looking. Will you look for me if I tell you to look?"

"Yes."

He frowned at me. "Then please stay unsmitten with our trial lady." He looked out his window. The snow now fell quickly and a strengthening wind mixed it with bits of leaves from the courthouse trees and roof. I thought about Florida or even south Texas.

I waited.

"Our unlucky lady is not without defenses," he said, moderating his tone. "Some things she says will differ from things said by the prosecution." He shook his head. "The last murder trial I had was that of a man who had killed his estranged wife and their children, age two and five. This one is different, very different. That man wanted to die."

I nodded. The judge's office smelled of decay, old books, and strong coffee.

"The prosecutor believes he has a good case," Daggert continued. "I heard a lot of that case in her alleged co-conspirator's guilty plea." He shook his head. "People hereabouts are suspicious of young women who marry men more than twice their age. This lady claims she's innocent. I'm told she will present physical evidence in my court of her innocence. We shall see what both I and the jury decide. Yes. We'll both watch and wait. Remember, she's innocent until proven guilty." He inspected me, his face lightening, but only a little. "What with Coulson leaving and you just beginning, are we getting behind?"

"Some juvenile hearings are accumulating, Judge."

He nodded. "Try doing them yourself. Get the child, the child's parents, and the child's lawyer in for a discussion. It's called pre-disposition and I favor the idea of it. If anyone gets persnickety with you, then tell me and I'll hold hearings. You'll likely be able to dispose of most of the juvenile cases by agreement, and I'll back you up on those agreements. Use the library for meetings. If you get stumped or confused, ask Annie. She's been my good right hand as court reporter and she's a most perceptive woman. Or, ask me. Send me a note into the courtroom."

"Yes."

"And listen to the trial as much as you can. Watching it will be a good experience. A young lawyer can learn a great deal from watching good trial lawyers fight it out."

23

I suppose I looked surprised.

"Wait and watch closely," Daggert said. "It'll likely get more interesting as it proceeds. Both lawyers are good at the business." He smiled frostily. "Try to watch the *trial*. Don't stare too much at the defendant."

"She's very pretty. She reminds me of someone I once knew."

He looked out his window once more. "She is pretty. Let's wish a bit of luck to her. It's hard for me to believe she did what's charged, and those charges have yet to be proved. But in our city, outside this window, you hear she shouldn't have taken up with the handyman, even if he is, in a way, as pretty as she is."

"Pretty?"

"Yes. When he was in the local jail and back and forth to the courtroom, he drew crowds of women spectators. They apparently got their panties moist every time he appeared. I had to order the courtroom cleared when I sentenced him." He nodded to himself. "The sheriff intercepted letters written to him by the smitten. Ladies, young and old, tried to pass him mash notes in the courtroom, even after he pled guilty to murder."

"Why did they do that?"

"If I could answer that, I could answer everything. It's the way people are, Jim." He shook his head and picked up an order from his desk and began to read it. "You'll see it's a bad case. I may want you to do some looking just because all other looking has stopped. And I may not want you to do a single blasted thing." He looked up at the ceiling. "Watch and wait."

CHAPTER THREE

Ballinger visited my first hospital. My eyes were bandaged against the light. All I could remember, when I wasn't sleeping, was the sun. Sleep was filled with nightmares about that sun.

He sat by my bed and waited until all sound of the nurse's retreating footsteps had stopped.

"Some friends of ours took out that village with a gunship two days ago, Carlos," he said. "The Judge's little terrorist group is wiped out."

"All right."

He waited for a while, perhaps for my thanks. Then, when I said nothing, he patted me lightly on the shoulder. "Sleep, Carlos."

I remembered later there were a couple of hundred people, men, women, and children, in the village. Even if I was to live (or preferably die) in the dark, not all of those people had been involved in holding and torturing me. Some had just lived their lives in the village.

ON THURSDAY MORNING there were arguments on pending motions. After that, the attorneys made opening statements. The judge had earlier conferred with the attorneys on short preliminary instructions. The pace of the trial was ready to quicken. This was the day the evidence was to begin.

The snow had been trivial and the jurors arrived on time. I arrived before nine at my private office, but things quickly halted there. I hurried to the courthouse to observe.

Judge Daggert began proceedings by reading short preliminary instructions.

In his opening statement following instructions, Corner paraded his case. He'd dressed for this day in a dark grey suit. He wore a figured tie and a white shirt complete with French cuffs and the cufflinks he'd worn and self-admired on my visit to his office. He had an outraged look to him as he addressed the jury. *See me? I hurt for justice.*

"Ladies and gentlemen, I now ask you, as jurors, to listen carefully while I read the indictment returned into this very court where you now sit as petit jurors. That indictment was returned by a local grand jury against this defendant." He then read documents with feeling, pausing for effect now and then, looking down at the floor, then up at a ceiling heaven, and reading the conspiracy indictment first: "Shirley Kentner, with intent to commit a felony—to wit: murder—did agree with Jose Ramon Garcia to commit the said felony, namely murder Fiala Kentner, and the same Jose Ramon Garcia did perform an overt act—to wit: murder of Fiala Kentner—in the furtherance of the agreement with Shirley Kentner to kill Fiala Kentner." And: "Shirley Kentner with Jose Ramon Garcia did knowingly kill another human being—to wit: Fiala Kentner—by shooting the said Fiala Kentner with powder and slugs from a .22 pistol and stabbing him with a sharp instrument until he was dead. All contrary to the form of the statutes made and provided . . ."

He omitted the formal parts and then walked twice, up and down, before the jury.

"We're going to prove all I've just read. Each of you jurors have taken an oath to well and truly try this case. That's what we expect from you as citizens. Doing your duty will take some days from your life. We're sorry to use your valuable time, but what you do in court here is important. Justice must be served." He stopped and consulted his notes. "There's one witness I want you to listen to with particular attention. He's perhaps the most important of all the commonwealth's witnesses. Other witnesses will relate items of evidence and give expert testimony, tell you about fights and problems between the deceased and the accused. But only one person witnessed the murder of Fiala Kentner and knows all concerning it and the plans made to commit it. The witness I refer to is Jose Ramon Garcia. I've talked at length to that man. I've taken his statements and checked them with care against all the evidence. I believe every word he'll tell you will be the unvar-

26

nished truth. He'll tell you that at the urgent request of Shirley Kentner he tortured and killed Fiala Kentner, and he'll tell you exactly why he did it.''

He cleared his throat and continued: ''Jose Garcia became the lover of the defendant, Shirley Kentner, while he worked for her murdered husband. He'll testify that she was the one who conceived a diabolical plan to kill Fiala Kentner. Garcia will tell you he killed for love, but that she had him kill for money.''

Corner moved close to Shirley Kentner's chair. ''This woman, this defendant, ordered the killing because she grew tired of her ill and aging husband and couldn't wait to inherit his money.'' He looked down at the defendant and shook his head. ''This scheming woman bewildered Jose Ramon Garcia and caught him in her silken spider's love nest. This woman preached hate and exhorted Garcia to commit cold-blooded murder. This woman sought murder to hide often-committed sexual sins and also because she wanted her husband's money. Big money. More than enough, as you will hear, to kill for.''

The name of the killer surprised me. I'd forgotten that he was Hispanic, and I realized now he was likely Mexican. The name Garcia was a common one south of the Rio Grande, like Smith or Brown in the USA.

I glanced at Shirley Kentner. On this day she sat reading a large, black Bible. She had it opened as the prosecutor looked down at her. When Corner moved away from her vicinity, she saw me looking her way. She leaned toward her attorney and whispered something to him. He shook his head slightly and she went back to the Bible, eyes downcast.

Corner moved back near the jury and droned on. In time he finished. I watched all the way through. Shirley Kentner never looked at the prosecutor as he made his opening statement. I thought she might have been directed not to look.

Corner sat down.

Henry Lee made defense opening remarks. He was dressed in a dark blue suit and wore a conservative tie. His client closed her Bible and stared up at him. She nodded when he made telling points, but her face remained sad.

I found myself wanting to make her smile.

Lee's opening was pointed mostly toward concepts of "reasonable doubt, credibility of witnesses, and burden of proof." He reread preliminary instructions covering those points of law with emphasis on areas favoring the defendant. He stood gravely in front of the jury, his voice low: "You jurors have promised my client that you will wait until all of the evidence is presented before you make your decision. That's a promise you must keep. When you've heard all the evidence, you'll realize that Shirley Kentner did none of the hideous acts the prosecution claims. You'll see she's a pawn in a puzzling power game played by a brutal man who extricated himself from the electric chair by falsely involving her in a foul murder he admits having committed." Lee walked close to where Corner sat. "And although Mr. Corner believes his main witness, the question in this trial is whether *you* believe him. Mr. Corner is paid by the commonwealth to believe his witnesses in a criminal case. You are not."

Lee glanced up at the wall clock. For a moment I thought he would stop. He took a step toward counsel table and then turned for another try at the jury.

"Listen!" he ordered softly. "Listen to each word. Watch and examine. You'll see what I have seen about this case. A man has admitted to the murder of Shirley Kentner's husband. He plea-bargained and saved his life by involving Shirley Kentner. Family money and the division of the assets of the lucrative estate of the murdered man are involved. The children of the deceased are greedy for every penny in that multimillion-dollar estate. And remember Garcia tortured his victim and killed without mercy. Listen closely to this admitted killer. Listen to the children of Fiala Kentner and see their hate for their stepmother, their greed and need for the money their father left. Then, before you decide, hear Shirley Kentner. Evaluate all stories and the motives of those who testify. Once you do this, I believe you will rush from this courtroom to the jury room and soon return your verdict. You will help me save an innocent woman from punishment for a crime she neither committed, nor planned, nor condoned." He held up his hand. "Listen!"

He sat down, then reached out and touched his client's hand. She gave him a brave nod as the fascinated jury watched.

It was now almost noon.

"We'll take our lunch break now," Daggert announced. "Where will you take the jurors, Mr. Donaho?"

The bailiff approached the bench and mumbled something. Daggert called the lawyers up and told them where the jury would take lunch and ordered them to eat elsewhere.

A small crowd had been watching. They managed to slip out. I stood up.

Daggert smiled out at me and his suddenly empty courtroom. "Evidence begins this afternoon."

I nodded up at him. I still had substantial money from the bank loan I'd gotten on the basis of having a new job. I'd get paid my first small county check that afternoon.

"Lunch?" I asked politely. "On me?"

He shook his head. "Not this noon." I noticed his eyes were red and there was a tremor in his hands. "How about you take me to dinner tonight?"

"Fine." *He'd drink too much and I'd be his after-dinner driver.*

Was I his keeper?

He'd given me a job when I badly needed one. I knew he needed help of some kind, but I'd not yet determined what it was. I supposed I could assault his bartenders, waiters, and waitresses. Maybe that's why he'd made me his P.O.

From comments made pointedly within my hearing by others in the courthouse, I thought he'd caught heat on my appointment. Politics, in a small town, is a thing that office holders, even judges, don't practice alone. I wondered *exactly* what had been said in smoky local back rooms when I'd been given the job instead of either a deserving party hack or someone's dewy nephew or niece fresh out of Bellarmine, Grimsley U., or U.K.

Small towns abound in stories. People hate well. I supposed I was, to many Grim City people, a dark, foreign interloper. Maybe the remnants of the KKK, if one still existed locally, had already met concerning me.

The court reporter called and surprised me by handing me my first county paycheck for the few days I'd worked. Those for the office had been delivered early.

If Daggert had declined my invitation to lunch and opted for dinner, there was, downstairs, David Silver Estrada, "Silver." He was the IV-D deputy. He was also the only man in the prosecutor's office I viewed with any approval. He chased delinquent poppas (and sometimes mommas) who neglected to provide support for their children in and out of marriage. I figured Corner wanted *someone* to do that nasty job, but didn't want to personally do anything unpopular himself and maybe lose votes.

Therefore Silver. He was good at the job. He was intent, and hugely ambitious. He knew the town. He was old Grimsley County Catholic. His paternal great-grandfather had been Spanish, not Mexican. Silver was slim and darkly handsome. The family was accepted, despite lineage and religion, by all but the most bigoted. Silver owned the kind of face that looks back at you from the slick pages of expensive magazines—a cosmopolitan face, square-jawed, and resolute, seeming more suntanned than dark complexioned. I'd run with him in law school, where, first time I'd met him, I'd tried Spanish on him, and been disappointed. He spoke very little, and didn't understand much more. In law school he was a year ahead of me and four years younger than I was. He was unmarried. His father, before his death, had owned a mediocre Cadillac agency. My father had once worked for Silver's father, but had moved on by the time he was killed. Silver's mother was a well-dressed lady, a bridge devotee, a giver of parties to which I was sometimes invited. She summered in Grimsley City and wintered in a trailer court near Naples, Florida. She lived on social security, insurance proceeds, and a few stock dividends.

Silver was restless. He was constantly on the go. Once, in law school, after a night studying, I'd awakened in the front seat of his car a few miles south of Indianapolis, where "he knew some girls." He did know some, too. He liked me being with him because I was no competition.

He drove a Ford now. His mother had sold the Cadillac agency.

Most wished him well. One day I hoped the town would say of

me: "Singer's okay, even if he is kind of dark-skinned like you know. . . ."

They already said good things about Silver. He was Rotary and Chamber of Commerce, the newly elected president of the local bar association, a hard worker, a constant organizer. He liked long vacations in the winter and summer, weeks or months *somewhere.*

He'd gone away for a month last summer and I still didn't know where he'd gone. When I'd inquired, he'd smiled.

Sometimes his work and play seemed to me more frantic than controlled. It was as if he expected all to watch and applaud.

I'd exhausted Silver and his mother of any information they had on my father. All Marie Estrada, Silver's mother, recalled was that she'd been told my father was a quiet man, that he knew the car business, and that he drank more than a bit when he worked at the agency. Silver said he didn't remember my father.

Silver's courthouse office was in an alcove that once had been a part of the downstairs district court enclave until the commissioners had walled it away. Through door windows into the court, Judge Rainbolt, the taciturn judge of that lower court, was engaged in some kind of bench trial. Rainbolt, clad in a faded black robe, saw me looking in his window and frowned out at me. He had not liked my recent appointment and, believing I was the one who had falsely reported he'd been appointed to the state supreme court, didn't like me. I turned away and opened Silver's door.

"Lunch?"

Silver stared up from behind his typewriter. "You're not safe on this floor. Rainbolt will get you." He grinned. "He's still stewing and sure it was you."

I shrugged. "He's been a horse's ass with lots of people. Why does he think I'm the one who did a job on him? We both know it wasn't me and who it actually was."

"He'd never believe anyone else did it. The job was not done until you appeared on the scene. And you were the one he bit on most in court, remember?"

That was true. He'd made my life difficult. He'd appoint me, pick on me, and then refuse to pay me more than a pittance for hours spent working on criminal cases.

31

"Now that you have power, you're going to take notice of poor me," Silver said. "How jackassedly thoughty of you." He said it without a smile.

"Every time I've seen you recently, you were surrounded by crowds of young ladies tearing at your clothes. I did not, as an officer of the court, want to witness any illegal or immoral acts."

He nodded, still not smiling.

I went on: "And now, after the noon recess bell has rung, I find you still hard at work trying to obtain blood money from poor parents who fail to pay. Perhaps you seek such fortunes so you can embezzle same?"

He nodded, his eyes feigning craftiness. "I'll take off only when there gets to be a big chunk in the register. Until that day, our commonwealth's attorney likes me to keep right after them, especially during election year." He nodded. "I'm about like you, Jim. This job makes me barely enough for three squares a day and a tank of gas a week. But my time in the local, state, and national arenas will come. Soon."

"I doubt you eat *any* square meals," I said, picking on one point. "When you turn sidewise, I lose sight of you. You swallow a martini olive whole and I think you have a tumor."

"I eat heavy, but unlike you I'm the active type," he said amiably. "I chase girls and catch them instead of picking on poor prick Judge Rainbolt." He covered his typewriter and got up. "I'll do lunch with you if we can go strictly dutch. That way neither of us will be obligated. Besides, you eat more than I do. I'm careful about things like that. I'll tell you political things I know and ask you questions. I'll also relate, if you ask nice, tales about your uncertain future in my, and not quite yet your, town, ace."

He called the world "ace."

"Let's eat lunch," I said, agreeing.

"Should I invite Rainbolt to go with us?"

"No way, Jose."

Braxton's on the River was an old, run-down restaurant with recent delusions of grandeur. It had been, when I was an undergraduate at Grimsley U., a shabby place, saved by good food smells and pretty coed waitresses. Service had been slow and sloppy. Recent new owners had repainted the premises, installed huge overhead fluorescents, and replaced the name–gouged booth tables with fresh ones with ultra-hard surfaces. There was now a long salad bar, and salads were offered with everything—soups, sandwiches, and dinners. The food was good. There were new, brisk student waiters and waitresses. Still, aiding the place some, from out of large, new windows on two sides, there was an imposing view of the river to the north. From out of those windows you could also see the parking area where my father had been killed. I'd visited and examined that area, but not much was to be learned there. All it was, by day, was a parking-boating area. At night, when I'd watched it in the warm months, it had been peopled by night creatures, but never by just one single group of them. Some nights it had been motorcyclists, racing and roaring. Other nights it had been overnight boating groups cooking hot dogs and burgers. At times, high school and college-age kids had partied there. I had seen money bet and dollars openly spent on drugs. I had counted and memorized faces until the very numbers made all anonymous. Cars had cavorted, played bumper tag and chicken, running at the fences.

We arrived at Braxton's early enough to get a table with a view.

A nubile waitress led us to a booth, looked us over, and then took our order. She smiled and dawdled with the order pad, made small talk, and took reluctant leave.

"How goes the murder trial?" Silver asked, after we had admired her retreating derriere and nodded at each other knowingly.

"The jury's sworn. We had preliminary instructions and opening arguments this morning. Evidence starts this afternoon." I thought for a moment. "It's said the state has a damned good case against Mrs. Kentner."

"It's a damn shame."

"Do I detect a personal interest in the case?"

He nodded. "I know the defendant a little. She once came to see me about a divorce. There was, I suppose, a later reconciliation, because she instructed me not to file. I saw her a few times thereafter at political functions. She's astonishingly good looking." He smiled. "I admit I secretly wanted her to divorce that mean, ancient bastard, even if she is a tad older than me, and then I wanted her to throw herself, with wild abandon, into my arms and so forth. And, of course, bring with her the settlement from her divorce." He gave me a smirk and then looked out at the big, muddy river north of us. "Sweet and friendly."

"Was she into politics?"

"No. He was the political wheel. He'd usually be at the head table at party dinners, and he'd chair area finance committees. I think Kentner got his jollies from owning a young, lovely wife, taking her out in public, showing off his bride, and watching the envy. He was a crusher of a man, Jim. He had money. He had influence. I guess he had friends. But he was an owner-occupant. She was *his* wife, his personal property. He named the tune, paid all the pipers, and wanted every dance on her card. And he was ill, of course."

"How ill?"

"I don't know. Ask his doctors. I'd see him and he looked sick. He used a cane and one of those walkers to get around."

"How did his proprietorship suit her?"

"All I can tell you is that I did opening gambit on an unsubtle pass and she didn't respond. I never saw her play up to anyone else, and I watched. I'd hear things, though. Maybe she just didn't much like younger dudes."

"What things did you hear?"

"That she was running. That the handyman and she were lovers. That there were others." He shook his head. "My mother knew her through summertime bridge and cocktail parties. My mother watches the world carefully. She approved of Shirley Kentner. She didn't and doesn't believe that she had anything to do with killing her husband."

"Would many locals feel the same way?"

"Most people would believe what the papers printed and the gossipers spread."

"You liked Shirley Kentner?"

"Yes. How about you?"

"She's lovely. I've been informed I may be asked to do some detective work about her and the case."

"I warned you that might happen."

"Yes. I remember."

He lost interest in me, shaking his head. "She's beautiful."

"Yes. I want to help her if I can."

"She's got you, too."

"Possibly. Does she have you?" I asked.

Silver's infatuations were, to me, almost legendary in both number and intensity. He wore his heart on his sleeve, but the sleeve was readily changeable.

"She's been in jail for how long?" I continued.

"Over a year," he said. "A long time."

"Have you been true to her?" I asked jokingly.

"Out of sight is bad for me, Jim. I've found several new ways to waste time." He smiled widely. "Still, I'd give up all current diversions for a hack at her."

Our waitress picked that moment to arrive with food. She deposited it on the table. Mine was a cheeseburger, plus I could get salad bar. I now found myself ragingly hungry for green things after months of V-8, hot-plate-heated canned soups, crackers, peanut butter, and diet drinks.

Silver had ordered a large bowl of vegetable soup, plus salad bar. The soup arrived thick and steamy.

The waitress doled Silver many extra cracker packages. She examined him. "You need lots of crackers. And remember you can go to the salad bar more than once. You're cute." She shook her head and added sagely, "But you're too thin for your weight."

"Yes, missy," he said, smiling up at her. He dutifully opened two cracker packages while she watched. He dumped them into his soup.

The waitress smiled back. I watched. I'd seen this kind of conduct exhibited by women concerned with Silver before. Women usually wanted to mother him or marry him, and sometimes they yearned for both. He had the easy ability to make many love him on sight. It was a gift he sometimes did not use wisely. When he abandoned women, he had no knack for it. The women hurt.

The waitress scurried away. I saw her watching Silver proprietarily from across the room.

Most women saw nothing in me. Maybe they sensed I was a burned-out case. *The sun also rises.*

The nights of exquisite, continual hurts had taken away desire. Doctors had told me things could and would be restored.

Not yet.

The woman on trial had stirred me some, made me think *what ifs.*

We filled plates at the salad bar. I wolfed down my cheeseburger and ate all my heaped plate of salad. Silver, with less food, finished before I did. He leaned back. Outside, a lone towboat plowed upriver. The river water looked mud brown and winter frigid.

"My squad leader is going to run against your boss for circuit judge," he said. "I couldn't say that to you on the phone recently when you took the job, but now I can."

I nodded. I'd heard courthouse rumors.

"There's been bad blood between them for a while. The loser had best get his butt out politically."

"No room for a compromise?"

"I doubt it."

"Who'll win?"

"It's uncertain. Corner ought to take it in a walk, but I don't know. Daggert is old family, lots of relatives, maybe lots of friends. Some people think he's a good judge. My mother likes him, although with me in my present job she's quiet about it. Corner has power through the party machinery. His cronies run the precincts and he and the county chairman pass out road jobs and decide who'll do business with the county." He took a fork and drew an idle, soft line on the tablecloth. "It once was a big, happy family until they froze out Daggert and Fiala Kentner."

"Fiala Kentner?"

"Sure. He was a major cog in party leadership once. That was the way of it before you came to town. Once upon a time, back then, there were four men who ran the local party. About a year and a half ago the four became two. The doubles champs are Fred Gow, the party chairman, and Commonwealth's Attorney Lynn Corner.''

''What happened?''

''I probably should say I don't know, because I'm not certain. Maybe what I'll tell you now is right, maybe wrong. The word from those sympathetic to your judge is that something raw happened, something Daggert couldn't or wouldn't stomach. He pulled out. Kentner left with him. Kentner was the finance man. Kentner had plenty of money and was willing to spend it. The money came from his machines, games, some of which may have been machines that were slots and paid off under the table. The party got a lot poorer for a time, but they stuck a two percent on all workers and stayed well. Daggert fired Corner's people who worked in his court. He hired his own. Any appointments made by the court are now made by Daggert alone. Corner, in return, raided some places and picked up Kentner's illegal slots and had them destroyed. There's been cross-sniping ever since. That's probably why you got your job. Daggert would be suspicious of anyone who might owe the kingly survivors even a smile.''

I remembered Daggert had asked me if Silver was helping me politically. He wasn't. I'd never asked and he's never offered, other than in vague promises.

''I see. I know that Daggert's wife died. Tell me what killed her.''

''She had a rotten heart. She was terminal. There are lots of scandalous stories, but my bet is if Corner believed he could create problems harmful to the judge, he'd have already done it.''

I thought about that. ''Maybe he's waiting for the most opportune time. That could be just prior to the May primary.''

''I doubt it. There's nothing. Rumors and gossip. Daggert drinks. He was supposedly drinking before he came to the hospital that day. People saw him. He was sitting with his wife in her room. Aggie had a massive attack and was gone in seconds. She'd had heart problems and she was bound to die in days or weeks no matter what the doctors did for her. A transplant wouldn't have helped. Daggert admitted going to sleep. He was loud in self-flagellation and mea culpas. So the stories spread. But if Corner, as prosecutor, tried to make more than that out of it, he'd need Daggert's complete cooperation.'' Silver gave me a shrewd look. ''Could that happen?''

I remembered the judge's drinking habits. ''Maybe.''

''How's the judge doing now?''

''Not too well. His court reporter told me he'd recovered well for a time, but now he seems to be mostly morose.'' I decided not to mention drinking. I wasn't going to say anything that might cause Daggert problems. Not to Silver. He was Corner's man.

And I was Daggert's . . .

Another towboat appeared downriver. We watched it pass in shared silence.

I thought of something. ''If Corner files for judge, then who'll be the party candidate for commonwealth's attorney?''

''Quite likely it will be little old me,'' he said, grinning. ''It's not a done deal yet, but the two leaders have talked to me and talked to others. I said I was interested and that I positively intended to file if Corner filed for judge. I promised them some, but not all, of my blood.'' He nodded. ''Silver must go forward. I know how to do the job, and prosecutors get paid good. I guess I'm their candidate.''

''How good is good pay?''

''The same pay scale as judges. Good money.''

They could have at least interviewed me.

Silver leaned forward and lowered his voice. ''I have many ambitions. Prosecutor is only the first one. In a year you may not have the job you hold. You were appointed by the ghost of Daggert present. If Daggert loses, your ass is bluegrass. That's unless you work out things quietly with Corner in the meantime. Do you understand what I'm telling you?''

''I understand. Daggert, when I hired on, told me my job might not last.''

''Do you know Fred Gow?''

''I know who he is.''

"Talk to him when you can. Up the line I can maybe fix it for you if you stay quiet and things go well for me. I can give it a try anyway. You're an old law school friend. I want you to stay here in Grimsley City. I have plans for you just as I have plans for me. So soft-pedal what Daggert wants and do what's right and bright for you. Go through the motions."

I mulled over the situation. Silver had made vague talk in and since law school about plans for both of us before, but nothing had come of them. The idea of him being involved with two men deciding who and what would prosper politically in Grimsley County and City bothered me.

The thought of having Lynn Corner as circuit judge bothered me even more.

I shook my head. "I'll get by. I can always try practicing somewhere else."

Silver gave me an injured look. "Don't even think of that." He smiled and used something else we'd discussed. "Anything happening on your father's death?"

"Not much. No one seems interested and I'm not learning anything new."

"But you're still looking?"

"Some."

I recalled other reasons why I'd returned to Grimsley City. I remembered the town from my good times in undergraduate school here. I had no job offers of consequence when I got out of law school. I was treated well at Grimsley U. Pretty girls dated me and I was accepted by other students without question. I liked that. So I liked the town and I knew it. I called Silver and he thought I could make it.

He'd even been enthusiastic about it.

He nodded at me. "You will be accepted here in the city and county also, but that can only happen if you stick it out. I promise you'll make it if you stay and don't have a thin skin. About your father: Lynn Corner called around the other day, and folks were told to give you anything you wanted and supply any information you asked for."

"I have a new report sent me through the mail by the GCPD, but it's nothing new."

"Get me elected and I promise I'll look hard," he said, smiling.

"I'm looking now. I'm not looking *hard,* because I have no way to do that."

He shrugged. "I still will help. You have Corner and his cronies interested and curious about you. I'm told that strange federal types keep coming in and out of town checking on you. Corner wants to know why."

I felt irritation. "I'm not sure." It was all I could say. I couldn't tell questioners that the group wanted me back so I could go to Mexico and spy for them again. That would violate my oath.

"These guys—and there've been more than one of them—carry I.D. cards with big, impressive seals. They show gold badges. People tell me they carry guns. Don't you know who they are?" he asked, his voice earnest.

"I might if I saw one." *Ballinger's groupies.* "Possibly it could be someone I used to work for before I went to law school."

He shook his head ruefully and waited for me to comment further.

I saw our waitress flutter past. She no longer noticed me. She saw only Silver.

"Our waitress is interested in your wasted body," I said. "Maybe she'd like to be your special friend?"

"She's too young for a lawyer who just noticed two grey hairs last week." He shivered and I remembered that one of his expressed fears was of growing old. "Tell me more on the murder case before I go back to my always interesting job of chasing delinquent mommas and poppas."

"All I know so far is what I see in court."

He looked down at the table and lowered his voice. "I think Corner's quietly glad Fiala Kentner's dead. It cut his political enemies in half. Kentner's son and daughter need Corner to get a murder conviction because of the estate money. Corner thinks a win would boost his campaign." He smiled. "Wheels within wheels. Now you're working and practicing detection for Daggert, and Corner views you as an election imponderable. He wants to know where you stand.''

I waited and remained silent, seeing he wasn't done.

"This town operates on political gas, Jim. The city and county green up on combinations of rumors, slander, and scandal. Everything happening in county business is part of a deal. Fred Gow visited me to ask about my running. He was uninterested in my law school grades or my theories about how an efficient prosecutor's office could best be run. He wanted to know if I'd run as a stand-in in a scenario where Daggert beats Corner for judge. That way Corner could try for the cake, and still be sure of the pudding. I told him I'd not run as a stand-in and that I planned to run if Corner did not. That ended the first discussion.''

"They came back?''

"Yes. I worked in the party to make sure they didn't discover an electable patsy. I passed the word I was going to run and run hard. The second time our leaders asked: if they blessed me, could they name the people for my office jobs? I dickered some, but okayed most of that.'' He shrugged. "It's the way things are in Grim City.''

"Your employees would owe their primary loyalty and their jobs to someone other than you. And Corner, plus crew, would know every move you made.''

"Yes, but that's the way things are here,'' he said again. "I told them I'd fire anyone who wasn't competent or who violated my orders.''

"Whatever,'' I said. It was, after all, his call.

"If you decide you want to play under their rules, I'll ease things your way. You think lots of local people hate you, Jim. It's only that they don't know you.''

"Thanks. I'll still decline. I work for Daggert.''

He sighed. "Corner and friends worry about you, so I got delegated. I told them up front you'd not play games and that you're one stubborn bastard.'' He made a beckoning motion seen by our hovering waitress.

She ran to bring our checks. I left an adequate tip. Silver smiled nicely for the waitress and left a munificent sum on the table.

41

At the door he said: "We're friends, Jim, but I'm working with people who will want to end your job. So be careful. Do only what you must. Soft-pedal it. Don't make my people angry."

"Whatever, Silver."

CHAPTER FOUR

There were, Judge Daggert informed me during our first dinner, three main things about a jury's perception of criminal evidence. First, there was what actually happened. Second, there was the part of that happening that became testimony, and third, there was of the testimony received those bits the jury believed, remembered, and on which it based its eventual decision.

TESTIMONY BEGAN that afternoon. It drew a crowd of people. The courtroom smelled of wet winter clothes, because it had begun to rain hard by the time I returned from lunch.

There was time to sit by a big window radiator and do a little thinking about my situation. Maybe Ballinger was crowding me in my new life for the reasons given on the phone the night before. It was also possible he'd called and offered me work because we'd been allies once. Maybe he believed I was the one who needed help because I was now living as an alien in this small Kentucky town.

Or was it something else?

In the hospitals, I'd been questioned over and over about what I'd seen and said to my captors, and, more particularly, what questions had been asked. I remembered the questions, but not all I'd answered. What I recalled best was the sun. Perhaps Ballinger believed that memories of that bad time had lately returned to me.

Ballinger was a strange mix. He talked like a friend, but I'd never seen him exhibit real feeling towards anyone who worked for him.

Ballinger knew about my job. Ballinger knew all. Why was he sending his agents into Grimsley City and calling attention to the fact that I was of interest to his nasty little piece of government? I thought on that and could come up with nothing truly logical. I'd been informed, when I separated from the group, that if I did ever remember anything at all, I was to seek immediate contact. I'd never needed to follow that directive.

I looked out the courtroom window. I could tell that the jury was back from lunch and in the jury room because of the talking and laughing I could hear through the jury room door. I watched as squirrels played wet winter games in tall trees. Traffic moved through the Grimsley City streets, trucks hauling tobacco, cars full of joyful high school kids. Grimsley City was an old, poor town, but not to its kids. They knew no different place.

Where there was money in the old town, it was usually family money, acquired and put out to interest or invested in stocks down the years. Tobacco, oil, and bank stocks. One day I'd read a general file of probate papers mainly to learn how the papers were done. I'd occasionally been astonished at the amount of money bequeathed.

Daggert took the bench. The jury came in from the jury room.

I tried to understand the strategy of the prosecutor.

Corner first spent much time establishing, over and over, the date, approximate time, and place of death. More time was expended on proving the identity of the deceased. Items of evidence that had been collected by the police were introduced. Those items consisted partly of clothes removed from the body. The items were marked, a state trooper identified them, a chain of custody established, and then each was passed through the jury.

The prosecutor lingered over a holed sport coat and a bloodied shirt.

The jury seemed impressed by handling the clothes of the murdered man as the exhibits were passed gingerly along their hushed rows.

Also passed through the jury for examination were slugs in a plastic bottle and a small-caliber gun found at the scene of the crime. A state ballistics expert testified briefly that the weapon and the slugs in plastic had been the instrumentalities that had killed Fiala Kentner.

Lee, on cross, said: "No questions."

Soon came photographs taken at the crime scene and other pertinent places. By mid-afternoon, dozens of photographs had been

44

marked. I believed the jury was sooner or later going to see the corpse of Fiala Kentner over and over in both color and black and white.

The jurors waited and watched and I could sense their shared tension. The exhibits that had already been passed through their hands had interested them, but had not set well after their county-bought lunch. Horace Donaho, the vinegary old bailiff, had whispered smilingly to me as he took his seat near mine that most of the jurors had eaten the Rendezvous Grille luncheon special of southern fried chicken.

Corner now had a plain-clothed state police detective seated next to him at counsel table. The two men conferred in whispers from time to time. I recognized the detective, but couldn't recall his name.

I could tell that Shirley Kentner knew him. She watched him with an expression that failed to mask hatred.

Lee sat beside his client.

The state detective had a lean horseface and an ingratiating smile. He sat upright and correctly in his chair. I believed the jury, sometime during the trial, would be impressed by him. I'd learned from other lawyers that prosecutors and senior police officials instruct their recruits to sit straight, say "sir," and carefully think out answers. They teach officers how to shave closely, cut their hair short, and dress neatly. Maybe there are ancillary courses in appearing to be honest, unbiased, and sincere. I'd found it disconcerting to represent defendants and call witnesses who slouched, wore rumpled clothes, and said things like "yeah" and "you know" (over and over) in court hearings. My witnesses usually wound up being outclassed by the police.

I glimpsed some of the pictures as they were passed up from the court reporter to the judge after being marked. Fiala Kentner, from what I saw, appeared to be well nourished and in decent shape for a man in his sixties. He was moonfaced and strong-featured and was perhaps twenty to thirty pounds overweight. He either still had a lot of his own hair or wore a good hairpiece. His appearance in the photographs was marred by two bullet holes. The most evident was in the upper-left quadrant of his chest. The second was an executioner's entry wound in the back of the head. The wounds were small and there was no exit hole for either. They'd been inflicted by the stubby .22 pistol already in evidence.

More shocking than the bullet holes in the photographs were the large areas of bruising and lacerations on Kentner's lower torso and thighs in and around the pubic area.

Kentner's eyes, in the photographs, were glued shut. A bottle of some kind of double-stick glue, almost empty, sat with the items introduced into evidence.

The glue made me shudder inside. It recalled memories.

His eyes had been glued shut, mine had been taped open.

In a few pictures, I could see that Kentner was fully clothed above the waist. He lay face up in an easy chair. He wore no watch and no rings. A lamp stood beside the death chair. Behind Kentner *deceased,* there were shelves of books and albums of both country-western and classical music. In other photographs, Kentner's clothes had been completely removed and he lay supine on a morgue slab.

I recalled early attorney bickering about how many and which pictures of Fiala Kentner deceased could be admitted into evidence. That question had not yet been decided by the judge. Henry Lee sat impassively and let the prosecutor proceed unimpeded with his picture circus. Objections would come when Corner moved for admission of the death photos into evidence with the intention of passing them to the jury.

The exhibits were placed in neat piles on Daggert's bench. A young, uniformed state trooper named Steve Yennert was the identifying witness. He testified he'd taken the photos and collected other evidence on the orders of State Police Detective Abraham Owens. He then identified Owens as the man seated next to Corner.

The jury watched as this was done. No motion to admit the photos into evidence followed. The process proceeded efficiently, swiftly, and ominously.

Corner asked: "Is this picture marked State's Exhibit Twenty a fair and accurate representation of the scene you saw inside the home of Fiala Kentner on the night of his death, when you were called there?"

"It is." Straight-arrow look, and quick, sure answer. He could have worn his state police uniform to a Marine ball.

"And you took this picture from what angle and for what purpose?"

Trooper Yennert would explain at substantial length. I thought if he was asked the time of day, he might build the jury an eight-day clock.

Henry Lee sat quietly. Once I saw him yawn. If he was trying to convey to the jury that none of this was important, he wasn't succeeding. The jurors listened intently.

"And, once again, you took this photograph marked State's Exhibit Twenty at the request of Detective Owens and under his direct supervision at the scene of the crime?"

"Yes sir."

Good prosecutor's stuff, well done.

Occasionally I'd see a juror's eye move from the growing groupings of photographs on the judge's bench, to the holed shirt and sport coat with little patches of dried blood. Then the juror's eyes would move on coldly and appraisingly to Shirley Kentner.

I looked around the courtroom. It was now crowded. Most of the people inside were locals or news people. A few seemed different. In the far back, there were two males, one about thirty, the other perhaps forty; one large, one a bit smaller. They were Hispanics, well dressed, sitting carefully, watching the trial. Both had large, dark mustaches, black hair, and swarthy complexions. Both ignored my looks at them. If they saw me at all, they gave no indication.

I watched them, and a little drop of sweat ran down my back. To my knowledge Grimsley City was a little less than half black, and a bit more than half white, not many Hispanics, even if you wanted to include Silver and/or me, plus some professors at Grimsley U. and a few students.

These men weren't students. I knew several of the Hispanic professors at Grimsley, and these men weren't instructors.

The two watchers seemed harmless. Tourists perhaps. Maybe they'd wandered in from the streets. I chewed up a dry Gaviscon.
Relax.

When Yennert's own photos were done, he also served as the identifying witness for a set of five photos discovered un-developed, after the murder, in a camera in the Kentner bedroom.

''Yes, Detective Owens found the camera and asked me to de-velop the film in it. I did so under his orders and supervision. Thereafter I placed the resulting photographs in the evidence room at the state police post. They've been under my control since and have been in the evidence room from that day until this morn-ing, when I got them from that room.''

Chain of custody established.

The five photographs were marked and handed up to the judge.

I caught a glimpse of the top photograph. In it Kentner stood by a younger man, both of them smiling for the camera. The other man's features were darkly handsome. He wore a T-shirt, denim shorts, and sandals. Mexico is a land of many colors, a mixture of races. This man was dark, but his features were acquiline and reg-ular and his teeth stood out whitely as he smiled amiably at the camera.

I couldn't see the photo well, but I supposed the man in shorts and sandals was the man who'd confessed to killing Kentner. He was Mexican, the two watching in the courtroom were possibly Mexican. The warning bell rang again inside me. It was a bell I'd heard before. Mostly I had it subdued now, but I had lived for a time in a world full of alarm bells and I still listened for and heeded them even though the necessity seemed gone.

Time to run?

I found myself still nervously afraid, although I was several thousand miles from the scene of what had originally caused my fear.

The judge put the five photos in a special pile.

We took an afternoon break. Outside in the hall, I washed down two Bufferin with water from the fountain, mixing them with the Gaviscon. I hid out in my office until I heard the jury returning from their jury room. Then I walked quickly to the courtroom. It was cold and I pulled my old sport coat close around me and warmed my hands by sitting on them. I looked around the courtroom, but the two men who'd set off alarms had not returned. I relaxed a little. I was forever seeing people who brought nightmares and daymares.

I tried to visualize Fiala married to Shirley. I remembered Silver's ideas on the marriage. Fiala had married Shirley to show off, to let the world see that he could capture and hold a lovely, young woman. I wondered why she'd married him. She could pick and choose. There had to have been other suitors crowding her life. Yet she'd married a man thirty-plus years older than she was, then taken an itinerant wetback workman lover younger than she was.

Soap opera stuff.

I was on her side. Although I'd not met her, I knew I was infatuated with her. But why had she married Kentner?

The answers that came easily to mind were disturbing. I wanted Shirley to be found innocent, I wanted to help her, but I was filled with doubts. Fiala had money, Fiala had power. Fiala was a man who, in his ownership efforts, undoubtedly had angered Shirley. Maybe, in anger, she *had* conspired to rid herself of him. Maybe he'd driven her to it.

Murder happens. I read about it weekly in the advance sheets of the appellate courts, and daily in the *Courier Journal.* I saw it on the Louisville, Cincinnati, and Lexington television stations.

I shook my head. I looked once again around the courtroom. No two swarthy gentlemen. Vanished.

Late in the afternoon, I found that Shirley was carefully watching me, perhaps trying to gauge jury feelings from what she read in my face. When I stared back at her, she turned away, her eyes somehow even sadder than when the trial had commenced. I tried to catch her eye again so that I could smile encouragingly, but she didn't look my way again.

When the day finished, I assessed the results. Corner had established the following: Fiala Kentner had been murdered a year-plus ago on November 17—which oddly was one day after I'd arrived in Grimsley City. Kentner had died in his expensive lake home, perhaps in his bedroom, where small quantities of blood had been

49

found on a bedspread. But blood, old or new, had also been found in other rooms, so it was only certain that Fiala had died in or around his home. Shirley had played bridge that night a few blocks away. The murder had apparently taken place after nine and before ten.

Kentner's eyes had been glued shut and he'd been tortured.

His half-nude body had been dumped into and over a chair in front of a living room picture window, curtains open. There was little testimony concerning exactly where the murder had taken place in the house, because the police had found no definitive evidence that made any room a better place than the others. The bedroom and the living room were the favored, but not positive choices.

Why had the body been dumped where it could be seen?

Both a light inside the room and the outside lights had been left on.

Why, again? The obvious answer to me was that someone wanted the body discovered.

A killer who had also tortured his victim would attempt to gain as much time as possible for his flight. He'd not leave the victim in plain view, dumped in a chair with his pants off. That invited being caught. *Why, once more?*

The first day of trial finished with a flurry of local police officers—whose time on the witness stand averaged five to ten minutes apiece—testifying. Each testified to his part at the crime scene. An anonymous call had been made to the police at 9:57 P.M. saying something "bad" was going on at the Kentner home. Police had driven there, seen the body in the window, seen blood, seen the state of undress, and so entered the home without a search warrant.

No motions to suppress had been filed. I theorized that Lee had filed none because an unconstitutional entry wasn't a part of his defense. His defense was that his client had no involvement in the murder. He wanted this part of the trial starring the death of Fiala Kentner, the torture, the lower-body nudity, and the wounds quickly done.

The killing seemed stupidly brutal, done for a bit of money and some items of personal property.

Lee spent most of the long day saying over and over: "No questions." He did, however, gently elicit testimony from the police that Shirley had immediately told them they should look for their Mexican handyman, supposedly gone on vacation. She also had appeared, according to several officers, "upset."

I thought my theory on such defense was correct. Lee's lack of early combativeness was cost-effective. Why suppress evidence that was provable in other ways? Later Lee would have things to question and dispute, but not now. So far, in this stage of the trial, Lee appeared to be easy, bloodless, and waiting, but I'd seen him in legal arguments before the trial began and he was not that way. He was mean.

I followed Judge Daggert to his chambers upon our afternoon adjournment.

He peeled away the robe and stretched. "Long day. I'm tired. I think that earlier I invited myself to dinner. I'll take a raincheck if you want. One small beer and a TV dinner should do it for me tonight."

I had many questions. "No. I'd like to take you, if you'll go. I have trial questions. You pick the place. And I can drive if you'd like."

He brightened. "You can drive, but we'll want to use my car. I've seen yours and I wish you luck with it." He smiled.

"It was my father's car. It runs good."

"Oh?"

"My inheritance," I said, smiling only a little.

"I talked once to your father. He tried to sell me a Cadillac. He knew the car business."

"Thank you. Whoever ran him down did it in the river parking lot near Braxton's late one night a few months before the Kentner murder. Then the driver backed up over him to make sure he was dead. The car that hit him may have been a Ford product."

"Yes." He waited politely to see if I would say anything else, but I didn't.

"I've got this special eating place for us," he said, breaking the silence. "I think you'll like it. The food is inexpensive but good. And, on the way, I want to show you something you may need to see."

"What would that be?"

"I'll show you," he said, smiling.

"Okay. I got my first county check today. Thanks again for the job."

"The job may not last a year."

"You told me that before. I've heard that the prosecutor is running for your job. Thanks anyway."

He smiled some more. "What questions are bothering you?"

"There are things about the murder I don't understand. For me to look into it, I need some direction."

"I'm glad you're curious. I want you to be. Let's move out of here before the phone rings. Ask your questions on the road."

I walked along with Daggert. He was dressed in a fine wool suit. I thought about either a new suit or new slacks and a sport coat for myself after I cashed my county check. Shopping time.

We took the elevator down to the basement and exited into the parking lot. Henry Lee was unlocking the door of a shiny black Cadillac two cars away. He waved without much enthusiasm.

"I think Henry wears out after long days in trial," Daggert whispered. "Don't we all. Getting old."

Lee left the door of his car and walked to us.

"You're breaking your new P.O. in by having him watch my murder case," he said.

"Yes."

"Would it be agreeable with you to have him interview my client *before* the trial is over?"

Daggert hesitated a moment, perhaps because of the emphasis on the word "before," and then turned to me. "Would you want to do that, Jim?"

"Sure. If you told me to do it." I'd never heard of doing pre-sentence work *before* a guilty verdict, but if the trial judge ordered it, then I guessed it was proper.

"Do you find this case interesting, Mr. Singer?" Lee asked.

"It's the first murder trial I've seen. So far the prosecution has been in charge."

"That's how the system works. I eventually will get my evidence in. When could you talk to my client in jail?" He smiled without humor. "She has lots of time on her hands, and I know she'd like to talk to you."

"Whenever you'd like. Do you want to be present?"

"Not necessarily."

I was surprised. In all interviews I'd read in the files, the defense attorney was always present. I said: "In that case, I could do it either at the jail or at the courthouse."

"Fine. We'll wait until the state rests. Then, before we begin our defense evidence, you can interview Shirley at the jail."

I nodded.

He turned away and returned to his car. Once inside he gave us a jaunty wave and drove away.

I thought he also winked at Judge Daggert, but I wasn't sure.

We got into the judge's almost new Lincoln town car. It was huge. There was room enough for a table of bridge in the backseat. Daggert handed me his keys. I smelled his breath, and it was sour. I decided he might have been tippling at break times.

Each break, he'd retreated into his office and closed the door. When the break was over, the court reporter or transcript clerk would tap softly, and he'd emerge and retake the bench.

Time enough for an unwitnessed nip.

I followed Daggert's terse directions. We picked up the state highway, and then, at the far edge of town, Daggert directed me to take a side road. Soon, on my right, there was a large, blue lake. The water rippled in the cold, winter breeze.

I'd seen the lake before, but had never used it. I hated the sun. I had been to parties at a home near the lake. Silver's mother, and Silver, in winters, lived there in a small house.

It was named Lake Keel. We drove past a closed municipal public beach and into an area of fine homes. A brisk wind bent pines and whitecapped the water. A few winter birds scavenged lawns.

"The Kentners lived on this lake," Daggert explained. "I

thought you should see the home. Like other things in the trial, you may need to know more about the house they owned together."

I drove slowly. Some of the houses were huge, particularly those built on the lake side of the road. We drove past a small house I'd visited before: Silver's mother's home. It was a brick cottage, comfortable but not imposing, and far away from the water. Five blocks after passing Silver's home, we came to a house that was particularly fine.

"Pull over to the side of the road," Daggert ordered.

I did.

"The agreed story is that the Kentners hired this man Garcia to be a gardener and handyman. That was in the summer before Fiala was killed. When summer ended, he stayed on as a sometimes company employee and a sometimes chauffeur, despite the fact that he had no driver's license. He lived in an apartment above the garage. He's a striking young man. In the courtroom he appeared to have intelligence and some education, but I know nothing definite about that. He refused to supply your predecessor with any useful information. He would admit only to leaving Mexico and eventually winding up here. I know nothing about any family. That was another area in which he refused the probation officer's questions. He and Shirley became lovers. The length of time of the affair is disputed. Fiala soon found out about the affair. After he knew, he kept Garcia on, paying him minimal wages." Daggert smiled. "Fiala loved bargains."

"Was Garcia the man next to Kentner, the one wearing shorts in one of today's photographs?"

"Yes."

"Sometime, if it's permissible, I'd like to look through all the photo exhibits."

He nodded. "All right. Maybe it would be good to wait until the close of the state's evidence. Some will go in and others won't be admitted, but that shouldn't bother you. I'll remember and stick all of them on your desk one morning soon." He seemed not to think that my request was out of the ordinary. "What interests you in them?"

"I spent a lot of time in Mexico and I'm hooked on the trial." I shook my head, not sure of my own motives. "I didn't know I could start a pre-sentence while the trial was still in progress."

"Why not? The defendant's lawyer agrees and the court consents."

"How about the prosecutor?"

Daggert shrugged. "The prosecutor can grow his own beans. Lynn Corner has no trial rights we're violating. He's in court to win and that's what he's trying to do. He has a theory of this case and he is presenting that theory relentlessly. He doesn't want the trial to be fair. Have you heard something that makes you question my wisdom in allowing you to talk early to the defendant?"

"No sir." *But wasn't it a favor to the defense?*

"There are all these frigging rumors floating around." He looked out his car window and nodded at the big house. "The most prevalent one is that I favor the defense. I don't, but I do think that this defendant, any defendant, deserves a fair trial, particularly where guilt is hotly contested."

"Is there really a rumor that you favor the defense?"

He smiled. "Yes." He looked out the window. "But nevertheless I'll conduct this case as I see fit."

The house before us was enormous. There was a three-story mid-section plus two-story wings on each side. I figured a dozen or more large rooms. The house was mainly stone, with some wood and some brick. It rambled pleasantly over the middle part of a large lot that had undoubtedly, in itself, cost many dollars because of the waterfront location.

A woman came to the front picture window of the Kentner home and stared out of it at us. If Daggert saw her, he gave no indication. I could see the watcher clearly. She was heavily handsome, perhaps in her mid to late twenties, and dressed in green. Behind her, by the light of the setting sun and interior lights, I could see a dark fireplace.

With the picture window curtain open it was easy to see how someone driving past would immediately have noticed the body of Fiala Kentner.

"I'd like to ask about a piece of testimony that bothered me today: Why did Garcia leave the drapes open the night of the murder?''

"I don't know. They were open. The prosecution's theory is that it was a signal made to Shirley Kentner, showing that the agreed job was done. She arrives home from the bridge party and can see through her car window that Fiala is dead. She'd not need to enter the house to raise an alarm. That way she could avoid suspicion. And it was known that Garcia had left on vacation that morning.''

"I see.''

"As it worked out, there was an anonymous call before Mrs. Kentner got home. The police think that a neighbor or passerby saw Fiala laid out over his chair, pants off, privates in view, possibly drunk. The caller was worried or scandalized or both. So there was a call.''

"Male or female?''

"The police say the voice was muffled and sex was undetermined.'' He nodded to himself. "The neighbors would all know Fiala drank. But no neighbor came forward after the fact and admitted making the call. So we have a mysterious call. Lake Keel was annexed into the city for tax purposes, so the call was taken by the city police. Because of the call a police car was dispatched to the house. Then the circus began.''

"You knew Fiala Kentner?''

"We used to play golf together. We drank some and partied some before he became ill. We were friends.''

"And so, very swiftly, they caught your friend Fiala's murderer?''

"Yes. He fled in one of the Kentner cars, a Mercury. They caught him late the following afternoon in Tennessee, maybe two or three hundred miles south and west of here.''

"This was on a weekday,'' I said, remembering.

"Fiala was killed on a Monday night. Garcia was arrested late Tuesday afternoon south of Nashville. In the stolen car he had money, Fiala's rings, and his Rolex.''

"He moved along slowly for a man on the run.''

Daggert nodded. "Yes.''

"Anything else reported missing?"

"Nothing reported. Once again, there are many rumors that you may hear if you listen for them," he said.

"What sort of rumors?"

"Diamonds, coins, antique jewelry."

"I see. I keep wondering why did both sides, prosecution and defense, leave you as the judge?"

"Change was a choice available to the attorneys. In early hearings I made a record saying that I knew Kentner well and had met his wife. I also know many other people in this county well. No motion was filed for a change of venue. So I remain trial judge." He looked out once more at the house. "I'd have granted a change motion. Judges are supposed to avoid the appearance of impropriety. The commonwealth's attorney left me as judge. Now he passes on his scurrilous rumors. Henry Lee's delighted."

"Why would he be delighted when your friend Fiala Kentner was the man who was murdered?"

"Henry knows Corner's running against me—if I run."

"Will you run?"

"Maybe. I'll not decide until this trial's completed."

"How well do you know the defendant?"

"I knew Fiala well. Shirley was his new wife. So I knew her. Fiala was protective of her, even with an old friend like me." Daggert smiled.

I looked once more at the picture window. The woman in green had vanished, but I had the feeling she was watching us from a more concealed vantage point.

"There was a woman inside looking out at us. I don't think she liked us stopping to look."

Daggert smiled.

"Sure is odd about the open drapes," I said.

He shrugged. "When I heard the evidence in Garcia's guilty plea, there was mention then that the drapes were wide open, but no explanation, and no questions asked by the prosecutor." He nodded. "I predict Henry Lee will ask questions about those curiously open drapes."

"The house must have cost a bundle," I said. "It's lovely."

"Fiala built it for Shirley the year they married. Gossip sets its cost close to a million. A honeymoon bower for two, with fifteen rooms and five baths. It's titled in their names jointly on the deed. There's also big money in the estate. If Shirley's convicted, she loses her inheritance rights. That way four to five million and the house would be split between Fiala's two children instead of Shirley getting the house and a million and a half and the kids splitting the remaining three million."

"A lot of money."

He nodded. "Lots, for this town. The prosecution theorizes that Shirley wanted her share early. She made a deal with Garcia, and he killed Fiala. When things died down, the prosecution claims, she was going to head for Mexico. Many people in town believe that."

"Do you believe it?"

"It's not whether I believe it. It's whether a jury believes it."

"Not always. Judges can direct verdicts."

He shrugged. "I know. Watch the trial. Look around. Exercise your curiosity. Tell me what you find. Wait and see."

"What's her story?"

"Henry Lee says, speaking for her, that it wasn't that way. After her arrest she admitted to a quickie affair with Garcia. She said he mesmerized her and half-raped her. When Henry got into the picture, she quit answering questions about that because, I suspect, Henry told her not to answer them. When she was admitting the affair, she said it lasted a few weeks four or five months before Fiala was killed. Fiala's son got wise. There was a blowup and both Shirley and Jose promised it would stop. She claims it did stop. Fiala was apparently so convinced and also so parsimonious he kept Garcia on. It's said he liked Jose. That became a fatal mistake."

I smiled, thinking on that. "The boyfriend stays, the three of them live cozily together in and around Fiala's big house, boyfriend supposedly plots with wife and does in Fiala. He then gets quickly caught and confesses, implicating Shirley. Sounds more soap opera than fact."

He smiled. "And the woman is so lovely."

"Yes. The kind of woman men dream about."

"It may have been the prosecution's way," Daggert said. "There's a mass of circumstantial evidence and they have the testimony of Garcia. His plea of guilty before me was partly in English, partly in Spanish. The Spanish was translated by Detective Owens, who claims fluency in the language." He looked at me. "You said you were a French major at Grimsley. I assume you also are proficient in Spanish?"

I nodded.

"How proficient?"

"In my job for the federal government, I was in and out of Mexico for about three years. I passed as Mexican."

"I thought it was that way. That's good."

I couldn't read his expression. "Why?"

He ignored my question with one of his own. "What are you doing in my town, Jim? What brought you and keeps you?"

"My father died here. I didn't come here wholly because of that, but now that I'm here I hope to keep after the police to find out why and how he died, even if I have to do some of the investigating myself. And I needed a place to begin practice."

"All right. Is it all right I happen to think there's more than that?"

"There is more. I went to Grimsley. I played soccer and got through by taking a language major that was easy for me. I dated pretty coeds who didn't ask that I call for them at the back door of the dorm or sorority house. I drank beer, partied, and loved the town. We called it 'Grim City.' I hear campus kids and some townfolk still do. Later, when I was in law school in Lexington, my father moved here. I'd spend weekends with him. He wanted me to come stay with him. Then he got killed before I was scheduled to move. I wanted a place I knew. I looked around some. My grades weren't high enough for anyone to recruit me to work in a big-city firm. So there wasn't anyplace better to go. Besides, I knew Silver. He encouraged me to come. But I came also because of the way my father died."

"Was your father a native of Grimsley County?"

"Of Grimsley, no. Of Kentucky, yes. He was born near

Hazard. He moved around, an itinerant car salesman. He was in Louisville before he came here."

"Did he live here when you were in undergraduate school?"

"No. During my undergraduate time he was in Memphis selling cars. He always moved around a lot. He was a salesman, mostly cars. He drank some and lived by himself. When I was in law school, I remember he kept getting picked up for public intoxication. I'd dig him out and raise hell. He'd smile at me and promise to do better. He never did until right at the end. The last couple of times I saw him, he was cold sober, smiling, and happy. When I commented on it, he told me it was a surprise to him also." I shook my head. "He loved my mother. She died thirty-plus years ago. He never remarried. I think now that a lot of him died when she died."

Daggert nodded. "I knew who he was mostly from his trying to sell me a car. I told you I only met him once, but I saw him around more times than that, always by himself. He worked for Silver's family agency then."

"Yes. He was a loner. Maybe I inherited that from him."

"Did he desert you when your mother died?"

I nodded my head. "Yes. I spent a lot of boy time wondering why he'd left me behind in south Texas. I never understood it then. My present theory is what I just told you. My mother was the only person Pop ever really loved. When he lost her, he only half-existed for the rest of his time. So he wandered around, waiting for things to be over, drinking, moving on. At the end of his life, when we got a little back together, it confused him." I smiled, remembering. "When he got sober right at the end of his life, it confused me. I'd come to visit for a day and he'd be more happy than I'd ever seen him. He wouldn't tell me why. Then he got killed."

"I see."

I looked once more at the murder house. I thought I saw the woman in green again. She stood in shadows near the dark, cold fireplace.

I turned the ignition key and pushed a button that rolled down the driver's side window. I could smell the cold lake, wood smoke from fireplaces, and dead leaves. I shivered and my bad eye flickered. Sight vanished in it and then reappeared.

I blinked. I had good peripheral vision out of my left eye, but doctors said the macula, that area of best sight, would never recover. There was much flashing, and I'd been warned flashing could portend more problems.

I closed the window.

I was still a watcher, interested in what happened around me. And I thought that now there could be other watchers, watchers who watched me.

Ballinger. He was a man ungiven to jokes. He'd not liked a few I'd pulled, for I had once been a merry person. But he wanted me back.

What the hell for?

"Drive on," Daggert said, interrupting my self-inflicted paranoia. "I've heard the name of Grim City before. It fits our pretty town."

CHAPTER FIVE

Ballinger once told me, not in jest, that man knew cruelty before kindness. He added that cruelty was still the more useful trait. He told me that in the lean months before I went to work for Daggert, using one of his patented late-night calls to attempt to lure me back.

"I really need you, Carlos."

"No way. You've got a hundred like me."

"No. I've a few adequate people, but you were my best. You don't think like the rest. You do perfect imitations of what you see around you. Once, in Mexico City, you were waiting for dark before you came in, and I could see you outside. You never looked up at our building. You sat at a fountain and took your sandals off and washed your feet. Perfect cover."

"But I was caught."

"Someone gave you away. The man who did it is dead."

"I might believe you if you told me his name."

But he would not tell me.

THE RESTAURANT-BAR we drove to was in a village named Dumont. It was at the far southern edge of Grimsley County in hill country where the land rose far above the river. The winter rains and snows had washed away the "metal" from the gravel and broken-asphalt road. I drove Daggert's big car carefully because the road was slick in spots.

Dumont was a hamlet of perhaps a hundred people. I remembered it from undergraduate nights. I'd taken girls to the Dumont restaurant on a few occasions before sorority dances and proms. It seemed long ago.

The restaurant was in the center of town. A lighted sign jutted from the building announcing FOOD. The windows were bright beacons. We parked by the side of the building in a rutted lot. My bad eye picked up confused shadows that my good eye ignored. Dominance of the good eye was uncertain in the dark.

Inside, the front of the restaurant wasn't crowded, but there were a few patrons. There was a long bar with four customers watching non-Kentucky basketball on television. The bartender waved to Judge Daggert.

Old acquaintances?

I'm not a heavy drinker, perhaps because of my father, and I hold problem drinking against people. I watch people for clues that indicate difficulties with alcohol. Although I admired Daggert, I knew he suffered from the alcohol malady.

Daggert nodded back to the bartender. "This is where I sometimes saw your father, Jim. He was at the bar when I was at the bar."

I eyed the bar. Daggert led me on.

The interior smelled of good cooking. I was still hungry for rich food, for meats other than hamburgers and cold cuts, for fish and shrimp cooked or dipped in tangy sauces, and for bowls of vegetables. I'd had enough canned ham and sliced bologna and deli foods to last me for the rest of my life.

At one side of the long bar, down a hall, there were private rooms for diners. We were shown to one of them by a sixtyish, bosomy lady who knew the judge well. They exchanged hugs, and she examined me curiously over his shoulder.

"This is my new probation officer," Daggert said. "I'm sure you've heard scandalous things about him at political meetings. His name's Jim Singer."

The woman nodded.

"This is Maude White," Daggert said to me. "She's my longtime friend, and she's also the precinct committee person out in this area of the county."

I gave her a smile. "Nice to meet you."

"And also you," she answered. She gave me a return smile that warmed her face. "Your name was mentioned with heat at a recent central committee meeting. Our county chairman wants to make all job appointments. His henchmen and toadies predictably get mad when he gets mad. It might help you and the judge if you attended party functions. Both Lynn Corner and Fred Gow are try-ing to make a bad, big thing out of your job appointment.''

''All right.''

''Lynn Corner pines to be circuit judge,'' she continued.

''I'd heard some about that.''

She eyed me curiously. ''It ain't no secret, but it also ain't all over yet. Could I ask who told you?''

''Someone who'd maybe not want me to identify him.'' *Silver.*

Her eyes lost sureness in me at the answer, but she carried on: ''You could help out the judge here by going to party functions.''

''I'd like to do that. All I need to know is the when and the where.''

She nodded at me, encouraged, and smiled at Daggert. ''He looks like something off an old coin. Our single ladies and some of the marrieds will try grabbing him.'' She brushed at my disinte-grating suit once or twice and then gave it up. ''You're going to get a call from me the day before our next function. You got your-self a steady woman?''

''No.'' I'd had no woman in a long time.

''That's good.'' She smiled at both of us. ''Bring the judge along with you if you can get him to come.''

''What if I take up with a steady woman in the meantime?'' Daggert asked teasingly.

She shook her head ruefully as she turned away. ''I wish you would.''

A younger woman approached. She handed us menus and smiled us down the hall.

Our table was covered with white linen. The silver was worn. There was a vase of flowers. I touched the flowers lightly and found they were real.

''They have a greenhouse out back of the restaurant,'' Daggert explained.

The waitress took our orders for draft beers. I was surprised when Daggert ordered it, but I doubled the order.

''Do they serve hard stuff?'' I asked.

''Yes,'' he said without looking up from the menu.

I read the menu. It seemed usual enough. Steaks, chops,

chicken, fish. A small sheet clipped to the top of the menu announced the daily specials: meat loaf, baked whitefish, beef stew.

Outside our room window, a north wind blew tiny flakes of snow over the brown Kentucky hills.

"I did something in the office today I've not done before," Daggert said.

I waited.

"I had a couple of shooters during breaks. I thought I had to have them to get me through the day." He looked down at big hands that trembled slightly. "I had me a case of the courtroom jimmies. Nerves." He shook his head. "I intend to try hard not to do any courthouse drinking again."

"Is that why you're drinking beer tonight?"

"Something like that," he admitted. "My drinking habits have gotten beyond control and I need to change them. If I can't change them on my own, when this trial is done I may go to a place I know where I can get straightened out. It'll take my vacation and some of my sick days, but it's both effective and anonymous." He looked down at his hands again. Something he saw in the inspection made him grimace. "I'm not supposed to drink at all."

"Doctor's orders?"

"His advice."

He had to be a veteran of many trials, and yet he was upset with this one.

"Why does this trial bother you?" I asked.

"All trials bother me. Sometimes trials don't find the truth. This one, like a few others I've seen, could be that way." He smiled and looked away, and I thought he was tired of talking about the trial for now, but then he unexpectedly added, "And I'm sorry for the woman."

"Pretty lady," I said, remembering his words.

He nodded.

"The first time I saw her, I had the urge to knock down her deputies, grab her, and run."

"Yes," he said seriously.

"What's good to eat?" I asked, when the silence grew overlong.

"All the daily specials are good. The steaks and fish on the regular menu are better than ordinary, but the dailies are first-class."

"I think I'll maybe double what you order," I said.

He nodded, not caring. His eyes had become somber. "I was a social drinker until Aggie died."

"Your wife?"

"Yes. We had a lot of years together. We were kids when we got married. We wanted children of our own, but she couldn't have them and we didn't want adopted kids. She died suddenly. Some of my local enemies, like the prosecutor, like to say her death was my fault. Be that as it is, I wake up now to an empty bed in an empty house and I can't get myself back to sleep. I get up and drink. Alone. I used to walk miles, no matter what the weather. Now I sit in front of a cold fireplace and have no energy for anything other than fixing drinks and thinking." He sighed. "Maybe we should have adopted kids. There'd be someone left to talk to."

"Annie said you did pretty good for a time."

"Did she say that?" He frowned. "I don't know why. You can't bring back yesterday. All you can do is remember it."

"Would you like to try to walk this weekend? Tomorrow's Friday."

"Maybe."

"I could come past. How about I call Saturday or Sunday. We can walk. We can quit walking when you want to quit."

He gave me a slightly mocking smile. "I didn't hire you to be my goddamn walking companion."

"Sometimes I wonder why you did hire me. I keep hearing federal people have been around the area checking on me. Doesn't that kind of thing bother you?"

He looked away and then back. I tried to read his eyes and wondered whether his answer would be all of it.

"It's said that the federal people ask harmless, friendly questions about you. They aren't investigating you, they're only asking questions. Who are your local friends? Who have you represented in court? Are you okay physically? It's not like you've done anything wrong."

"I haven't. I promise and swear it."

"I believe you. You needed a job. I was short a probation officer. I didn't want to spend time sitting in my office interviewing party hacks and sweet college kids. I knew for certain you weren't owned by the peckerwoods backing Lynn Corner. You were an easy answer for me and I have hopes you'll eventually be a popular choice. I wanted a probation officer with some experience in life. Don't fret about Corner. I can beat his butt if I decide I want to. I don't like him and he hates me. Fiala Kentner was once a friend to both of us. In a party split, Fiala stuck with me. That past history is a local, ongoing, and not-so-secret joke, what with Corner prosecuting this murder and me judging it. Maybe it *is* funny. People do laugh and wonder out loud what will happen. I wonder too." He sighed. "I miss Fiala."

"I still think it's curious that Corner, running against you, let you stay on as judge to try this case."

"Why not?" he answered, agitated. "He knows I'll be fair. I try to be fair even when the people in front of me are my enemies. When the evidence is completed, Corner knows I'll be the one who understands more than the jury. No one owns me, Jim. Corner wants me to be fair and at the same time wants me to make mistakes in this case that will help him beat me. Maybe I will and maybe I won't. Anyway, I saw no reason to get out."

"Yes sir," I said soothingly. "I agree recusing yourself is your choice. Maybe it's just that I don't like Corner and don't want him to be circuit judge."

"Do what Maude asked then."

"I'll sure do that. Corner would fire me his first day in office."

Daggert nodded absently, probably not caring about what would happen to me if he ran and was beaten.

I wasn't affronted. I still didn't think he'd told me all his reasons for hiring me. Maybe he didn't know them himself. So far the job was routine. There were probationers who came to the office to report, and scores of juveniles in major and minor difficulties. There was lots of record keeping. But the job was easy enough other than for the woman and her trial.

Our waitress returned with beer and big glasses of ice water, and we ordered. Daggert took beef stew, so I asked for the same. I sipped at my beer. The food came swiftly and was good. It was served with fresh slices of warm rye bread, slaw, a mound of mashed potatoes, and a side of green beans. Daggert ignored his water and ordered another beer. I put my almost full beer aside and drank water.

He ate most of his dinner and seemed in better spirits.

I paid the moderate bill and left a substantial tip. At the door we both waved good-bye to a watching Maude White.

The bartender added his own wave. I decided I'd come back and talk to him about my father.

Daggert and I shared silence as I drove him home. I parked his car in his garage and handed him the keys.

I thought the chances were good that he'd forget earlier resolutions and go inside his big house and drink the night away. I walked with him to the porch.

"Come in for a drink," he said.

"I guess not. It's late. See you tomorrow," I said.

"There's a thing I meant to tell you about your father," he said softly. "I asked the chief of police about him and about what they had on his death. I was told that he was run over at least twice. Whoever hit him likely then stopped the car, got out, and made sure he was dead."

"How did they figure that?"

"Your father died instantly. Someone turned him face up and pulled out his pockets. The pockets were not bloodstained. If they'd been left inside for a short time, there'd have been blood on some of them. So it was done just after he was killed."

"Thank you for asking."

"Yeah. Sure, partner." He opened his door and entered.

At his porch steps I hesitated and stared for a few moments out into the night, watching, thinking I'd seen something moving. There was nothing. I heard music from inside. The "Warsaw Concerto," I thought.

I walked from his house to the courthouse to pick up my Mustang. The night was cold and quiet. Once, a police car passed me. It slowed and officers attentively looked me over. I waved and they resumed normal speed, perhaps recognizing me. Pedestrians, as Ray Bradbury once tellingly wrote, are suspect in these years of the auto, particularly after dark.

I wondered if anyone else watched me. I'd lost the fine edge of ability to keep watch around me. If there was someone out there, friend or foe, I'd seen no sign.

Near the courthouse I did see one car that kept going by and then reappearing. It was a nondescript five- or six-year-old Ford. It would pass and then come around again. It could have been several different cars. After I began to watch in earnest, it disappeared.

Someone who really was after me would now know my routine. Why bother to track me when they could lay in wait and know I'd soon be back in my apartment?

The Mustang sat on the courthouse lot. I checked it over to make certain that no one had tampered. I removed a bent twig I'd placed in the windshield well. The habit of placing one there remained with me. I'd been taught it.

When I couldn't find a twig I put tiny rocks on the hood where they'd fall off if someone tampered.

I was alive.

I was home by ten. My efficiency was in a building with forty efficiencies. Most of them were occupied by young marrieds attending Grimsley U. Sometimes, on football and basketball nights, there were parties, but things were mostly quiet.

I watched out my window for a while after I'd turned out the lights. I saw no one out there. But Ballinger was near and I found that confusing.

Why are you screwing with my life again, Ballinger?

I turned on my tiny black-and-white television set and flipped through. On several stations I could watch late-night gibberish. On one station a Louisville lawyer hawked his services. Cowboys and Indians, fractured sex, and mysteries were available. But on this night, I found Streisand doing *Funny Girl*. I listened to her fine trumpet of a voice until the movie was over. I then turned the set off, undressed, and got into bed.

69

My phone rang when I was near the crest of the hill of sleep. I got up and answered it.

"Yes?"

Nothing. I listened hard and thought I could hear someone breathing on the other line.

"Who's there?"

The caller said nothing. The receiver at the other end was hung up.

Someone.

I lay inside my blankets. I put a hand over my bad eye and watched the ceiling. I put a hand over my good eye and saw the edges of the ceiling with a black chasm between.

Quitting my watcher's job had become inevitable even as my health improved. The group hadn't wanted me to do it and had sent doctors to tell me I needed more hospital time, more counseling. I was told that I should (must) reconsider. Medical doctors, psychiatrists, psychologists, and ophthalmologists hired or commissioned by the group had flitted in and out of my hospital room, some of them trying hard and paid to convince me.

I'd left the last of the hospitals against medical advice. I'd walked away and visited "home" in Texas. Things were lost and distant there. My grandfather, old, fat, and alone, sat basking in the sun I now despised. He ate and smiled and talked some in Spanish and some in English, but no longer knew who I was. His words held no meaning. I sensed that those who cooked and cleaned for him did not want me around. They waited for me to leave. Sometime soon the old one would die and there would be an additional room in the old house for more poor family to come up across the Rio Grande. It wasn't that they hated me, but I was alien to them, a mixed-blood love child.

I left Texas. I called now and then still, but those who answered were vague with me. Yes, he lived. No, he knew no one. It was said that I should not come visit, but that I would be expected at the funeral. It was implied that money would be useful.

I went to law school. I used job-saved money for tuition, books, and food. There'd been enough money, what with part-time work, to get me through three years of law school plus the time waiting for the bar examination results. But the money was gone when I'd arrived in Grimsley City.

The group wanted me back. This time Ballinger promised that my job would *mostly* be behind a desk. I now believed that some-place out in the government's world they were working hard and dirty at recruiting me, at pressuring me to return. I was being watched and they were responsible.

Or was there someone else?

I wondered, as I'd wondered at each arrival, if the group was also responsible for my anonymous slashed-eyes letters. It seemed more than possible. *Perhaps to shame me?*

Ballinger had told me that my law degree's only meaning to him was the group could now legitimately pay me more in the job. Lots more. He'd added that this could and would happen even if he personally believed that lawyers were people who couldn't find anything useful to do with their lives.

He'd laughed when saying that. He didn't like lawyers.

Ballinger promised I'd be a senior officer. I'd work behind a desk. I doubted that would be the way of it. I had been good at what I did and they needed me to do similar jobs. Once I signed their contract, I must do what they told me to do. I could do rea-sonably well behind a desk, but I also could move into any Span-ish-speaking city and quickly become part of it. I could be landed on a deserted beach or be parachuted in by airplane. I could live off the land. In an uprising or revolution, I could pass as Mexican. I could watch and report on that changing, dangerous land.

There are many below our border who despise the gringos. There are those who plot and plan and wait patiently and impa-tiently to do us harm. They delight in feeding our drug habits, they gleefully kill and rob our Yanqui tourists when they can, and they watch and wait. Most of what they plan is foolish and will never happen, but not all. I knew the hate because I had seen and heard it. I knew how poisonous it was, how unthinking and ingrained.

Thinking on going back made my eyes nervous. My bad eye was now probably as good as it would ever be. I'd never have more than peripheral vision with it, but if I lost my good one to illness or accident, I'd still have something. I'd not be blind.

I feared blindness. I feared it because I remembered what it was like. I remembered, after weeks of darkness, the day the bandages had come off my eyes and the question of sight was answered in my favor.

The fear of blindness that I owned was so compelling that when I woke up during the night I always found my right hand over my good eye, shielding it from possible hurt.

The idea of going back to the group made me sweat and caused my hands to shake with fear and self-doubt.

Thinking on what I wanted and didn't want also made me realize I didn't want to be in this insular, winter-frozen town being a county probation officer. Actually I was not even probation officer, except officially. I was a judge's lackey, driving his fine Lincoln car, listening to his problems, and delivering him from bar to home because he was lonely, alcoholic, and in political trouble.

I realized I had no stomach for being a functioning part of what seemed to me to be an inevitable process that would send a lovely woman on to prison.

I wondered if she was the judge's girl? *There was some sort of relationship.*

I slid over the edge of darkness and into sleep. With sleep came familiar nightmares. I fled before swarms of angry, shouting men. They chased me and caught me and that part of the dream was true.

By hanging about, being a part of the village background, and becoming useful to them in labor, I'd infiltrated a mountain group in the high peaks near Monterrey. In six months I was a trusted member. The group was hard-edged and dreamed and talked great plans of Yanqui destruction and death. It had automatic weapons and plastic explosives. It had maps showing savings banks in Laredo and Eagle Pass. A man from Jordan and a hawkeyed warrior lady from Iraq were on loan from Cuba. When they weren't in bed with each other or seeking out other partners, they planned grandiose efforts against the Yanquis. I bedded the hawkeyed lady with exuberance and she liked it and I did also.

Somehow someone found me out, perhaps when I slipped away to send a message. Ballinger now said I'd been betrayed, but that was no certainty. I never asked my captors exactly how I was discovered, mainly because I hotly kept protesting my innocence.

I knew only what I'd heard from friends and acquaintances. Yes, I knew Mexico City, and yes, I had worked there. Yes, I called relatives and friends there. Yes I knew Yanquis and yes I had done work for them, unskilled work, and so I could speak the language some.

But I was innocent.

For a time my captors kept me, thinking I might be of informational value. But drugs and small tortures could not dredge up much more than I willingly gave them. They then printed up a ransom demand and sent it to the embassy in Mexico City. It was, of course, treated in the usual fashion.

Ignored.

But my associates in Mexico City then knew for certain that I was a prisoner. And they knew generally where I was.

I argued with my captors. I confused them. I was, in turn, angry, logical, and pleading. My hawkeyed lady listened and shook her head.

She told me stories of a leader I'd never met. One summer day soon, he would come see and examine me and make my final life/death decision. She said he came "almost every" summer. He was called "Judge" and he was, to his mountain followers, a supreme being who knew all things. It was said he intuitively knew good from evil and that he could tell Yanqui spies by their very smell.

She said his word was good and never broken. Some detractors smiled and whispered to me that he was Yanqui or English himself, but others claimed he was the coming of a cruel Aztec god who, in old times, had snatched out the living, bloody hearts of those who offended.

When he made his ruling, that ruling would be the law.

At times those who guarded me were old acquaintances who thought I was still their friend and who believed the others who ordered me held captive were stupids.

We waited for the Judge to come. I waited for rescuers, but no one came.

I escaped the camp.

They were quicker in their mountains than I was after my months of forced inaction. This time more were sure. I still protested. "Would you not run if you thought that crazy people were about to take your life on a fool's whim?"

They tried stronger tortures and more powerful drugs, taking what they could from me. It was not much. There was a telephone clear number that changed after each call. I was only a reporter, a watcher. Some deep, hypnotic instructions the group had done took over inside when I was rendered unconscious. I could see my captors were confused, but confusion didn't mean I was innocent.

I heard them whisper around me in the nights. Some counseled swift death. Others wanted more. That second group, some of whom had been my friends until I ran, won. The hawkeyed lady avoided my eyes and stopped touching my body when she visited.

For long, hideous weeks, I spent days and nights with parts of me hooked to things electrical. Somewhere during that bad time I lost ability and became impotent. My doctors after rescue insisted function would return in time, but it never had.

I was beaten with clubs and "executed" with unloaded guns. We played cruel night games where I was always "it."

The Judge came. I never saw him, but I did hear his distant voice speaking Spanish far away in the night, the last night I lay in the prison hut with rats and insects feasting on me. In reality or in dream, I heard him speak my sentence.

He ordered that I be fastened to rocks very high up in the mountains. I was left there exposed, to die where I could be seen and have my hours and days of dying observed by others who might consider future treacheries.

The Judge was the *law*. Once I had been sentenced, that sentence would not change. The lady I'd once joyfully bedded had told me that.

I was cleverly and securely tied. I was stripped nude and laid flat out to the sun. Each night, at first, I was untied and returned to the village and questions were again asked, the electrical things again applied. During the days my head was tied so that I could not escape the sun's rays when it was high above me. But I could, until the thirst came, look away. And instinctively, even when I was semi-conscious, my eyes avoided that blazing sun.

The hot rays seared my skin despite the fact that I was of dark complexion. Soon I could see nothing and no tears would come when I willed them.

The first day, they taped both of my eyes wide open, pulling the skin around them away. That tape was never removed. I could not thereafter close my eyes. Early on, there was a rain of tears that dried quickly in the sun. Then the tear ducts went dry.

Water, water, water.

I was left exposed on the mountain for what seemed many eternities before I was rescued. I remembered a lot of the first few days and nights, nothing thereafter.

I found out in the first days that I could turn my head a fraction and so escape more of the fierce sun in my right eye than my left. And I could also look away from most of the sun until I grew unaware. I then lost my ability to control where my eyes focused, but instincts of survival remained.

After I was rescued, a jovial group doctor told me early that I could still see light and shadow out of that right eye upon their first exam, and that that was ''encouraging.'' One more day in the brutal sun, he thought, would have ended all chance of sight. Therefore I was ''lucky.''

The nightmares and I were now old acquaintances. I'd endured them before. In the nightmares I was always stone blind and searched for a way to see. If I could not see, I could not fight. I wanted death. People savaged me. A hawkeyed woman whispered softly about fires larger than Hiroshima, about invented diseases deadlier than AIDS. They would deliver those things to us goddamned Yanquis soon.

The dream Judge laughed again at me, told me that his given judgment, never to change, was that I must die. He whispered stories in English and Spanish about new ways for me to find blindness, impotency, and death.

Next time.

75

I awoke and was cold. I'd kicked away the blankets. I shivered and pulled them back around me. After a time, sleep returned. This time, mercifully, I dreamed of a blond woman, sweet and lovely, a woman for all the years.

When morning came I had my usual spartan breakfast. It was Friday. TGIF.

I knew that law school and a year in practice had softened me. Once, long ago, I'd been in shape. I could run all day then. I could live off a desert land. Now I was over thirty and old.

I would walk to the office. That would help.

The morning outside tried to change my mind. It was crackling cold. The sun hid behind black clouds. Pelting sleet rattled roofs and struck me with small, sharp blows as I walked.

The day smelled of winter. The cold attacked my nasal passages, making them feel as if they would freeze shut. The cold also made my eyes, both of them, sting and water. I smelled the big Ohio River north of me as I walked through icy streets. I tried to stay under overhanging roofs. A few cars passed me, moving slowly, tires spinning on the ice. When I got downtown, merchants in their windows nodded and waved to me.

I doubted anyone was following or watching me on *this* day.

Nevertheless I felt them out there. Someone . . .

My "practice" still consisted mostly of collections and bankruptcies, but a few things had come in. I was working on a minor's claim from an auto accident. I was writing a contract to sell real estate, plus two wills for an aging husband and wife. I still did my own typing, because I couldn't afford a part-time secretary. I'd been asked to represent several divorce seekers, but had refused. I could ethically take divorce cases, but it would require a special judge to hear them. So before I did take them, I wanted to talk to Daggert. I'd decided to wait until after the ongoing trial was completed to do that.

Without my probation officer's job, I'd still have a difficult time eating regularly.

It became a triumph to arrive unfallen at the courthouse. I

managed it, slipping and sliding, but upright. Inside the front door, it was warm and dry. Inside I could look back out windows and see the accumulation of ice I'd journeyed through. I believed that the weather would interfere with the ongoing jury trial, but I wasn't positive.

I rode the creaking elevator up to the circuit court floor.

CHAPTER SIX

Each courthouse is a separate country. Many people scheme for control. Control changes (or remains the same) each election.

IN MY OFFICE, Bailiff Horace Donaho waited for me. He was a vinegary old man pushing carefully along and nearing eighty. He drove a newish Buick that always seemed to have just been washed. He was originally from Italy. His skin was dark, but not as dark as mine. He had a tiny, simian face, was small of body, and slept a lot. If Daggert noticed his sleeping, he seemed not to mind, and Donaho, to his credit, was a silent sleeper. He dressed in dark grey, blue, and brown suits and wore soft shoes which were highly polished. He blended into the background of the courthouse and was always listening.

I'd been told that he and the judge were close political and personal friends by several courthouse workers who disliked and feared him.

"Don't trust him," they whispered. I thought that some of those who told me that were also telling others not to trust me.

Horace believed he was my work superior even though I was paid more money than he was and worked half days while he worked (or slept) full time. He enjoyed issuing orders to me like, "Clean up your desk before you leave," and "Don't stack your shit on the floor." He also tried, now and then, to enlist my aid in moving books about in the law library, projects that usually failed to come to fruition. A few times we'd moved minor sets of books and I had thought mischievously about returning later and moving them back, but I'd not done it. I'd thought such conduct might confuse him even more than he was now confused.

He was a small, sour man who'd lost open rage at the world around him and now watched most things with silent hate.

I put up with him. Confrontations are always available. The world teems with opportunities for them. Getting along with others isn't easy. I smiled at him and was continually civil. I did one thing he didn't like. I called him "Horace" rather than "Mr. Donaho." It appeared to be acceptable, though it wasn't agreeable to him. He'd sometimes give me a hard look, but he'd answer.

On this frigid morning he was wide awake and visibly upset. He breathed hard and his color was bad.

"What's happening, Horace?"

"Someone entered your damned office last night. Maybe they got in other offices too." His voice quivered. "Was you the last out yesterday?"

"I don't know."

"I think maybe you was." He smiled a superior, indicting smile. "But I ain't dead sure, so I ain't pointing no accusing finger dead at you."

"That's decent of you." I waited, knowing there had to be more.

"We bad needs for you to tell the judge about someone getting inside."

"Did this someone break in or enter because a door was left unlocked?"

"Yours was the door that was left unlocked. That's what I'm telling you."

I refused to take offense. I looked around my small office. There was nothing worth stealing. Copies of most of what I did daily were in the clerk's office in the full files there. Everything official I did typewise was in triplicate or more, usually one copy to my file, one to a master file in the clerk's office, and one to Judge Daggert.

"Did they take anything?"

"I don't know. You best look. And then you maybe better look some more, hard, both here and in the other offices. How many damned exhibits has old shit-in-the-face, the persecutor, introduced so far?"

I thought for a moment. "Thirty-two have been marked, if my

memory's right. Only a few of those, maybe seven or eight, have been introduced and are in evidence. None of the photographs are admitted into evidence yet.''

"What's it look like to you here in your office? Anything missing?''

I looked around. My desk was clean, but I'd cleaned it off yesterday before leaving. I opened my center drawer. It seemed neat. I opened other doors. Nothing appeared to be out of place.

"Everything looks okay.''

"Your door was wide open and flapping in the morning breeze when I got here early. So you better check good and also check them exhibits in the judge's chambers, if they're still in there.'' He nodded. "You count them. It ain't my job to do no damn legal stuff. I figure that job has to be yours. You're the lawyer.''

I hung my old coat on a hook. I put my gloves in the pocket, stuffing them tight, making sure they'd not fall through.

"Maybe them exhibits is what they was after,'' Horace said darkly. He nodded at his reflection in the window. "There's more to this murder case than meets the eye, young Jim Singer.'' He had become calmer, having shared his bad news.

"Sit yourself down, Horace,'' I said, interested. "Tell me what you know about the case. I need to get filled in by someone who knows more than I do. My bet is that's you.'' I motioned him to the chair across from me and sat down behind my desk.

He sat and smiled a little, liking what I'd said. "Money,'' he said. "Bushels of money. Lots of dollars for Grimsley County, where most folks are poor as evicted church mice. Them kids of Fiala's, particularly the son, have just got to get his wife convicted of murder.''

"For the money?'' I asked.

"Yep. Unconvicted, Mrs. K. gets a lot of Fiala's dollars, plus the big, new homeplace. If she gets convicted, then the kids get it all. That's what they want. Not that I was all in favor of Fiala marrying her, but that don't mean she had him killed. Maybe yes, maybe no on that. You can't trust wetback words.''

I nodded impassively. I figured I was, to Horace, mostly wetback myself, both a foreigner and a countryman of Jose Ramon

Garcia. Therefore I was not to be trusted. Still, I worked for the judge, *his* judge. That meant I was to be watched carefully and reported on. But I also was to be made a part of the office. A knotty problem.

"I knew something was going to happen from the time Fiala whispered to me and the judge he was going to marry that woman," he continued. "If it hadn't been for that greasy Mex dinking her, then there'd have been someone else. I think there was more than the Mex. Hot woman. Looks blond and cool, but she's hot as a heatin' stove on a January day. A bedful of woman."

"How well did you know Fiala and Shirley?"

"I was thick with Fiala. He worked for me for years. Then we was partners for a while. Later, he bought me out. I fished with him. I played cards. I drank some with him back when I was able. Him and the judge got to be political pals because I put them together years ago. I knew Fiala and his kids didn't get along good and I knew why. They wanted to take over the business I sold him fifteen years ago."

"It was your business before it was his?"

"Sure. Jukeboxes and them computer-game machines. Good to own around this pee-dad town, what with university kids wasting money and time on foolishness instead of on learnin'. I sold out to Fiala when it wasn't much and he built it to big stuff. So I said, 'More power to him.' I wasn't jealous." He smiled his monkey's smile. "Not much, anyway. He was good with machines. Magic hands. All I ever knew was how to plug them machines in and empty the cashboxes."

"And so Fiala made lots of money?"

"Sure. But only after he worked hard and built it up. When he got sick, his kids wanted that money, all of it. The son gambles and the daughter, she just wants it all because she wants it all. They turned green as May tomatoes when Fiala married Shirley after promising them he'd not marry her."

"Did he promise that?"

"You bet. He promised but I guess he never meant it. One day he upped and married Shirley. I knew about her, but I didn't know her personal. He'd been after her for a while. Maybe he did it partly to fix his two kids." He shook his head. "But she sure is one pretty lady." His eyes dreamed impossible dreams.

"You said there might have been other men for Shirley?"

"Sure, other men," he said reluctantly. "Maybe more than a few. There were stories about her before and after she married."

"What stories?"

"There are men who chase in every town. You'd hear her name linked to them in gossip."

"What men?"

His eyes closed a little. "I ain't sure. I won't mention any names."

"All right. What else do you know you *can* tell?"

He leaned toward me and lowered his voice. "No one's saying anything, but there's a wad of money and other stuff missing."

"How much money?" I remembered the judge had said there were rumors of missing estate assets.

"The business I sold is a funny business. Let's say you put your machines in some restaurant or bar and there's five hundred dollars in the cashboxes after a week. So you and the owner of the spot wink at each other. You declare you took in a total of three hundred dollars and you split the leftover money and don't report it."

It didn't sound like a lot, but I nodded. "A hundred each, untaxed."

"Times a hundred spots now, some taking in more money, some less." He smiled while he calculated. "Could easy be five or ten thousand a week."

"Was Fiala doing that?"

"He was if the Pope's a Catholic." He crossed himself. "He never let anyone watch when he collected. He did all that alone. At some places I'm sure he'd report every quarter in the cashbox. But if the owner wanted to skim, then Fiala would oblige. I taught him about that when I first took him out on the route. And I taught him to sell the quarters from the cashboxes to the spot owners so that he'd not have to cash in change and make a tax trail for the damned federals."

"Even with paper money in big bills there'd soon be lots to hide."

He nodded. "He used to buy collector stuff. Coins and stamps. Antiques and old watches. A couple of years back he told me he'd stopped that. There were too many big eyes watching. Coin dealers and collectors were turning each other in. He quit going to coin and stamp shows and went instead to flea markets, pawn shops, and estate sales, but he kept what he'd accumulated. At flea markets he could buy with no questions for cash. He did a lot of trading also. Once he showed me a sack of expensive rings, mostly diamond. He said he was going to take the stones out of them and then trade the gold back in on the next batch of jewels. The stones were easy to hide."

"Go on."

"By then he was putting up with federal tax audits, but he was still stealing off the top. He said that once the feds sent a man with him to watch collections, but he fixed that by sneaking out late at night and doing pre-collections. Them tax boys did make him nervous, though."

"How much would he have hidden?"

"It would be big money." He smiled. "The odd thing is that no one but the federals are seriously looking for missing property."

"How about his two kids? Wouldn't they know and be interested?"

"They'd know," he said. "They never got on together until Fiala got killed. Now they're real thick." He smiled. "And *they* do the collecting now. The federals are watching them."

"Does Henry Lee know that Fiala's estate is short?"

"Sure. Lee's no dummy. Shirley would have known and told him."

"What else?"

"Let me think some more on it. I already told all this to the judge. As to Persecutor Corner, a man in his firm, a man who shares his office building, is the attorney for the estate. Fiala swore he was going to make up a new will after the political fallout, but he never got to it. That surprised me. Them two kids *lived* in Corner's law office after Fiala got dead. They wanted Shirley indicted. So Corner's associate, he opens the estate, and the kids got themselves a quick grand jury and prosecutor. The two kids also got appointed co-executors. That's so's they can watch each other.'' Horace showed me a scandalized face. ''Bad, but the Grimsley world knows that Corner would do anything for a buck or a vote and that them two Kentner kids would steal anything not screwed down.''

If Horace was correct, the estate situation could be a problem in greed. It also could be another reason Corner had not rocked the boat by asking for a change of judge. For him to be prosecuting a person charged with murder while a lawyer he was even loosely associated with settled the estate of the deceased seemed a possible ethics violation. But problems in ethics only emerge when someone complains, and then only after a disciplinary committee looks into that complaint. Horace could be exaggerating the connection between Corner and an associated lawyer.

The urge to take the chance might overwhelm lawyers because of the estate fee. But how do you do a fair job of prosecuting a presumed killer when you are, at the same time, gaining monetary advantage from the children of the deceased, who need that presumed killer found guilty? And why would you look hard for missing assets when finding them would confuse the criminal case?

''Anything else?''

He shook his head.

''It was my door you said was open. Could we go out in the hall and you show me exactly what you saw when you got here earlier today?''

He bristled at my suggestion, so I added: ''I mean we need to do it so I can explain exactly what happened to the judge.''

''Okay,'' he agreed, subsiding. ''You follow me.''

He led me into the hall. He showed me how far my private door had been opened. Once inside my office, an intruder would then have access to any other offices if inner connecting doors had also been left unlocked.

Horace had found my door open. I experienced a peculiar feeling about there suddenly being yet another shadowy someone who left things wide open after the fact, just as Fiala's killer had parked him where he could best be seen. Why not just close the door (or draw the shades) upon departure and avoid discovery?

Nothing seemed disturbed. Nevertheless, the intruder could have read the files, except for the daily "working" files. Those files came up each morning from the clerk of the courts when a trial or hearing was ongoing and were returned each night to be locked away.

"How about the custodians? Maybe they were up here cleaning?"

"Custodians don't clean up on this floor when they's a trial in progress," Horace answered scornfully. "One time the head custodian and Daggert got into it hot. The head custodian and his people report to Fred Gow. Daggert thought they were nosing into his things, so he issued an order. No cleanup during trials. No custodians upstairs during trials unless requested by the judge. There was a squabble about it and Daggert ordered the commissioners and the custodians up here. He told them he'd put anyone in jail for contempt who violated his order. What happens now is that I clean up the jury rooms after the jury goes home. I take the trash downstairs, tear it up, and spread it around in the alley containers. Sometimes, if it looks like hot stuff, I take it home and burn it. That way they's no damn nosing."

I thought about it. Someone had or could have come into the court offices. But then that someone had left the door of entry open so that we'd find out. Why?

"You'll tell the judge," Horace ordered.

"Yes. And you say he knows the other stuff you told me?"

"He knows it. Ask him, if you don't believe me." Telling me his message had relaxed and relieved Horace. His eyes were sleepy. He gave me a yawn, turned away, and wandered on. At this time of day he normally slept in an upholstered chair that guarded the jury room entrance. He headed in that direction. I watched him go and thought more about what he'd told me.

When the judge arrived I told him what Horace had discovered.

"Let's look," he said calmly.

We then went over the exhibits with Anne Melville, who knew

more about them than we did. The numbers were correct when we counted numbers against exhibits. Nothing appeared to have been disturbed, except the tapes of the trial were out of order.

"Sometimes I'm not neat," Anne explained.

"Or maybe a reporter got in here and listened to the tapes," the judge said.

Anne smiled at both of us when the counting and checking was completed.

"Sometimes, laddy boys, old Hoss gets up from bed out of sorts with this cruel world. Maybe, to make the morning worse, his wife burns his morning toast or overcooks his Eggbeaters. Hoss then has to figure a way to get even. Sometimes he'll eat a forbidden sweet roll, sometimes he'll use sugar in his coffee instead of sugar substitute. He has galloping diabetes. He likes to shake all us troops up and maybe the open door was his way of doing it for today." She gave me a keen look. "Was anyone with him when he discovered your open door?"

"I don't think so."

"Then maybe there was an open door, maybe not." She smiled up at me. "Jim, you've now been put on notice by Mr. Hoss that you're to make sure your door is closed."

"I'll make certain that's done in the future. But maybe someone did enter, listen to, or view what he or she wanted to hear or see, and then moved on."

"Could be," she answered sweetly.

There was not to be testimony this day. Weather in the county was reported to be even worse than in the city and some jurors lived on farms. The office phone began to ring as jurors called in to report impassible roads, trees and limbs down from icing, and recalcitrant cars.

Anne Melville instructed each juror to try hard to make it to the courtroom. By ten o'clock seven jurors and one alternate had arrived.

The attorneys conferred with Daggert in chambers. The jurors in attendance were admonished, telephone calls to those absent were made, and the matter was continued to Monday.

Horace caught me in the office as I was leaving.

"You told the judge about your door?"

"I told him."

"Well, what did he say?"

"He was upset," I lied. "We then checked and nothing was missing. He was glad you'd discovered the open door."

"You think maybe he'll post a guard? He could order someone over from Sheriff Riggs' office to check over the weekend." He smiled, liking the idea of causing Sheriff Runner Riggs personnel problems. I'd heard he hated Riggs.

"I guess he could."

"Maybe you should suggest it," he said, smiling some more. "He seen you was pulling out and he sent me to tell you he'd like to talk to you before you took off."

"Thanks."

Simon Daggert smiled from behind his desk. His wide face had better color and his eyes were brighter than they'd been the day before. I noticed that his hands were steady.

"You said you'd like to get some walking exercise this week-end?" he asked.

"Not if weather stays like this."

"It's supposed to warm up overnight and be in the high forties tomorrow. No wind, no snow, sleet, or rain. Kentucky sunshine, Jim-boy."

"Then I'm your man."

"Afternoon would be the best time. We'll drive out to Lake Keel and walk there. It's a grand place for walking. Would two o'clock tomorrow afternoon suit you?"

"Sure." *Back to the lake for a second time.*

He turned slightly away from me and looked out his window. Outside, Grimsley City still suffered from the aftershock of icy weather. The streets appeared deserted. I remembered that in my four years in Kentucky I'd learned to hate Januaries. January was a nothing month haunted by the skeletons of bright decorations of

Christmas past, most still mounted on light poles, a few tattered in the gutters, thrown there by Christmas revelers or casual vandals. It was a long, dull month.

Daggert nodded out his window, his eyes not meeting mine. "The weather today gave us a small trial reprise. Next week is forecast to be unseasonably warm. This case could finish then." He shook his head. "Quick for a murder trial."

I waited, somehow knowing there was more.

"I'd like you to do an extra job next week while you watch the trial."

"Of course, Judge."

"I still want you to watch everything, but I'd particularly like your opinion of Garcia when he testifies for the prosecution. Garcia understands English. He both reads and speaks it. In his plea he said a few things in his own language, in Spanish. I got translations that day on what it was he said from Abe Owens, the state police detective, who claims to understand the language. I'm informed by prison authorities that Garcia has been intensively teaching himself English in prison. I'm also informed that Corner and Lee have agreed that Garcia's testimony in this trial will be all in English. What I want you to do is watch Garcia. I want you to listen to this man and give me your opinion on his truth and veracity. If he says anything on or off the record in Spanish, I want your translation. To me this man is a foreigner and a wetback. To you he's more of a known quantity."

"All right," I said hesitantly. My impression could have no legal significance unless Daggert took the case away from the jury by ordering a directed verdict. Was that going to happen?

"How about the other witnesses?"

"Watch all," he said darkly. "Just like I said." He shook his head. "Something's not right."

"What's not right?"

He gave me a sharp look and ignored my question. "I want reports communicated to me privately. I don't want anyone else to know."

"Yes, sir."

"Listen to Garcia. Try to understand him. God knows I

couldn't figure the bastard out when he jumped guilty in court. He told his story and I listened. Afterwards, when I sentenced him, he sat there grinning at me like I was full of all the extra shit in the world. The prosecutor's witnesses know what he said then and will say now, and they'll tailor their stories to fit his. A woman's freedom depends on what the jury thinks of Garcia's story, but her freedom might also depend on what I believe.''

I knew he was again thinking of a directed verdict. The defendant, through her lawyer, would routinely file a request for a directed verdict at the close of state's evidence. Just as routinely such motion would almost always be overruled.

But a judge *could* grant the motion at any time after it was filed, saying there was not enough plausible evidence to convict the defendant. He could then prepare a finding of ''not guilty'' and order the jury to vote. Such a ruling would leave the prosecution only an appeal. Even if an appeal later overturned the judge's decision, such would not affect the appellee defendant, in this case Shirley Kentner. She would walk free.

Daggert would likely lose any future election.

I thought again of Horace. ''Are we going to have a deputy checking the courthouse over the weekend? Horace is worrying himself about it.''

He shook his head. ''Horace wants to screw up the sheriff's office. Go read advance sheets or something. Unless you've got appointments set for this afternoon, then you're off until Monday. But I will see you tomorrow for some educational walking.''

I departed. Once outside the courthouse and inside my private office, I carefully checked things. No one had been prying there or, if someone had, I found no detectable signs of it.

I caught up on mail. Mostly I disposed of the formidable stack by sitting, wastebasket in front of me, dropping opened mail inside. Everyone either wanted to sell me something or get something from me free.

I wrote a few severe collection letters and then had a blue plate special at a downtown lunch counter.

In the early afternoon, with only one late appointment facing me, at three-thirty, I ''found'' a men's store on Main Street after depositing my county check in the bank, taking some back in cash. Inside the store I bought a grey herringbone sport coat and two pairs of navy wool pants. Winter clothes were on sale. I worked my way through the sale racks, continuing to look even after I'd found what I wanted.

Half price.

I eyed a lined, heavy raincoat longingly. I could buy it and eat mostly soup for another month after paying rent, utilities, and gasoline. My old overcoat was doggy, but still serviceable. I still had a mouth set for lots of fresh vegetables and cheeseburgers through the garden. A new coat was not that wanted.

It would be two weeks until next pay and I'd likely run short before that happening. Vegetable soup and crackers again.

I waited and looked around the store while the pants were being cuffed. I paid cash and took my purchases with me. The streets were mostly clear, and the ice was fast melting on the sidewalks. A warm wind blew the skies clearer.

An aging, affable merchant bowed me out his door after having told me how lucky I was to be working for Daggert, who he claimed was a personal friend. In return for his affability I let him extract enough of my history to enhance both store and home gossip.

My afternoon appointment for Friday was with William Cannon. It was my first appointment with him, but I'd read his juvenile and adult records. He was twenty-five years old and a part of the local drug scene. He'd been into it for almost ten years. He'd both bought and sold. Mostly he'd consumed.

The early probationers I'd seen had been wary of me, careful of what they said and asked. They'd waited for my questions, answered them as innocuously as possible, then hurried away. I thought by now the telegraph of the town had taught others reporting what it was best to say and do.

The sun had come out and it shone through my window. I put my clothes packages up on a filing cabinet and waited.

He came five minutes late. Down below my window I saw a tall young man look up at the clock on the courthouse cupola and adjust his watch. I thought it was Cannon, and it was. In a few moments I heard the elevator door open and close, and there was a tap on my door.

"Come in," I called.

He entered. His face was a friendly mask. His ears were small and his features were tiny and childlike. A pretty baby in what was now a man's body. He nodded at me. "You the new P.O.?"

"I'm him. Jim Singer." I rose and shook his limp hand. "Take your coat off and have a chair."

"Yeah." He took his coat off and held it nervously in his lap. He sat across from me, a strong-bodied young man-child who'd had many troubles and likely was destined for more.

"It says, in last month's report, that you thought you might have a job soon. Did you find a job?"

"Still looking. I'm staying with my folks. I'm in by ten, sir. I don't go into bars, pool halls, or anywhere there's trouble. I don't party."

I nodded. I knew from the files about his family. His father was an executive at one of the local factories, a smart, ruthless man according to what William had told Coulson, the previous probation officer. There were two older "perfect" sisters, both now married. There was a mother who drank too much and too often. And there was William. (Willie? Bill?)

He was dressed well, but most probationers dressed well when they came for their monthly visits. He was well-spoken, and that was unusual.

"There's no requirement that you work, but it would likely be good for you."

"Too many people know me around here, sir. No one will hire me. Grimsley U. won't let me back in. I reapplied and got turned down. I'm thinking about going to school somewhere else. If I found somewhere else, maybe another university that would accept me as a student, would you transfer me?"

"What courses would you be taking?"

"Business. I had three semesters of it from before my last troubles. I'm hoping to get into U.K."

"I'm sure we'd approve transfer. You'd probably have to show us something to convince us that you'd been admitted." I looked down again at his record. He'd spent a long time in the Grimsley County jail and been granted a suspended sentence (time served) for dealing marijuana. I noted his jail time had been served during the time that Garcia was in jail.

He was nodding and smiling to himself at my answer. I read hope in his eyes. I remembered pessimistically that Lexington had more than its quota of drugs and druggies.

We watched each other. He smiled at me easily, wanting to get along. I thought that if he was tested for chemicals right now, he'd likely fail the test. His hands were shaky and he had a tic near his right eye. Drugs or drink.

Probation is not a cure. It does nothing but set up a casual watching by authority. I could threaten him, I could advise and recommend. I could check on him at his house or on the streets of Grimsley City. He'd agreed to personal searches when he accepted probation. I could write reports. If he was arrested and charged, I could make the decision, along with the court, as to whether or not probation continued or whether he went back to jail and/or on to prison.

Probationers stole, used drugs, broke into houses, drove drunk, and sometimes killed with only slightly less frequency than before being placed on probation.

"How long were you in jail?" I asked, knowing.

"More than five months. My father could have bonded me out anytime. I guess he and Mother decided not to do it." He shook his head and I could detect faint bitterness. "I get into it bad again I'll get no help from them. Nothing." He smiled gently. "Maybe it was time for me to find that out and do some time."

"Are you using now?"

He shook his head, seemingly shocked. "No, sir."

We both knew he was lying.

"You were in jail with Jose Ramon Garcia. We're trying a case out of that murder now."

92

"I read it in the paper," he said, relaxing a little. "That would be the Shirley Kentner case."

"Yes."

"I don't know anything about her, but that Garcia guy shook me bad. We all walked carefully around him in the jail. For one day and night they had him out in the tank after he pled out, but then they quick put him back in a cell. Some big, older dude in the tank said something to him about owning a cute ass. We thought that maybe he put a move on Garcia's body after lights out. I don't know for sure. All I do know is next morning they put Garcia back in a cell and the big guy crippled around quiet for the rest of his time until they shipped him on to prison." He smiled. "And he never said nothing to anyone else about having a cute butt."

"Did Garcia talk much to you or any of the other prisoners?"

"He talked to all of us when we were together in the tank. He was friendly enough, but we were in one place and he was in a distant, higher one. I listened to what he said, and I didn't ask any questions. He talked about the pigs, about jails, and lots about women. He didn't talk at length, but when he spoke, everyone in the tank listened."

"Did he ever mention Shirley Kentner?"

"No. No specific women. Just about screwing women here and there in various countries. Big puss man." He looked down at his watch, wanting the interview to be done.

"Okay. Come back in a month." I smiled at him. "And next month try to be on time."

"My watch was wrong."

I nodded. "I saw you resetting it."

He smiled at me and told another lie. "I reset it with the court-house clock."

"Sure you did."

He moved on. I waited for a few minutes and then I also moved on.

I went to my apartment and watched television. On the small screen, confident salesmen tried to sell me cars, life insurance, and things that would make me desirable to the opposite sex. Since my time in the sun, my sex life had been nil. The electrical appendages had killed desire. Even when I saw the woman in court, there was only a faint stirring.

She was the only female who'd excited me for a long time. A woman to dream about.

I smiled to myself. She *had* to be innocent.

CHAPTER SEVEN

"Probation officers may be appointed by the courts as necessary. The judge of the court where the probation officer shall serve is the appointing authority. Except as hereinafter provided no more than one probation officer shall be appointed for each circuit court."

ON SATURDAY MORNING, after a combination of television watching, sleep, and nightmares, I awoke to find that Judge Daggert was right about the weather. Overnight warming from south winds had cleaned the ice from the streets. Instead of yesterday's biting wind and teen temperatures, this day was January spring complete with a bright sun and white, fluffy clouds. By two in the afternoon, when I rang Daggert's doorbell, the temperature was in the low fifties. The sun on my Mustang roof had been warm enough to induce me to turn off the heater in my car.

I believed in spring again.

I wore a long-billed cap to keep the sun out of my eyes.

Daggert answered his door wearing a lumberjack shirt under a lined windbreaker. He had on cord pants and walking shoes. If he'd had a drink to bolster him, I saw no sign of it. From the inside of his house I could hear classical music.

"Keel's the best place to walk," he said with enthusiasm. "Lots of folks walk by the lake in the summer, but there won't be many today. Is that okay with you?"

"Fine."

"Give me a moment to turn things off inside."

We drove to the lake in silence. I parked the Mustang in a semi-deserted parking area near the municipal beach. I looked for a tiny stick, but found none, so I satisfied myself by placing tiny pebbles on the hood.

"Why are you doing that?" Daggert asked. "Do you think someone will bother your car?"

"No. It's just an old habit, hard to break."

He nodded. "Once, when there were coal strikes, we had some local bombings, but none since then."

"I was trained to be careful." I looked away and out at the lake. "Sometimes, if we were found out, there'd be no warning anything was wrong."

A few walkers, most of them striding along the shoreline, were hard at it. There were also joggers.

I saw a familiar face. Silver. He ran along the shoreline with several female companions. All of them wore sweats.

They saw us and ran our way.

Daggert nodded.

"Yo," Silver called. "You want to run with us?"

"We're walkers," I answered. The girls with him were handsome, but unknown to me.

"We're part of a pack," Silver said. "The Lake Keel Running, Submarining, and Chowder Club."

All of them were running in place as they talked.

"Run on," Daggert said.

One of the girls smiled at me and I had a sharp feeling of loss. Sometimes, at nights, things still happened, but after failures, I'd not been with a woman for more than four years. I no longer badly missed it. There was no money to spend in the chase, there was no real desire. Only the woman in jail had made me dream.

The runners turned away and ran back to the shore. I watched and saw them join a group of other runners.

"Silver's mother lives out here," Daggert said. "Small house across the road from the lake."

"I've been there."

"It's said around that Silver's why there are so many female runners in the Keel group."

"Sure," I said.

"Unusual man. Very ambitious."

"Yes."

"I notice you don't date?"

"No," I answered shortly.

He let it go.

Across the lake from the parking lot I could see Fiala Kentner's mansion. The back of the house, the side that looked out at the lake, was mostly brick and glass. People pay big money to see oceans and rivers and lakes from their windows.

"We'll walk to Fiala's house and back," Daggert said. That will be about two miles. Okay? Both educational and good exercise." He seemed intent and positive.

"All right."

I let Daggert set the pace. At first he walked swiftly, but then he slowed and I could hear his labored breathing.

"Go easy," I advised. "You've not been getting much exercise. You can't start a walking program by trying to do ten-minute miles. No one can."

He stopped and looked up into the bright sky. He then gazed across the lake.

"Last night I didn't have a single drop. No booze, no beer, no wine. It was my first time to bed dry for a long time. It made for an eternal night." He shook his head wryly. "Lately I've been pouring a couple of shots of vodka into my morning coffee. Then I chew breath mints to cover it up. This morning I only had the mints." He looked up at the sky again. "New leaf. Same sad sinner, but a new, green leaf. I decided it was time to stop mourning for what once was and mooning about what could have been."

"Good for you." I looked him over and knew I was not only grateful to him, but that I also liked him, even if I did not always understand where he was coming from.

He gave me a careful look. "Thank you for believing in that, Jim. I'll re-ask you a previously asked question. Why are you here? Whether you're allowed to say anything about it or not, half the courthouse knows you were some kind of CIA man or something. Some people, local law enforcement officers included, think you took leave and came or were sent here to catch and punish the person or persons who killed your father. That's silly, but others think you came under cover for more than that, that you're here to look into local corruption and maybe tax evasion. There's another story that you're hiding here because bad people want to kill you."

"I'm a private citizen who used to work for the federal government. I retired from that job. It was a medical retirement. My job, when I worked it, had nothing to do with any murder, corruption, or tax evasion. I worked outside of the USA, almost always in Mexico. I got injured on the job. For some reason, the people I worked for are still interested in me and still keeping an eye on me. I don't know why. They say they want me back. Maybe, instead, they suspect I've gone rogue. But all I want to do is practice law and be the Grimsley County probation officer. I have an interest in my father's death, but that's not why I moved here. Moving to Grimsley City was my plan and his plan for me before he was killed. I knew Silver in law school. I talked to him about the town when I got out of school. He thought I might make a living here."

"You said he'd never helped you?"

"That's not all the way true. Sometimes I meet people through him."

He nodded. "I've had some recent calls on you. I suppose I'm permitted to tell you that. A person you worked with told me you were very good at watching and figuring things when you were in your previous profession."

Ballinger. "Who said that?"

He smiled. "I'm not sure that person would want me to give you a name."

I found I was getting a little angry.

"Please listen to me, Judge. Ask Ballinger or anyone else who calls to explain exactly how I'm obligated to the government or any of its branches. I promise you I'm not. I worked for a semi-secret government agency for a time. I did as I was told. I hope I was good at the job. But when I left the job, I didn't leave it in any kind of situation where I could be recalled back. I was strictly a civilian employee, an employee for a term of years. I'm not some kind of reservist. I had a contract and the contract said I could resign when my time was up or I could be fired at any time if I

98

didn't do my job. I resigned partly for medical reasons. I draw a small pension. I quit four years ago. I wasn't under pressure to resign, but I did resign, by the book, and when my time was up." I looked down at the road. "I had to walk away from a hospital to make it stick."

"I see. Let me ask you one more thing. Is someone else looking for you?"

"Not for certain."

"Little rocks on your hood," he reminded.

"An old habit."

I wasn't positive he believed me and so I continued: "I could make a good case in federal court against whoever is doing the looking, the investigating, and the calling. If they call you or come to see you, tell them I'm considering doing that." I doubted that I in fact could go to court, because of things I'd signed when I'd terminated my employment, but I liked making the threat.

He nodded. "The call I got wasn't unfriendly, Jim. It was just a call. The caller wanted to know how you were doing. I asked if the federal government had an objection to you being my probation officer. There wasn't any objection. None at all."

"But someone called and I was the principal reason for the call?"

"One of the reasons."

I decided to say no more. In a moment he nodded at me, having regained his wind. We began to walk again, this time at a slower pace. He slowed and stopped when we came to a fine ranch house halfway to our goal.

"This is Fiala's daughter's home. Ruth Thacker. I've heard it said she'd like to sell it and move into Fiala's home." He shook his head. "Seems to me that this one she now owns would have enough room, what with her being divorced."

"She's divorced?"

He nodded. "It got filed out of this county after Fiala died. All worked out. Clean and simple. Henry Lee represented her husband. No contested trial. She and her hubby even settled custody and visitation. Her husband got most of the custody."

"How's that?"

"He has their kids most of the year."

"Does the husband get anything out of Fiala's estate?"

"I think not. They'd separated before Fiala died. Some people don't like sharing, Jim. Some people want it all and will plot and scheme to get it all."

"Do you suspect her of murdering her father?"

"It could be, but neither of the Kentner children are indicted. Shirley Kentner is."

We kept walking. We were moving slower than my usual pace, but all walking is good. I stayed alongside Daggert.

Four or five city blocks further he stopped in front of an attractive two-story brick-and-stone that looked to be worth many dollars.

"This is the house where Shirley Kentner was playing cards the night Fiala was killed. The bridge game was two tables, eight ladies, and was hosted by Belle Trempen, Doc Trempen's young widow. See how the west room looks out over the lake? Witnesses will likely testify that you can see Fiala's house out of that window. That's from the room where the eight women played cards. Some of the lady cardplayers may or may not testify that Shirley kept watching her own house that night. Others will deny it."

"What would it mean either way? If I had a house like Fiala Kentner's, I'd watch it every moment I could."

He shrugged.

It was easy to see what he meant about being able to view one house from the other. The shore of the lake curved away from the Trempen home. Looking through the gap from where we stood, I could see the Kentner house. I looked back. You could see Fiala's house from his daughter's house also.

"Shirley Kentner watched out the window. When the outside lights came on, the theory is that she knew Fiala was dead. Is that it?" I asked.

"That's the state's theory."

I laughed a little. "What that does is fit the facts with a theory to cover them."

"All criminal cases do that. Prosecutors have little mercy. We're not trying Shirley Kentner because there's much hard evidence against her. We're trying her because a confessed murderer says she helped him plan her husband's murder. We're trying her because the prosecutor promised not to seek the death penalty against Garcia if he'd name his co-conspirators."

"It's a dumb murder," I said. "I still want someone to tell me why Fiala was dropped into a chair in front of a picture window and the curtain opened and lights arranged so as to spotlight him after the killing."

"Wait until you hear Garcia testify next week. There'll be questions and answers about that."

"Monday?"

"No. Not Monday. More likely the middle of the week or later. First we'll listen to Fiala's children, then Owens, the state detective. We'll hear some of the bridge ladies, and whatever else the prosecutor can throw in. Garcia will be the state's late star. After him, there'll be doctor's depositions and then, finally, for the defense, Shirley Kentner's case."

"I see."

"Did you know that some of the torture marks on Fiala Kentner's body were made after death?"

"Why would he be tortured after he died?"

"I don't know, but he was. When Garcia pled out, he said he continued with his cigar and knife because he hoped Kentner would snap back from unconsciousness."

"That sounds cruel."

"Yes, cruel. Garcia's not a big man, but he's strong and, in his way, handsome. His eyes are about the same color as yours, very dark blue or maybe black. He moves like a ballet dancer or a bullfighter and his voice is good. I heard him tell his story about the killing of Fiala in his plea of guilty. The story made my blood run as cold as yesterday's weather. It was as if Garcia was standing away from a picnic campfire and telling a horror story about someone else, a story he wasn't personally involved in. The killing was an incident in the story and meaningless to him. Now a woman's life and freedom depend on whether a jury believes a man like that or a woman like Shirley Kentner."

"It's not a death penalty case."

"It's a slow-death case," he answered. "Put Shirley in prison and she'd be like a caged, wild bird."

"And you don't want that to happen?"

"Not if she's innocent."

"Was all the questioning during Garcia's plea hearing done by the prosecutor?"

"Yes. Garcia told his story. That was all. Some of that story may or may not have been the truth. People have amazing capacity for evil, lust, and hate. And they do lie. They always lie, Jim. That wetback man had nothing. So, for openers, he seduces his benefactor's wife, maybe using force, if you believe Shirley's story. When caught in the act, he manages to convince his benefactor that what has happened will never happen again. Later he tortures and kills this man." He shook his head in puzzlement. "The question is, Why? From what I've seen in and out of court, I can't believe that Garcia ever seriously thought Fiala's woman would run away with him. Maybe he had hopes that she'd follow behind, but you'll see even the prosecutor soft-pedal that."

"Why?" *I'd not seen Corner soft-pedal anything yet.*

"Because Shirley Kentner never made any discoverable preparations. Let's say she planned to flee and join Garcia, early or late. She'd have done things, traceable things. Maybe bought luggage, maybe applied for a passport, possibly bought traveler's checks. She might have bought or borrowed library books on Mexico. She might have taken a refresher course on her high-school Spanish. The prosecutor would have put the people who could so testify to those actions on his witness list. There are no such witnesses."

"You don't believe she conspired with Garcia," I said.

"I'm not saying that. I'm the trial judge. What I'm doing is recognizing holes."

"Did Garcia, in his confession, say she planned to join him?"

"Yes." He shook his head. "My guess was then that he didn't believe it. I thought, when he pled out, that maybe, just maybe, he was sorry he'd not killed Shirley also. But that would have made his trial a different situation. Multiple murderers seldom can deal their sentences. Most multiple murderers wind up on death row. And this guy stood in front of me and smiled sweetly when I sentenced him to a long term. Like he knew something I didn't know."

I stood silently, sensing he wasn't done.

"The state seeks to make all things simple. Garcia says he did his killing because he loved Shirley. He says he did it because Shirley wanted Kentner's money. Garcia says it was done to please her. But if she wasn't going to run with him, what's Garcia's reward? And why did he torture Fiala before and after death? Why run at all? Why not, instead, drop a weighted Fiala's body into a deep part of the river? Garcia would then have had days to escape and hide without any instant pursuit." He shook his head.

"Lights on, curtains open wide," I said.

"Exactly. Still, we have Garcia's confession, and it's powerful. You'll see him repeat it for the state next week. Very impressive. If he's lying, then *why's* he lying? That's what the defense must combat. It's like fighting the rain."

I had a sudden moment of understanding. "You like Shirley Kentner a lot, don't you?"

"Maybe. Don't you?"

"I've never talked to her, but I do like her and want her to win. Can she win?"

"So far I've not seen anything that makes me certain she's guilty."

"Or innocent either? How well did you know her?"

His voice went stiff. "Her husband was my good friend."

"She's beautiful," I said. "I see her and I'm stirred. A woman like that . . ."

He shrugged and quickened the pace. A cloud covered the sun and the day became a little colder. An old, yellow dog frisked in a nearby yard and eyed us with friendly interest. When we passed, he followed us.

"Is the job okay?" he asked. "Remember there's a test in a couple of months."

"The job's fine. I'll try to be ready for the state test. And the salary's a great help."

"How about probationers? Any problems?"

103

"I had one in yesterday who told me a tale about trouble in the jail with Garcia. My probationer was a prisoner in the jail when Garcia was there."

"I never heard anything about jail trouble," he said. "When did that happen?"

"Right at the time Garcia pled out. The probationer's William Cannon, a druggie."

"I know him and know of his family. Again, I never heard about jail trouble. Ask Sheriff Riggs about it. Tell me what he says." He shook his head, his eyes troubled. "I don't like for things to go on within the system and me not know them."

"Yes, sir."

"Anything else?"

"Not on probationers. The few I've had, come in, report, and go. I try to be obliging. A lot of them, male and female, are stick people, lost in a nasty world, unable to cope. I tell them I have to know exactly what they're doing for my monthly reports. I tell them they must look for jobs, but I know most employers won't hire them. Even if jobs were offered, many of our probationers wouldn't accept one."

He smiled. "And do they lie?"

"Yes, sir. They lie. I know also that some of them, once outside my office, go back to what they know best. If they were burglars, they break into places. If they were drug users, they try hard to get into the sales or transportation end of the business, along with using. Sooner or later most of them will get caught again. So we'll ship the worst of the worst to prison and try the rest on probation again."

"Anyone now you think should be revoked?"

"No one in particular—yet."

"Bend the rules. If you know you've got a bad apple, bend rules so he or she goes to prison. Separate them from us for a while. If a bad apple comes through on a plea bargain, tell me so I can turn Corner's proffered plea bargain down. Conversely, if you get people worth giving a second or third chance, then bend the rules to help them."

"All right." My probationers were wary of me because I was

still an unknown. It was encouraging to know there was no hard line the judge wanted me to follow.

The yellow dog had moved close to us, trailing along. I held out a hand and he came to it, sniffing but wary. He let me give him a scratch behind the ears.

"Shirley Kentner was working as a registered nurse at the hospital when she met Fiala Kentner," he said.

I nodded, knowing that vaguely.

By now we'd arrived in front of Fiala Kentner's house. It looked both lifeless and magnificent at the same time. It was the largest house we'd passed on our walk.

We stood in the road and looked at the house. The south wind was brisk and I could smell the odor of fish, and sand, and fireplaces.

"When we drove past on our way to dinner, someone was inside," I said.

"That was Ruth Thacker. I saw her. I'm told that she looks after the house with a vengeance because she wants it badly. Shirley won't sign anything over, so the house remains in limbo. If Shirley's found not guilty, the house is hers."

"What happens if Shirley's convicted?"

"If she's convicted and the conviction's affirmed, then she can't inherit from her husband or benefit from his death. But there's some law to the effect that she'd still own half of the house." He shook his head. "I don't know what would happen. I've never researched it." He smiled. "Ask Ruth Thacker. I'll bet she knows and can quote verbatim either the statute or the ruling case."

"I've been keeping up on advance sheets. Most criminal appeals seem to be routinely denied."

"I know some appellate judges who'd get highly irritated hearing that kind of statement. Persons charged with crimes want perfect trials. They want each of their motions granted and the state in shackles come trial time. After they get convicted, they then want to nitpick all that happened. When their attorney loses, then they want to complain about his poor, inadequate defense."

"If Shirley Kentner is convicted, would she have much chance at the appellate level?"

He shrugged. "Reversal would be possible, but unlikely."

"How do you think things are going now?"

"Too early to tell. The final question is whether the jury believes Jose or Shirley." His eyes seemed sad. "If they believe him and she's convicted, then she could be inside for a lot of years. I don't believe she'd survive prison."

"Makes you think on the justice system," I said carefully.

He nodded.

We stood looking at the house. There was no one looking back at us from inside the house today.

"I don't believe there's a soul around," Daggert said. "It would be a good time for you to walk up and take a look through that picture window."

"Why would I want to do that?"

"Because you're curious about this murder. We both know that. And you have, just now, an inquiring look on your face. Go look." He smiled without true humor. "I'll act as your lookout. And I'd like you to look."

I experienced again the notion that he wanted and expected me to be more than I was. But why not look? It would please Daggert if I did.

I walked up a cobbled center path. The grass was stiff and winter-short. The big window lay to the left of the path behind small trimmed bushes. I stepped in between two bushes. The picture window curtain was open to the sun and the inside was visible. I could see an easy chair, one of the kind that reclined. It was, I believed, probably the same chair where Fiala Kentner's body had been dumped. I imagined, without seeing anything, blood stains on the chair. Along a wall, there was a big stereo. A stopped grandfather clock gave the time as 9:50. I wondered if the clock had stopped the night of the murder or run down afterward.

There was a high, broad fireplace with a closed screen. Some items of furniture in the room were covered with drape cloths. Other items were not. Along one long wall, there was a long sofa with a white sheet covering part of it. The sofa was upholstered in rich leather.

A contraption stood near bookcases. It was made of metal. I thought I should know what it was, but I couldn't call its name or use immediately to mind. It looked to be fabricated out of light, tubular metal, legs bolted together strongly, with an opening at the top. I remembered seeing something like it at my grandfather's house in Texas.

The door to the hall was open. I could see yellow tape hanging limply down outside that door. It was the kind of tape used to denote a crime scene. The room had either been officially reopened by the police or been reopened unofficially by others.

I speculated silently about how close the room was to what its condition had been on the night of the murder. The drape sheets would not have been present. And, again, where had the deceased been killed before being dumped half-nude in the chair? I'd heard no telling testimony. The exact place of death in the house was shrouded in vagueness.

The carpet was inches deep. The house and furnishings were rich. There were cases full of stereo records and compact discs, although I could see nothing to play them on. A few compact disc boxes stood upright on a table. Country-western and Boston Pops. My bet was that Fiala had been the country fancier, Shirley the Boston Pops.

I still wondered why and where Fiala Kentner had died.

Garcia had admittedly killed Fiala *somewhere* in the house. He then had openly advertised the killing by dumping the body into the reclining chair and opening the drapes. Then he'd highlighted the completed act.

I took one final look inside. I heard a car approaching from far away. Judge Daggert stood motionless at the edge of the road. I walked back to the road. As I arrived, a car passed us.

Daggert waved jauntily to the occupant of the car. She had slowed to perhaps five miles an hour and she gave us a long, hostile look. On this day she was dressed in dark red.

The yellow dog barked at the car.

"That's daughter Ruth," Daggert said to me out of the side of his mouth. "You almost got caught in the act."

"Hey now, maybe I left identifiable footprints in front of the picture window."

"I'll go your bail if you're charged," he answered.

The car turned into the drive. A woman got out of the car and stood looking at both of us. Her face was dark and angry. The car was large, new, and foreign. A Mercedes, one of the big ones.

Maybe from pre-spending her inheritance?

We turned and began the journey back toward the beach.

As we walked, the incident began to seem funny to me. I watched Daggert and saw his mouth twitch. He whooped and then I whooped, and we shook with shared laughter. He beat me on the back and I responded.

The yellow dog watched us carefully, perhaps having witnessed human insanities before. He moved off and ranged through nearby yards, abandoning us.

We walked back to my Mustang without further incident, except that every once in a while I'd laugh and Daggert would be infected by the laugh and we'd whoop together all over again.

I asked him one more question before we parted: "When Garcia pled guilty, was there any mention of the stopped clock?"

"Yes. He said he damaged it when he was searching for money."

Later, when I was back in my apartment, I remembered what the name of the metal contraption in the murder room was. A "walker." A tubular aluminum aid used by people who'd suffered a stroke or been seriously disabled. Lean on it and it would help walking.

It was Saturday night, date night. I had no date and was long accustomed to not having one. I satisfied myself by ordering in a small pizza. I gorged on it and diet cola.

That night I had a new locale for my nightmares. There was a lake and a big house. People watched me from shadows. All I saw were bits and pieces, like flotsam on the Ohio River.

In the morning I walked to the sheriff's office and interrupted lackadaisical Sunday routines there.

I entered the jail's side door and a bell went off somewhere inside. I could smell the odor of too many bodies packed into too small a space. It was a smell of dirt, rot, feces, and disintegrating canvas shoes.

A sign directed me to the check-in counter.

A mean-looking lady deputy who likely outweighed me idly worked a wall full of radio equipment in the alcove behind the counter. She saw me come to the counter, but ignored me while trying to raise Unit Three. She had three chins, and her upper arms were thick. She had a pencil stub and she made stab marks on a paper in front of her. I thought she might be one of the women who daily delivered Shirley Kentner to the courtroom.

"Unit Three, Unit Three, this is home base. Come in now."

I waited.

She tried a couple more times and then gave it up.

"Damn road warriors are into biscuits and gravy at Hardy's. Easier to call on the telephone than raise them assholes on the radio Sundays." She nodded at me, upset I was still there and listening. "What do *you* want?"

"Runner around?"

"Our late-night-blooming sheriff has only recently risen from his slumbers," she said sarcastically. "He will be at morning coffee down the corridor. What do you want to see him about? And who are you?"

"Business. I'm Jim Singer, the circuit probation officer."

"Oh yeah. I heard they got them a new one after Buck Coulson quit, and I seen you in court. Go on back." She smiled and forgave me for bothering her. I smiled back. It cost nothing.

Big woman.

I walked down the hall. In a big room to the right, there was a sink and a stove. Something boiled ominously on the big stove. It smelled more like washing than cooking. A stainless steel coffee machine was in another corner. Beside it, there was a tray of fried doughnut halves. Runner Riggs, the fat sheriff, was hard at work eating doughnuts and washing them down with steaming black coffee.

He nodded at me affably. He was a man who tried hard to stay on the good side of everyone. He was up for re-election in the fall. He'd been reticent about my father, but friendly about all else. His department was reputedly good at serving papers and delivering prisoners to the various courts.

"Come in, Jim. Come on in. Want some coffee and maybe a doughnut or three?"

I declined. The doughnuts smelled good. I thought if I started eating them, I might continue through noon. And I already had last night's lump of pizza hanging fire inside.

"Runner, I'm checking some stuff from the court files. I got a report that just after Garcia pled out last year, there was some trouble here in your jail. You remember anything about it?"

"Who told you that?"

"A chance interview with someone who was inside the jail when it happened. Now we're worrying that maybe Garcia will use what happened inside the jail to his advantage up the appellate line."

"Shit, Jim-boy. Garcia ain't going to do fuckin' nothin'. I'll bet you a thousand to a hunnert on that. All that happened is that a big, ass-kickin' dude named Hawkins from up around Covington was, because space's a problem, in the big dayroom. We put Garcia in there also. It was a mistake. Hawkins put the make on Garcia. He likes them dark-skinned." He held up a hand. "Happens now and then. Garcia kicked Hawkins in the family jewels and said a few hard words to him. A jailer saw it, told me, and we quick moved Garcia back into a private cell. Hawkins drew five years for warehouse burglarizing. He's still inside. I think at Eddyville." He laughed a huge laugh. "I'll bet it was a long time before he made a move on anyone at Eddyville. Great big dude, bigger'n me. And Garcia's weighing about two-thirds of him. Garcia's not large, but he's a hoss."

"You have any other trouble with Garcia?"

"No. Once he was inside, he just sat in his cell and smiled at us, real polite like, a waitin' man, used to it. He did what he was told and he didn't smart-mouth. He read the magazines, he watched the tee-vee. He never complained. I think our jails was better than them he'd known south of the border.''

"Did he say he'd been in jail before?"

"No. But he had. I watched him. There's things that old jail-house hands do. They keep soap of their own, they hide their matches and money deep, or they carry it with them always. They don't eat much or say much. They sleeps light. My bet is that he'd been in lots of jails before he saw the inside of mine.''

"And no one punished him or threatened him for kicking this guy?"

"For him nuttin' Zeke Hawkins? Hell no. The jailer who saw it said some real complimentary things about Garcia. Said he was quick and mean. Said he might have killed Hawkins, but he seen he was being watched. Kicked Zeke a couple of times and called him some things in spic and American and then let it go.''

"Thanks, Runner. Where do you house Mrs. Kentner?"

"She occupies our ladies' penthouse suite,'' he said, smiling. "Nice lady. She's clean as a cat. Her cell is always perfect. She smells nice because she washes lots and she's polite as pie on a plate to my four lady deputies. I don't know about whether she's guilty or not, but I do know she's a special favorite around here.''

"Does she have any visitors?"

"Her lawyer."

"That's all?"

He nodded. "No others. Her close relatives are all dead. All she has left around are cousins. They don't visit. I guess she had some friends, but none of them have come around callin' since the trial began. She's been inside too long.''

His answer offended me. "She hasn't been convicted yet, Runner.''

"I suspect the town thinks she will be.'' He lifted a hand and grinned. "To make up for it she has admirers who stand in the alley and look up at her window, hoping she'll come to it and they can see her. Every time she goes back and forth to court, there'll be a crowd of men waiting for their look. One of the men who comes every day is a merchant, married, with two kids." He shook his head. "Hard to understand."

Not to me.

I knew that if I felt love for Shirley Kentner it had to be the strangest relationship in history. I'd never met her. Our knowledge of each other came from exchanging glances.

A performer assured me that a multimillion-dollar jackpot would soon be mine. I wondered how many dollars were being spent on *that* promotion. After that, there were ads for the various lotteries.

Dreams. Like mine of Shirley.

I ate Campbell's reliable vegetable soup, but I had carried in an Arby's roast beef to gobble down with it.

The phone rang twice during the night. Each time, when I answered it, no one answered me on the line.

Someone wanted me to know he was watching. I had no idea who it was.

CHAPTER EIGHT

*Each morning I'd awake and try first the good eye, then the bad.
Every morning I'd hope for some sort of miraculous recovery.*

*I was happy to be able to see, but I wanted to be as I'd been
before I spent mountain sun time.*

*I'd given up on my other area of injury, but now and then,
mornings, all seemed well.*

I SLEPT BADLY that Sunday night, but that was not unusual. I kept
coming awake and thinking of the beautiful lost woman who
haunted me from her jail cell. I watched the smirking town waiting for the inevitable finish to the ongoing courtroom debacle.

I kept hearing over and over what Daggert had said about jury
trials not coming out "right."

I walked to the courthouse from my apartment. Today it was
cool, not cold. The world usually is either alive, dying, dead, or
coming to life. On this day it struggled to decide exactly where it
was. There was a dim sun and thin clouds.

I waved back at locals who waved at me. The town was beginning to recognize me.

Spic lawyer. Looks real dark, don't he?

All seemed normal in the courthouse. I returned some calls
from probationers and talked to those whose day it was to come in
and report. I'd changed the schedule so that probationers could
report any day, not just Fridays.

Horace Donaho, having decided temporarily to like me, nodded amiably in the hall as he searched for a quiet resting spot.
Anne Melville beat a tune on her computer-typer. She winked upward when she saw me. Judge Daggert conferred with various
lawyers in chambers. He looked up, saw me, and waved me
inside.

"Look these over," he said offhandedly. He handed me a sheaf of photos, large and small, marked with numbers.

The proposed trial exhibits.

I carried them back to my office. For some reason I felt like closing the doors, but I didn't.

I found photos of Garcia, and I examined them intently. In the best of them he smiled out at the camera, all dark complexion and white teeth.

I'd fantasized, from previous brief glimpses of his photo, that maybe I did know him, that perhaps he was a recognizable part of my past, but nothing about his photos meant anything to me. In my times in Mexico I'd associated with high-born and low-born revolutionaries, people alienated from the often rotten and corrupt Mexican political system, ones who'd go to any length to cripple or destroy that system and the all-powerful government to the north, called the United States, that both tolerated and aided it.

I remembered a thousand faces from those days.

Garcia's wasn't one of those faces. But there were ten thousand faces I'd seen and had no memory of. And I'd never seen the face of "Judge."

I looked through the rest of the photographs.

I sensed someone watching. Anne Melville was looking in my door, waiting patiently.

"You concentrate well," she said. "He wants those back if you're done. We'll need them in the courtroom."

"Yes," I said, having seen enough. I gathered them and handed them to her.

It was still half an hour to trial time.

I caught up with messages, mostly about juveniles in trouble. A boy-girl high school youth group had formed a sex club and been caught showing pornographic films in the home ec room. Two juvenile boys, ages fourteen and fifteen, had broken into a Holy Roller church and vandalized it. A sixteen-year-old boy had been caught aiding his adult brother in a house burglary. I sighed and made notes. I then walked down the back steps to the clerk's office. From my office I'd smelled coffee below. I waited the pot out and stole a cup, black and strong. I gulped it, then left the courthouse. I hurried to my private law office and checked the phone recorder. No calls.

I was glad. The trial and the woman obsessed me.

I walked back. I was now "at home" in the courthouse. There was a divorced lady in the county clerk's office with whom I kidded about dates. There was another girl in the auditor's office. I knew who brewed the best coffee, what office had the friendliest staff, and where to hear the latest gossip. I knew the methods of doing my job. I wasn't sure I'd ever know "how."

My civil practice remained sporadic and I wasn't hotly interested in its immediate growth.

Trial began again at ten and I was in place.

Lynn Corner called Alfred Kentner.

By rumor's telegraph the word had spread throughout town and county that things were heating up in the murder trial. The courtroom was crowded. The Grimsley City *Trumpet* had two reporters in attendance instead of one. I saw new people I thought were from the big-city dailies, Lexington, Louisville, and Cincinnati, come to cover expected juicy testimony.

Alfred Kentner was a pudgy, juvenile version of his father, unholed and alive, thirty years younger. He was at least forty pounds overweight. He was moonfaced like his father and he wore thick glasses that softened imperious eyes. His hands were his best feature. They were oversized, strong, and capable looking.

Prosecutor Corner had dressed for the day in a dark brown suit, white shirt, and muted tie. He moved up close to the witness after Kentner had been sworn. He was careful not to block the jury's view of his witness.

"State your name, occupation, and your place of residence," he began. He quickly led Kentner through the preliminaries.

"You are Fiala Kentner's oldest child?"

"Oldest living child," Alfred corrected primly. "My parents had a girl born two years before me. I remember her a little. My sister died when I was three."

"Ahhhh," Corner murmured sympathetically. I wondered, being both suspicious and a lawyer, if that question and answer had been rehearsed.

115

A couple of jurors nodded, perhaps knowing some Kentner family history. Jurors are cautioned over and over not to read anything outside the courtroom about the case. They're told not to talk to anyone. They do read, they also listen to radios and televisions. And they talk, and talk, and talk.

"Is your mother alive?"

"No. Mother died of cancer nine years ago come August. My father married his second, childless wife three years ago in June."

I saw Henry Lee flinch, but he didn't rise to object. I approved. The folksy questions and answers weren't hurting much. To object and be sustained and then hear the answers given again to more direct questions would hurt. "Second, childless wife" was a legal term that Corner had likely inserted into his witness's mind.

Listening, I became certain that almost all of what I was now seeing had been carefully rehearsed. There was nothing legally wrong with such rehearsal, but jurors, upon discovering it happening in the midst of a criminal trial, usually didn't like it.

"Did you and your sister approve of your father's second marriage?"

Alfred smiled. "We both wanted my father to be happy. However, his new wife was much younger. We believed there would be problems. We were right."

Once again Lee looked up, wounded.

Corner nodded and stepped away from Alfred. He went to his counsel table and opened a file. He looked in it for a long moment while the jury waited and digested what it had already heard. I thought it was stage play, but I was now beginning to understand what Daggert had meant when he'd told me that watching the trial could benefit me as a learning lawyer.

"Did your father and his new, young wife eventually employ a man named Jose Ramon Garcia to work for them at their home?"

"Yes. At a new home my father built."

"How long ago was this new house built?"

"Just after my father married Shirley. Jose came along later."

"Did your father build an *expensive* home?"

"Yes. Lots of money." Alfred's mouth turned down, disapproving.

116

"How long did Jose work for your father and Shirley?"

"He worked until the night he killed my father."

"I mean, how many months or years did Jose work for your father?"

"I'm not sure. More than six months, less than a year."

"And on the night your father was murdered, were you called to his new home?"

"Yes. I was called to check things. I discovered that my father's billfold was gone, as was his Rolex watch. One of the family cars was gone also. The Mercury Sable wagon."

"Did you later find out who had taken those things?"

"Yes. Jose was caught in Tennessee by troopers. He had the watch and my father's billfold."

Hearsay and subject to objection, but Lee sat stolidly, refusing to rise to the bait.

"Where was Jose caught?"

"In Tennessee, like I said. South of Nashville on Interstate 24."

I thought vaguely about routes south. If Garcia was fleeing back to his land of birth, would he be going *that* way? Interstate 40 or maybe I-65 would be better ways south and west to Texas and Mexico.

"Before this time did you ever see this man and your stepmother talking together or interacting with each other?"

"Yes. Many times. Shirley had some high school Spanish. Jose could speak English, but when I was around the house Shirley liked to give Jose orders in Spanish. Clean this, fetch that. Cool and efficient." Alfred smiled.

"Did you ever see anything going on between them which would indicate they were other than master and servant?"

"Not early on."

"Did a time come when you personally discovered that something different than master and servant was going on between Shirley and Jose?"

"Yes."

I could feel the sense of expectation among the spectators in the courtroom. The reporters hovered over their ballpoint pens. The audience leaned collectively forward, salivating.

Dirt.

"Exactly what happened?"

"I caught them in bed together in my father's new house."

"When was this?"

"About four months before my father was killed."

"Tell the jury what you saw."

The jury waited along with the spectators. It was like being at your back fence and having a neighbor tell you eyewitness sex stories about another neighbor you'd always suspected of being both a window peeper and a sex nut.

"I got sent to the house for some papers Pop had forgotten to bring along to the office when Jose delivered him that morning. I drove my car to the house. I parked away from the drive. I had Pop's key and I went in quiet. I could hear them before I saw them. They were in the bedroom. Jose had all his clothes off except for his socks and Shirley was nude. They were at it in the bed. They were so hard at it they didn't see me when I first opened the door and stood there."

"What were they doing?" Corner asked.

A male juror tittered knowingly.

"Having intercourse."

"Normal intercourse?"

Alfred grinned. "Looked normal to me. Lots of noise and lots of movement."

"What happened when you interrupted them?" Corner asked, pursuing a good thing.

"Well, they both scrambled for clothes. She didn't seem to mind that I'd caught them. Jose put his on quick and went out the front door. I fetched what Pop had forgotten and I drove back to the office. I think Pop could tell when he saw me that something was wrong. He asked me about it and I told him what it was."

Henry Lee was finally up. "Objection, Your Honor. Part of the witness's answer is inadmissible. I'd like the entire answer stricken and the jury admonished concerning it."

Daggert nodded. "That's right. Let's exercise some care, Mr.

118

Corner. It's apparent to the court that you and this witness have conferred. I'll ask now if you need *further* time to talk more with him and let him know what is and isn't admissible in this court.''

Corner shook his head. His eyes seemed unconcerned, but I knew he'd been wounded. Daggert, in a few short words, had hurt the prosecution's case as far as this witness was concerned. But the jury also had heard that Alfred's father knew of his wife's treachery, and no admonishment would take that away. Something good, something bad.

''I've not coached this witness.''

''Perhaps not,'' Daggert answered severely. ''If you haven't, then someone else must have done so for you. The answer of the witness is inadmissible for several reasons. Because of that the court will strike the entire answer. The court will further admonish the members of the jury to completely disregard the last answer of this witness and not consider anything said in that answer to be a part of the evidence. Is that admonishment sufficient for you, Mr. Lee?''

''Yes, Your Honor,'' Lee answered disdainfully, making the best he could out of the situation. He could move for a mistrial, but I doubted one would be granted. Even if it was, his client remained in jail.

No win.

''Proceed, Mr. Corner.''

Corner smiled carefully and went on. He had Alfred Kentner describe the bedroom in living color. He asked what furniture was there, what items of clothes lay beside the bed, what size the bed was (king-size), how rumpled were the sheets, the color of the walls, the temperature outside, and the kind of day it was, sunny or cloudy.

''Did these two people say anything to each other while they were dressing?''

''Not a word. He dressed on his side of the bed and she dressed on hers after they got unhooked from what they were up to. They didn't look at each other.''

''Do you know how old Garcia is?''

''He told me once he was twenty-nine. That was more than a

year ago. That would be a little younger than my stepmother." He looked up at the courtroom ceiling. "I guess that would be right. Them Mexes are hard to tell ages on."

"Were you personally present when your father and step-mother discussed what you witnessed?"

"No, but I heard about it from Pop."

Henry Lee was on his feet.

Corner smiled piously for the jury. "This court has ruled that you can't testify about things your father said or conversations you had with him, Mr. Kentner."

Daggert leaned ominously forward. "The rules of evidence are the guidelines disallowing such dead man's testimony, Mr. Corner. Would you care to send the jury out and argue them? Should those rules continue to be ignored by you there might soon be a reason to excuse this witness, grant a mistrial, and set a new bond hearing."

The prosecutor nodded and smiled, but his neck was now beet red. "I understand, Your Honor," he said agreeably. He retreated to his table and read his notes again, giving the jurors time to forget the exchange.

"On the night your father was killed, where were you before you were called to your father's house?"

"I was at my sister's house on the lake. My father came past there early. There were some business things we met to discuss."

"When did your father arrive at this meeting?"

"Like I said, it was early. His part in the meeting got done soon and he left about six to go back to his place."

"Did he drive?"

"No. Shirley brought him to my sister's house and later came for him in the Cadillac. Jose was supposed to be off on a short vacation."

"How far is your sister's home from your father's place?"

"Not far. They're both out on the lake," Kentner said. "Maybe half a mile."

"Tell the jury what this business meeting was about."

"It concerned my father taking a smaller share of the company profits. He no longer worked full time in the business. He wanted to come and go as he pleased. So we asked him to take a smaller share and let us do the work of collecting."

"Was a new written agreement signed that night?"

"Yes."

"And did you see your father sign it?"

"Yes. We all signed it. A lawyer had prepared it for us."

"Did the lawyer draw the agreement up at your request?"

"Yes. It was my sister's and my proposal."

"And the agreement was signed?"

"Yes. We went from Pop taking half the profits to each of us three family members taking a third. Plus we would take over collecting the routes. And he could set his own hours, come and go as he pleased."

If what Horace had told me was essentially true, then that meant that the untaxed money had started to flow in a new direction the night of the murder.

Corner had a document marked. He got it identified by Alfred, gave it to Lee for inspection, and then offered it into evidence. Lee looked it over and allowed it in without objection. Copies of the document had been prepared for each juror and alternate. I could see the document was three pages long. The copies were passed and each juror read his or her own copy.

I decided that Corner was now trying to show the jurors that neither of Fiala's children had any urgent reason to kill him.

The jury stolidly read through the copies. When they were done and the contract copies collected, Corner went back to more questioning. He had Alfred describe hot arguments overheard between Fiala and Shirley. Lee and Corner fought battles about admissibility, but most of the witnessed arguments got into evidence, covered by different evidentiary rules.

Corner finally ran out of questions.

"Your witness," he said to Lee.

Lee nodded. He stood and looked up at the wall clock. "I may be lengthy," he said to Daggert. "I'd like not to have to break up cross-examination of this witness."

The clock read quarter to twelve. Daggert nodded, found out where Horace would lunch the jury, and notified attorneys and witnesses to eat elsewhere.

I decided to drive to Dumont and have a long lunch. I wanted to talk with the people at the restaurant about my father and see if I could find someone who remembered him.

I called and found that the restaurant had opened at eleven.

I drove the Mustang, careful on the road because my tires were worn. At some point I noticed the dust trail of another car behind me as I drove the winding road.

I parked where I'd earlier parked Daggert's car and walked on inside.

A tall man cleaned glasses behind the bar.

I sat on one of the stools. He smiled at me. He was fiftyish. He wore small, rectangular spectacles hung precariously on his nose. He had on a clean white shirt and bib overalls.

"Get you something?"

"Diet cola or iced tea. Can I order a sandwich here at the bar?"

"Sure can. I'll hold off on the drink until I get you a lunch menu."

I waited until a young girl came out of the kitchen and delivered the bartender a menu. The menu was typed, but things had been crossed out and written over, prices had been changed.

I heard another car pull up outside, but no one entered.

"We don't do much lunch business," the bartender said. "A few locals. Later in the afternoon I do some bar business."

"How about a cheeseburger with lettuce and tomato, fries, and some iced tea?"

He wrote it down on a pad and carried it down the hall.

I waited until he returned.

"Did you ever do any business here with my father?"

"Who would your father be? I seen you before, but I don't know your name."

"I was out here with Judge Daggert. My name's Jim Singer."

He nodded quickly. "I know Simon." He held out a hand and I

shook it. "My name's Del Canfield. My family owns this place."

"My father was Allen Singer."

"Sure. Car salesman. Got hisself killed a while back. He was your dad?"

"Yes. Did he come in here?"

"Some. He'd come in and drink. He'd drink enough that I'd worry about him getting back to town. Then, right before he got killed, he'd come in nights and drink lemonade or Sharp's or O'Doul's. He'd leave for a time. Later he might come back to pick up his car."

"Who would he leave with?"

He shrugged. "I don't know. Pure and holy as he got about it, what with no drinkin', I thought maybe he had him something treed, but I never saw her."

"What kind of car would she drive?"

"Just a car. Sometimes it'd be one car, then maybe something different."

There was a noise and we both turned to the door.

The two Mexican-appearing men I'd seen in the courtroom entered. I froze. They took a seat at a table by the front window. They watched me carefully.

"You want drinks or lunch?" the bartender asked.

"Both," the older of the two said. He was burly and strong-looking and maybe in his forties, fifty pounds heavier than me. His hair was two A.M. black and needed combing.

"I'll get you a waitress."

"Sure. Do that."

The bartender vanished down the hall again.

I watched the two men from the bar and they watched me.

"I believe I earlier saw you gentlemen in court," I said, recovering.

"Did you now," the younger man said. "Would you care to come sit with us a bit and talk about the beauties of Mexico?" His English was unaccented.

I shook my head, wary of them.

The bartender returned with menus resembling the one I'd seen. He gave one each to the men.

"Come join us," the older man ordered.

I again shook my head.

He smiled. I saw a bulge under his coat. "Maybe soon," he said. His voice threatened me.

The younger man laughed. "Soon or late."

The waitress came and took their order. I wondered what would happen if I tried to leave. I got up from my stool. "I'll come back another time."

The younger man got up and walked to the door, blocking my exit.

Del Canfield had moved behind the bar again. He polished glasses, looking first at me, then at them, reading the problem. He bent and put the glass down. When he came back up again he had a double-barreled shotgun. He pointed it out into the room and cocked both hammers.

"I don't know what's going on, but I don't want it happening here." He moved the shotgun in the direction of the man at the door. "You sit back at your table." He nodded at me. "You can go. I'll eat your burger and fries." He smiled at the two men. "You'll have your lunch and then you can go also."

The man blocking me looked at the older one and received a nod.

I walked on past them, opened the door. I said to the bartender: "Thank you."

"Don't be a stranger," he said, grinning.

There was a big Chevrolet parked next to my Mustang. I wrote down the plate number.

I watched behind me all the way back to town, but no one came.

At the sheriff's office I asked a deputy to run the plate number. He looked at them, then at me, and said: "It's a rental."

"Ask Runner to find out who rented the vehicle, lessor and lessee. The two in it kind of threatened me." I told him what had happened.

He began to smile before I was done. "Del Canfield used to be a state trooper. His family owns that restaurant. I'll give him a call out there. You wait."

I waited. The deputy used the phone in the sheriff's office. I saw nothing of Runner Riggs.

The deputy returned. "Del said they ate their lunch civilized, paid and tipped handsome, and left peacefully. He took their license number also. I'll tell Runner about it and we'll check where they rented the car and what names they used."

"Did Del say anything else about them?"

"Only that they'd never been in before."

CHAPTER NINE

A few days after I began practice in Grimsley City, I drove to the parking lot on the river where my father had been killed. In daytime it was a huge area that had been set aside by the city for the use of boaters. Boaters could pull their vehicles into the lot, back the boat trailer down a ramp into the river, unhook and float the boat, then park the vehicle.

It seemed an innocuous area.

But not at night.

HENRY LEE scored the first effective points for the defense during the afternoon. His cross-examination was forceful and he couched his questions so that the jurors were always aware that he didn't believe the answers of the prosecution witness.

"Mr. Kentner, I'll ask you to try to be frank with the hardworking folks on the jury. Will you admit to them you hated your stepmother?"

"Well, *hate,* that sure is a strong word, sir. I don't much like Shirley, but I don't hate her, because I try to be a Christian person. I didn't trust her as far as my father was concerned. Pop met her when he was ill and in and out of the hospital for tests and treatments. At first we thought it was a harmless flirtation, but she sure didn't let it stay that way."

"She pursued your father?"

"Not like you're trying to get me to say. No, he was the one doing the chasing, but my opinion is she was making sure he stayed close after her."

"You say your father was ill. How ill was he?"

"Pretty sick."

"He was sick enough to die, wasn't he?"

"I don't know. I'm no doctor."

"Tell me how sick you thought he was?"

126

"Some."

Henry Lee smiled, scenting trial blood. It was apparent to me that the witness was evading the question, and I thought the jury also sensed it.

"When you began to think your father's relationship was a problem, did you ask your father to promise he'd not marry Shirley?"

"He promised that on his own."

"And you and your sister had nothing to do with him making that promise?"

"No."

I saw two jurors smile knowingly.

"Let's move ahead to the night your father died. You had your meeting, all three of you together, one big, happy family. Where was Shirley?"

"At the big house, I guess. It was just my father, my sister, and me. The business partners."

"And one of those partners was almost a dying man, wasn't he?"

"I'm still no doctor, sir. Far as I know, he was sick, but not dying."

"Okay," Lee said amiably. "What time was it when your father left your sister's home?"

"Early. Shirley maybe picked him up as early as six in the evening. Certainly no later than six-thirty. He waited until the food was out and he'd had a few bites. There were cold cuts for sandwiches, plus baked beans, and potato salad. I remember he managed a tiny bit of each, even though we could tell he didn't feel well." Alfred smiled for the jury. "Pop dearly loved picnic food and my sister's a good cook."

Lee attacked. "All right, Mr. Kentner. So your father loved picnic-type food and now will picnic no more. You've slyly let the jury in on that closely kept secret. How late did *you* stay at your sister's house?"

"I'm not certain. Not too long after Pop left. We got the papers all signed and everything done. I'd been home an hour or two when the police called."

"Was anyone with you at your home?"

"Sure. My family. That's my wife and my two kids."

"And did you leave your sister alone in her house when you left?"

"Yes."

"Was she married then?"

"Separated."

"Let me submit to you then, Mr. Kentner, that either you or your sister, or the two of you in league, could have gone to your father's house and assisted Jose Garcia in the murder of your father and the search of the house."

Someone on the jury moved and the chair squeaked.

Alfred Kentner nodded coolly. "I guess we could have, but we didn't. Or at least, I didn't."

"I doubt you'd admit it if you did. But will you concede that there was time for it to happen if you'd wanted to kill your father that night?"

"I guess so, but I didn't kill no one."

"Who gets your father's money, all of it, if your stepmother is convicted in this trial?"

"My sister and I."

"Every bit of the money? All the real property?"

"That's what I'm told."

Lee moved away from the witness chair and took up station to the right side of the jury so that jurors could better observe the witness.

"How much money?"

"I don't know for certain. There's estate expenses. There's inheritance tax, both federal and state. There's attorney and accountant fees. There's all sorts of things."

Lee's face didn't change. "Three million? Four? Five?"

"Could be."

"Did you graduate from college, Mr. Kentner?"

"Yes. From Grimsley."

"What degree do you hold?"

"I have a degree in business—accounting."

128

"And aren't you, along with your sister, a co-executor of your father's estate?"

"Yes."

"Let me ask you again if you don't know, more than a year after your father's death, almost to the penny, how much money is in your father's estate and how it would split up with your step-mother involved in a share and how it will be if she's convicted and cut out?"

I saw jurors smile again.

"The accounting isn't done and won't be for a while."

"You mean it can't be done and your share figured until your stepmother is convicted?"

"I only want justice for those responsible for my dad's murder."

"Yes, good old apple-pie justice. Let's move to a minor point that might interest the jury. There was a clock in the room where your father was found dead in his home. I'm told that the clock in that room was stopped at ten until ten. Did you see the clock when you went to your father's home the night he was killed?"

"I saw it."

"Was it stopped at ten to ten?"

"I think so."

"Had you noticed that clock before?"

"Sure. It was Pop's favorite." Alfred Kentner smiled. "It was expensive and had big gold numbers on the face."

"Had you ever seen the clock when it wasn't in working order?"

"No." Alfred leaned forward in his witness chair. "My father was a perfectionist about machines, Mr. Lee. Anything he saw broken he fixed or had fixed. That clock, to my best recollection, was working until the very night my father was murdered."

"Do you remember when you last noticed the clock before the death of your father?"

"I'm not sure. Maybe a day or a week or a month before that night my father was killed. But I'll bet it worked if it was in his house."

"Would it be a good assumption to say that your father was likely killed near the time the clock stopped?"

"It sounds okay."

Henry Lee turned back toward the defense table. Shirley Kentner watched him. She sat in her chair, Bible open in front of her.

Something was to her liking. She smiled faintly and Lee acknowledged the smile with a tiny nod.

Lee moved close to the witness.

"What are your hobbies, Mr. Kentner?"

Kentner's words seemed carefully chosen. "I play some bad golf. I swim and walk. I like spectator sports—football, Kentucky and Grimsley basketball, the baseball Reds, Cardinals, and the Braves."

"How about horse races? Trotters and pacers and Thoroughbreds?"

"Sometimes."

Lee smiled for the jury, alerting them to the fact he was heading towards a goal. "Do you bet on horse races or other sporting events?"

"Yes."

"Large or small bets?"

The prosector had risen. "Objection, Your Honor. What's being asked is far removed from any questions asked this witness in direct examination."

Daggert nodded solemnly. "Mr. Lee, is there some reason for your pursuit of this line of questioning?"

"Yes. It will likely become apparent, even to our concerned commonwealth's attorney, if the court will allow me to proceed onward a bit."

"All right. Objection overruled. However, please get to the point."

Lee nodded, unoffended. He turned back to Alfred Kentner. "Are you deeply in debt from heavy gambling losses, Mr. Kentner?"

The witness looked at the prosecutor's table, but there was no movement there.

"I owe some money. Yes."

"How much money?"

Alfred Kentner shrugged lightly. "I'm not sure. I intend to pay it all soon."

"You mean you'll pay it out of your share of your father's estate?"

Kentner shuffled his feet against the floor. "Out of that and my normal income." He smiled apologetically at the jury to minimize the problem.

"As to your normal salary, how much did you make a year over, say, the last five years before your father died?"

"Good money. Six-figure dollars a year salary plus bonuses and dividends of eight to ten thousand a year."

"Can you approximate for the jury how much you owe in gambling debts, Mr. Kentner?"

"I'm not certain."

"A thousand? Ten thousand? A hundred thousand? Many hundreds of thousands?"

"Yes," Kentner answered, voice low.

"I didn't hear you, Mr. Kentner. Answer again."

"I bet too much and too many times. I finally made myself quit gambling."

"But you owe hundreds of thousands of dollars?"

"Maybe. It could be that much."

"And didn't you and your father fight many times about your gambling habits and losses?"

"We talked. He made me promise to quit."

"You argued bitterly about gambling in public more than once, didn't you?"

"A few words. He was right and I was wrong. I admit it now."

"Your father accused you of stealing money from the business, and you, in turn, told him publicly that he was the thief when he collected. You told him he was stealing from coin boxes to give the money to the 'bitch in heat' he'd married. Didn't you use those very words?"

Kentner sat silently.

"Wasn't that the argument and those your words?"

Kentner nodded slightly. Someone on the jury sighed.

131

"The record doesn't pick up nods, Mr. Kentner. Answer my question so that the jury can hear."

"Yes. My gambling was a thing we argued about. And I was sorry later because my father wasn't well and didn't need extra worries."

"And now would you like to answer again the question I asked earlier about whether you hate your stepmother?"

"She had my father killed."

"Did she now? Didn't this argument on gambling occur only days before your father was murdered by a man you could have hired as easily as you seem to believe your stepmother hired or sex-bribed him?"

"They took place in that time period, but I didn't hire anyone."

Lee kept on. He went through theories about what happened on the night of the murder, different scenarios from those the prosecution favored. Alfred sat low in the witness chair and found strength to deny all wrongdoing beyond heavy gambling.

"How much money?" Lee asked again and again.

"I don't know. A lot of money. I owe it numerous places. I owe some people in Louisville and Lexington. I owe some in Nevada."

"I submit to you that you do know exactly how much you owe, Mr. Accountant. I further submit to you that the amount is obscenely large. I believe you know, almost to the penny, how much you will receive from your father's estate in every scenario. I also submit to you that the people you owe this money to don't want to wait for their dirty gambling dollars. Maybe they are waiting now because they know your father is conveniently dead and believe they'll soon be paid. But you were the one who needed your sick father dead, Mr. Kentner, not his second, childless wife."

"I didn't want my father dead," Alfred Kentner answered faintly.

"Can you deny that your owing money in many gambling places didn't precipitate, whether you were involved or not, the murder of your father?"

"Of course I deny it. Your questions are wrong. I owe money

to *gentlemen.*" He looked at Shirley, who was watching intently. "She got him killed," he said, pointing. "We all know that."

Lee smiled. "Do we all now? And here I thought and hope this jury thinks, because of their earlier promises, that the death of your father and the reasons why he was killed were subjects this jury was to determine."

Kentner subsided and sat silently.

Once more Lee moved close to the witness chair. "I have copies of the estate inventory in my files, Mr. Kentner. Will you admit that those papers show a gross estate of about four and a half million dollars?"

"That sounds right."

"Just four and a half million dollars?"

"Yes."

"Isn't there a great deal of missing money?"

Corner rose again, but he only stood and waited.

"I don't know anything about missing money."

"Didn't you accuse your father of taking money from the Kentner Amusement Company and hiding it?"

"Maybe I did when we argued. It didn't mean anything."

"Was your father the only person who collected for Kentner Amusement until the day he died?"

"Yes. He did the collecting. We changed that the last night of his life."

"And don't you believe that he took some of the money from the weekly collections and kept it for himself?"

"I was never certain of that." Alfred Kentner took a handkerchief from his pocket and rubbed it over his forehead.

"How much money did your father steal from the company collections, Mr. Kentner?"

"Objection," Corner said softly. "Asked and answered."

"Asked, but *not* answered," Lee said.

"The witness may answer," Daggert said calmly.

"I don't know for sure that there was any money taken. If Pop did take some money, then it was a tiny bit, just pocket money."

"Who collects for Kentner Amusement now?"

133

"My sister and I collect."

"Are collections up in volume since your father died?"

"Yes. Business seems a little better."

"And is someone from the IRS now accompanying you and your sister on your collection route?"

This was something I'd not known about.

"A man did for about six months. He doesn't now."

"How much are collections up since your father died?"

"About twenty percent. We feel that business is better now. More kids in school, more people with leisure time."

"How much were total collections in the last full year when your father was the sole collector?"

"About three million."

"And how much a month are collections now?"

"It varies from month to month, but last month it was in excess of three hundred thousand."

"So your father could have been skimming six or seven hundred thousand dollars a year from cashboxes, untaxed so far, and unaccounted for?"

"We don't think he did that."

"Does the Internal Revenue Service?"

"I suppose. They always do."

"Is the IRS claiming money from his estate?"

"Yes."

"What law firm is handling your father's estate?"

"John Phillips."

"And whom does Mr. Phillips practice with?"

"Well, he shares offices with Seth Ellison and Mr. Corner."

"How convenient," Lee said sarcastically.

"Your Honor!" Corner said indignantly.

"The same firm or association of friendly lawyers that's handling the estate of your murdered father for you is prosecuting my client, and not you, for that murder. Is that it?"

"Your Honor, we're prepared to show that John Phillips, Seth Ellison, and I share only an office building we bought together. We don't share incomes," Corner said heatedly.

Daggert nodded at Corner. "I agree that this testimony may go out if your outcry of unsworn explanation means you're objecting to it.''

Lee said: "We'll then want to make some offers to prove to preserve it and what would or could follow from it.''

"You may, Mr. Lee,'' Daggert said smoothly.

Corner and Lee went to the bench. They whispered up there for a time until Lee nodded, satisfied.

The trial recessed at about five. That was an hour after the jury had left for the day and after the completion of offers to prove by Henry Lee concerning the legal association of Corner and John Phillips.

Corner offered to bring in and file with the court affidavits from Phillips, Ellison, and an accountant showing he would and could not benefit in any way from the estate of Fiala Kentner. Lee smiled and agreed politely to allow those documents in, but also reiterated his original statements. "For the record,'' he said. "The fact that the prosecutor claims his office setup is a legitimate business arrangement still affects my client, her indictment, and this trial.''

I smiled. The jury had heard what had been said in their presence, and the careful, bloodless admonition of Judge Daggert after the happening. I thought, for the first time, that Shirley Kentner had a chance.

I watched her. Her eyes seemed brighter, her face had more color. She caught me watching and I smiled and was thrilled when she smiled in return.

The last thing I heard Henry Lee say was that he was done with Alfred Kentner, unless the prosecutor asked him anything on redirect.

Corner said, "I have nothing more for him. Tomorrow I have some of the ladies from the bridge game on the night Fiala was murdered and I have Fiala's daughter, Ruth Thacker. After that there'll be Jose and I'll tie everything together sometime with Detective Owens, just to introduce and show the state's exhibits. Plus the coroner's deposition.'' He nodded at the man who sat silently at counsel table and then smiled coldly at Henry Lee. "Do you intend to accuse Mrs. Thacker of also being involved in the murder of her father, Henry?''

Lee smiled in return. ''Perhaps. Don't attempt to plan my case for me, Mr. Corner.'' He nodded up at the judge. ''We also want the coroner's deposition and two doctors for the defense, but all of the doctors are by deposition.'' He looked up at the ceiling. ''And then we might have the defendant. Who knows?''

I visited my office on the way out to get my coat. There was a phone message on my desk from Maude White, precinct person, and the judge's restaurant pal.

It read: ''There's a political meeting set at headquarters for 7:30 tonight. Be there!!!''

Whoever had taken the message had underlined the three exclamation points.

''My'' political party, in good times past, had bought an old fire station for its local headquarters. I'd had the purchase story told me by a young, pretty secretary I'd taken on a single, long-ago date.

Grimsley City had gone from volunteer fire departments to paid, full-time firemen in the nineteen-sixties. That had left most of the neighborhood fire stations unused. The largest of those fire-houses had been mid-block in the poorest and most depressed part of Grimsley City. My political party and hers, my date said, had decided it would be good business to put headquarters there, where the Grim City poor could see and be uplifted by the choice we'd made for headquarters and so vote the straight party line.

Parking places nearby were sparse. I found a spot a block-plus away. I locked the car. I then did one more thing. I picked up a medium-sized twig and put it, bent under pressure, into the windshield-wiper well, between the hood of my car and the windshield.

I looked around. No one was watching me or following me. I felt silly, but I also still suspected unseen eyes. Those eyes could be a block or a mile away. The happening at the restaurant at noon had unnerved me.

136

The neighborhood was made up of aging frame houses, most of them shotgun in style, one room behind another. Many houses were built flush with the sidewalk. There were tiny sideyards, brown and bare in winter. I smelled the odor of coal smoke mixed with those of garbage and fish from the nearby big, muddy river.

Double doors opened into headquarters. I'd been there for chili suppers before, so I boldly opened the doors. Inside the door, two women sold dollar chances on half the money collected (with the other half to the party). I recognized the women from the court-house. I handed over a dollar for a ticket. I hung my old coat on a wall peg, thinking no one would have the bad taste to steal it.

A crowd of women fussed together over the arrangement of re-freshments on folding tables. There was a bubbling coffee ma-chine and a lighted, warm popcorn popper. There were big plates of cookies and finger sandwiches, some wrapped with wax paper, some already uncovered. There were full bowls of dip with crack-ers and chips heaped beside them. An uncovered half barrel of iced-down soft drinks stood nearby, mostly ignored for now.

The headquarters smelled of good food, liquor, and tobacco smoke.

The men stood together near far tables. Behind the busiest table, two aproned men worked diligently at serving drinks, pull-ing beer taps, pouring whiskey into glasses from bottles. I could hear discussions on weather, football, U.K. basketball, baseball trades, and even political talk.

I saw Maude White come in headquarters' doors. She looked around and brightened when she spotted me. She beckoned to me subtly.

I walked to her.

She was rouged and powdered and looked younger than she had in the restaurant.

"You're in the stronghold of the enemy, Jim. The judge won't be here. He despises these things. If anyone asks if there's some-one here to speak for him, could you hold up your hand?"

"Sure. If you think he'd want me to do that."

"He does. I called him and said I'd asked you to be here. You smile at everyone and say the judge is still considering whether or not to run and will let his friends know soon."

That sounded simple. "All right. Can I ask you something?"

"Sure."

"Did you know my father, Al Singer?"

"No. But I heard you were in the restaurant this noon and Del told me to tell you that the rental car that followed you in was rented by a man named Ramirez at a Lexington car rental agency at the airport."

"Thanks."

"Del's my half-brother," she said.

"I may need to hire him to bodyguard me," I said. "I admired his double-barreled shotgun."

She smiled up at me. "Whatever. We'll now introduce you among the ladies. If I hold up my right hand a little when I make an introduction, that means the lady's married. If I hold up my left, it means I've heard she's taken. If I don't hold up either hand, then the lady could be, as far as I know, available." She gave me a wink. "Some are all three at once. Okay?"

"Fine."

She took me into the busy group of women of various ages. Some smiled at me. A few did not, but I smiled at all of them.

Not many of the women were hands down. That was all right.

One name had a special meaning for me. "Belle Trempen." She was a hands-down lady. She was also, I remembered, the lady who'd held the bridge party in a nearby house on the night of Fiala Kentner's murder: "Doc Trempen's young widow."

She was a short, handsome woman who I guessed was no more than forty years old. Her clothes were bright and flashy and she wore big dinner rings on both hands. She seemed energetic and smiled prettily. I liked her looks.

"I saw you at the trial today," she said. "I've been called as a witness." She gave me a coquettish look.

"I remember reading somewhere that Shirley Kentner played cards at your house the night her husband was shot."

"Yes. There were eight of us girls. I don't know why anyone would want me as a witness. We just played cards. It was like a

138

thousand other bridge nights. Both sides have taken statements from me. Shirley was second high. She got no telephone calls and she didn't seem nervous. I never saw her even glance at her house." She looked around. "Am I supposed to tell that around?"

"There's a witness separation, but that wouldn't affect me."

"I won't say anymore anyway. But that's what I'll testify to on the stand." She saw Lynn Corner watching us. She patted my hand lingeringly and moved on, looking guilty.

Maude White also moved me on. When we'd run out of handy ladies, Maude motioned me aside.

"Now you go on back where the men are. Maybe someone will take you in hand there, but be careful. The judge has lots of quiet, good friends. Our prosecutor has lots of backslappers who talk one way and vote for who they hate the least. Help Daggert where you can."

"Is Daggert going to run again?"

"He has it in mind or he'd not let you say a word. His wife's death took the stuffing out of him. He drinks too much and knows it. He broods over what's past and worries about the future. I worry about him, because he's a good man." She nodded earnestly up at me, her eyes bright. I liked her a lot.

I walked back to where the men congregated. By now there were maybe a hundred people in headquarters, with others still arriving. The noise had intensified. Men shook hands, yelled friendly and unfriendly insults, beat on each other, and damned the other party for all of humanity's ills.

The smell of cigarettes and cigars overwhelmed food smells. A man I vaguely remembered nodded carefully to me and I tried to recall him and succeeded. Fred Gow. Party chairman. I'd seen him several times around the courthouse. He was a big, fleshy man wearing heavy-rimmed glasses and sipping hard and often at a Bud Light.

Tonight he seemed affable. "Thanks for coming, Jim. We can always use new blood. How's the job going?"

"Well enough. There's a jury trial in progress. I'm finding it interesting."

"I heard they was trying Kentner's blond bitch," he said

sourly. "Are you willing to donate part of your salary to the party?"

"Sure, if my boss says okay. Whatever's customary, as soon as Judge Daggert approves."

"He'll okay it. We're not that far divided, no matter what you hear." He smiled. "How about collecting for us?"

"Not just now," I said. "I'm sure you already have someone doing that job and I'd not want to tamper with the existing order of things."

He smiled some more. "We do have a someone. She'll be around to see you soon for your fair share. I just wanted to know if she could ask you to fill in collecting for her now and then. The party always needs money."

"I heard when Fiala Kentner was involved in finances, it didn't need a lot."

"That was then. This is now. Will you help collect?"

"That might be okay. But right now it could upset courthouse people if a newcomer, one who took a job others wanted, began trying to collect from them."

"You have a point," Gow said. He looked around the crowd, some of whom seemed to be watching us. "Let me introduce you to some people."

He led and I dutifully followed. Once again I smiled, shook hands, and made small talk.

Eventually Gow and I wound up in a group with Lynn Corner and one or two others. I believed that Gow had purposely led me there.

U.K. basketball was being discussed. The team, as it almost always was, was having a strong year.

"How about you, Jim?" Corner asked. "I remember your name from somewhere."

"I played a little soccer."

"Sure," Corner said. "You played for Grimsley."

I nodded.

"You made all-American," Corner said, either remembering or using something he'd saved back.

"Second team."

Gow examined me and said humorously: "Fuck soccer."

"Fuck all sports," I answered, grinning back.

He bristled. "Soccer's for grade-school punkies and pussies."

Corner shook his head, stopping my planned reply that football was for big-assed, microcephalic boys and basketball for over-grown idiots. "Not so, Fred. Soccer draws more fans, worldwide, than damned near anything. Anyone who believes the game's for kids hasn't seen it played." He looked hard at the much larger Gow, dominating him. "I went to soccer games. I remember Jim-boy here playing for Grimsley. He put our local school on the map in the sport." He watched me, working hard at being ingratiating. "You were good."

"Thanks."

"For nothing," he said. "It's God's truth." He eyed me with interest. "You and I need serious talk before long. I'll want to know whether or not you want to continue being probation officer next year."

"I work for Daggert. I've heard around you're going to run for his job. Are you offering to continue me if you win?"

"No. I can't, by law, make such an offer." He smiled carefully. "I think you know that. But if you've got an interest in continuing as probation officer should I run and be elected, then I want to plan concerning that contingency."

I decided that if I indicated any interest, then we would talk carefully about what was, in return, wanted from me.

I smiled. "I'm unsure. Could be, by the time this year is done, I'll no longer be interested. The money helps some now, but I may not need it in a year as my practice grows. And I don't want to bite the hand that feeds me."

He took a step closer. "Why is that hand so interested in the murder case we're trying?"

"Is it?"

He gave me his prosecutor's look. "I hear it is. I hear that he, along with you, were twice caught skulking around the scene of the crime in the Kentner case."

141

I laughed out loud and found I was alone in the laughter. "We drove past the house once and we went walking around Lake Keel last Saturday for exercise."

"The Kentners are suspicious of Daggert's motives and also yours," Corner said severely. "They see you, the probation officer for this county, and the circuit judge hanging around where Fiala Kentner was murdered. They then wonder, openly and publicly to me in my official capacity, what the hell you were doing."

"Driving past. Walking. Curiosity on my part might be an added answer."

"It would be intelligent on your goddamn part and his goddamn part to walk and drive elsewhere."

His tone of voice riled me, but I smiled. I refrained from telling him I'd walk where I damn well pleased.

"You planning to indict us?" I asked.

Corner subsided. He smiled and shook his head. "Of course not."

"Are you helping Daggert the drunk in his campaign to be?" he then asked.

"I don't know for certain he's a candidate," I answered truthfully.

"Let's hope he damned well isn't. Lots of good people around here think he ought not run. Daggert drinks like ten fish, and lots say he had something to do with helping along his own wife's death."

"Tell me about his wife and her dying."

"His wife fucking died funny. She was sick, but he was supposed to be watching her. He was shitfaced drunk in the hospital room. She died and it was half an hour before a doctor or nurse knew she was dead."

"Sounds interesting," I said. "What with me working for Daggert, maybe I ought to tell him your story so he can decide about running?"

"Good damned idea," Corner said.

"Okay if I mention you're the one who told me the story?"

Corner stepped back a little. "No. Don't do that, please. I don't want any more problems than I already have with the judge, even if he has less than a year to go.''

I nodded. ''Glad I asked then. So I guess I should ask him questions and not reveal my source for them?''

Up front, Fred Gow, having moved away from us and to a podium, interrupted us, saved Corner's answer. Gow tapped on the podium with a beer bottle I hoped was empty. ''I'm now going to introduce our declared candidates. First off, for circuit judge, Lynn Corner.''

Corner turned away from me and waved at the crowd.

There was mild applause.

Corner smiled at the crowd. His voice was loud: ''I don't know yet whether I'll have opposition. The two-term incumbent hasn't deigned to tell us where he stands. While he remains silent, I'd like to take this opportunity to ask your support in my run for circuit judge.''

There was applause again, but I saw some people sitting on their hands.

Fred Gow looked around. ''Is there anyone here representing Judge Simon Daggert?''

I turned so the audience could see me. I put my foot on my folding chair.

''My name's Jim Singer. I'm a lawyer and I'm also Judge Daggert's brand-new probation officer. I wasn't born in Grimsley City, but years ago I came to Grimsley U. for college and I liked the town and the people. Now that I'm back here, I plan to stay. I hope none of you are too upset with me because Judge Daggert appointed me.'' I smiled for effect. ''I was hungry and needed the job. The good judge wanted me to tell his friends here tonight that he's considering whether or not to run again. He promises to make that decision soon.''

''I can hardly wait,'' someone yelled in friendly fashion from the back of the room.

I grinned and joined in laughter. I sat down to scattered clapping.

I listened idly to more candidates. In many cases there was but one candidate, probably party-blessed, for the office. In a couple of cases there were two candidates, each proclaiming his or her great worth and pleading for support.

I came back to life when Silver was announced as the solo candidate for commonwealth attorney. I'd not known he was there. He walked to the podium to make his remarks. I stood and clapped with others.

"I plan to file on the first filing day," he said carefully. "I hope to be this party's only candidate and this party's commonwealth's attorney for the next term. I want your help." He smiled ingratiatingly.

Someone in the crowd called: "Go for it, Slim Silver."

I laughed with others. Silver saw me standing and gave me a tiny wink.

"I want all of us together in the fall no matter what happens in May. I want our party to win the courthouse, the statehouse, both houses of Congress, the White House, and even the outhouse." He leaned a little on the podium and waited out the laughter. "I want it all for us. Work for us and we then will work for you."

There was much applause.

Silver sat down ten rows from me. Lynn Corner moved close and sat by him. They conferred.

I'd wanted to talk to Silver, but I decided against it for now.

I watched some more. They had the ticket drawing for the money, half to the party, half to the winner. I was not upset when I didn't win and I learned something useful when the winner, one of two candidates for auditor, gave his half on to the party, a popular move.

Maude White came to me when the meeting concluded.

"You did okay," she whispered. "Now move on. Some of Corner's boys, the rough element, road and garbage truck workers, will lift a few drinks and might try to start trouble with you if they can. So move on."

In the back of the room I saw a man look hard at me and then whisper something to a companion.

"Okay," I said. I found my old coat and fled into the night leaving the sounds of revelry behind me.

144

CHAPTER TEN

Ballinger, after I signed on, sent me to Quantico and I did "boot camp." When I finished, I got sent to a Navy base near my boyhood home in Corpus Christi, Texas. There an intense old man taught me things about explosives.

WHEN I ARRIVED at the place on the street where I'd parked the Mustang, I could still hear loud sounds coming from behind me as other loyal party members departed. I stood in the darkness and listened. I smiled and smelled the icy odors of winter. I felt exhilarated in that I'd ruined Lynn Corner's night.

My Mustang sat in darkness. I let my eyes grow accustomed to the lack of light. I waited and watched around me. Nothing. In a few moments the clouds parted and a sliver of moon allowed me to see my car more clearly.

I stepped close and saw that the twig, while still in the well between the windshield and hood, was not as I had set it. It had been sprung away so that now it was no longer under pressure. My heart jumped within me and I looked around, certain there was someone lying in wait for me.

There was no one.

The surface of the car was dry. If there was an appreciable breeze, I couldn't detect it. Yet the twig was sprung. Maybe it had happened naturally.

At first, and almost telling myself that all was well, I unlocked the car door to release the hood and do a check. I remembered there was a flashlight in the glove compartment and the batteries had been live when I'd last checked them.

But I thought better of opening the door. I backed away from the car and stood watching around me for another long moment. I left the car and walked eight blocks to the sheriff's office. I found Riggs at the booking desk. He shook his head at my story, made notes on paper, and then contacted both the Grim City police and the state police. I thought, were I not the probation officer and someone who'd had other trouble that day, that he might have laughed and sent me on my way.

In half an hour I was back with Runner Riggs and others near my car. Riggs had a spotlight from his car shining on mine. Two state troopers, wearing bomb gear, were taking a look under the Mustang with curious instruments, lights and mirrors on long poles. There were yellow tapes up, and Grimsley City officers and deputy sheriffs kept a small crowd, some of them departing the political meeting, away from their nearby cars and mine.

"What makes you think there might be a bomb in your car?" Runner Riggs asked.

"I'm not sure there's a bomb. But no wind. No rain."

He looked perplexed.

"I put a twig in the crack in my hood windshield well when I parked the car. The twig had been sprung when I came back. The outside of the car was dry and there wasn't much breeze. I think someone lifted the hood and thereby sprung the twig, but maybe I'm wrong."

"Couldn't we unlock the car, open the hood with the hood release, and check?"

"I'll give you the keys, but would it be all right if I move further away?"

Runner smiled without humor.

One state trooper now had his long pole under my car turning it left and then right.

The sheriff watched them and me.

"Opening the door, opening the hood, or getting into the car could set it off," I said.

"What the hell do you know about this kind of stuff?" Riggs asked suspiciously. "You some kind of expert?"

"No expert."

The two state troopers near the car waved to the sheriff. He walked that way and conferred with them.

"Could be timed also," I called out to the assembled group.

One of the state troopers frowned and shook his head at me and said something, low-voiced, to Runner.

Runner Riggs listened to the armor-clad state trooper and then returned. ''They see something wired on top of your engine block and maybe hooked to the battery. They ain't sure if the battery is all that can set it off. So we're going to evacuate the neighborhood and leave your car and the other cars near it alone. They've called on the radio and they're flying in a bomb guy from Alcohol, Tobacco and Firearms in Louisville to take a look.'' He smiled, liking me better now that I wasn't a wolf-cryer. ''Unless you want to take a crack at it.''

''Not me,'' I said.

''Go home then, Jim. I'll call you when it's safe to get your car, assuming we don't have to blow it up along with the bomb.'' He looked me over. ''I got a question. I'm interested and the state guys are interested: Who's after you, Jim?''

''Someone new, someone old. Maybe the two men I saw in Dumont today.''

''But why?''

''I'm not sure. Even if I was, I probably couldn't say.''

He waved me away.

I walked home.

From outside my building I could see my lights were on in the apartment. At my door I could hear my television blaring. Whoever was inside wasn't trying to take me unawares.

I opened my door carefully and looked in.

Ballinger sprawled comfortably on my bed-couch. He'd opened himself a diet cola from my tiny refrigerator. I buy all kinds of soft drinks, opting for whatever is cheaper over the ones that have the best and most blaring ads on television. *Uh-huh.* I'm not impressed by claims. They all taste pretty good to me, because once I was dry. Very dry. Cola is cola, orange is orange.

In his lap he held my ''blind'' pictures, the ones taken from magazines and then savaged.

''Interesting set,'' he said. ''All from U.S. magazines.''

''Yes.''

"Where you been?" he asked, grinning whitely. He was as big as an NFL lineman and he looked strong. But he was old, over sixty, maybe over seventy. His hair was sparse and white. His eyes were black and watchful, the whites bloodshot. He had a mouth like an old prune.

"I had to walk home from a meeting," I said. "Someone stuck a bomb under the hood of my car."

"No shit? What kind of bomb?"

"Not sure. They said it's on top of the engine block. Whoever laid it in opened my locked car door and then unlatched the hood to do the job. The sheriff said he might call me or I can try calling him later to find out more."

"What's going on, Carlos?" Ballinger asked, smiling only a little.

"What am I still into from times spent with you?" I told him about the two I'd seen in Dumont earlier and what I'd learned about them.

"Two guys?"

"Two *Mexican* guys."

He shook his head. "Those two would not be my people. Have to be from someone else. I thought things were done when we razed the village where they held you prisoner. Lots had moved on by that time, of course. And we gave the villagers time to get out, which might ease your pious mind." He gave me a level look. "Do you remember anything at all now you couldn't recall when we questioned you in the hospitals?"

"Nothing. Other than the pictures in your lap of happy gentlemen with their eyes slashed out. That's new. They came by mail, maybe once every month or so."

His eyes flickered. "I also saw the envelopes. You'd not told me this before."

"One reason is I thought maybe you were the one doing it. You, or one of your people. A joke. Maybe an advertisement for the job you keep wanting me to take. A way of calling me chicken."

He sipped my diet cola. "If it's being done by my people, no one has told me about it, but that's possible. There are people in my office who know your history and know I want you back.'' He shrugged, dismissing it. ''I'll take the pictures and inquire. Anything else? Had you ever seen either of the men before?''

''No. Except in court.''

''And that's all?''

''Yes. Maybe if your people asked the same questions again, they'd find something new and exciting.''

''We could and will try if you, in your exalted civilian status, would hold still for it,'' he said. ''Would you?''

''Sure. Why are you sending your people in and out of my town and why do they ask questions about me, questions where you already know the answers?''

''Checking. That's all. Strangers in your courtroom and a bomb in your car might indicate why.'' He nodded at me.

''More than that, Ballinger. Your people were around before the bomb or the strangers.''

''I will tell you a little. Bad stuff has been coming out of Iraq and maybe Iran. Most of it came out in the months after our troops went in and spanked the Iraqis. The British found a two-ton shipment in Belfast. We intercepted another, similar shipment on your river. It came up from Mexico.''

''The Ohio River?''

''Yes. What we found was some nerve gas hooked to antipersonnel bombs, time-fused. Let one explode and it'd take out maybe a hundred yards on all sides, killing everything. Then there's some nuclear junk, made in Iraq. We think it would take expert workers and technicians years to assemble and make even a crude bomb out of the stuff and it still might not explode. But maybe some could be used as a poison added to a conventional bomb.'' He looked down at his black hands. ''I'll swear under oath that I never told you any of this. But it's part of why I need you back with me and most of why you're being bothered by us— me.''

''Could one of those nerve gas bombs be what's under the hood of my car?''

He calculated in his head and then nodded his head. ''It could fit.''

"You want me to go back down into Mexico and try to find out who, where, and why?"

"Exactly."

"I can't do that sort of thing anymore, Ballinger. I worry too much. I'd be language rusty and I'd get caught quick. Besides that, when I was caught before, how many people who got away before you went back and razed the village saw and would remember me if I turned up elsewhere?"

"Plastic surgery," he said. "A tuck here, a bit of bone there. Maybe a tattoo or two, even some new scars. We can make you look different." He smiled. "And I can promise for the benefit of your sex life you'd look more interesting than you now look."

"I have no sex life. You know that."

"Yes. We checked around. You would have one if you came back to us. The doctors who treated you say you're physically okay."

"Can you give me back my bad eye along with sex?"

"No. You know I can't. I'm sorry about what happened to your eye, Carlos. But our doctors could treat your other problems." He waved an arm. "I think you left us to punish yourself, to live poor, to live without women. You felt it was your fault you were caught. You still feel that way."

"Why, when you knew where I was in those hills, did it take so long for you to rescue me?"

He shrugged eloquently. "It was the way it was. I think you know that someday you will work for us again once our doctors give you back your *cojones.*"

"Forget sex. I have. Without both eyes what you'd have working would be half a man, a man who spends nights sleeping light and cradling his good eye behind his hands, a man who has both nightmares and daymares and breaks into the blue sweats when he discovers someone has installed a bomb as new equipment in his car."

"You'd be okay back with us. The fear would only make you better and more careful. You'd never get caught again."

"Maybe, but I won't go back into Mexico for you, Ballinger."

"We need you. I need you."

I shook my head. "Maybe we can help each other some way, but not your way."

He shook *his* head stubbornly. "I send amateurs down there and the local assholes laugh at me and mine. They know who all my people are, they know who's watching and being watched. We try to infiltrate them and our agents vanish. We try to use Mexes and the bastards buy them out from under us with stolen or terrorist-provided dollars. They bomb our safe houses, they shoot and knife my Mex employees when they can't buy them. I'll bet the two guys you had your problem with today came from down there. And each day there's more stuff coming from Iraq, Iran, and Libya and wherever else, some bought, some free. We hear whispers about bad happenings to be, but we can't get a handle on them. We hear there's new money around and more coming from the States."

"Let me talk for a moment and you just listen. No interruptions."

He did let me talk first and then we both talked for a long time.

In the morning, still tired because sleep had never fully come, I met Ballinger for breakfast. The sheriff had never called me, so I called him.

We drove Ballinger's car, an anonymous black Chevrolet, to the breakfast meeting place the sheriff had named as a rendezvous, at the edge of the Grimsley campus. "Call when you get there," he'd said.

I asked for grapefruit juice, biscuits and country gravy, and hot, black coffee. Ballinger ordered city ham, three eggs, and decaf.

"Screw the cholesterol," he said.

"Screw caffeine," I answered.

I called Runner Riggs's office and told the deputy who answered the phone that Ballinger and I were in place and waiting for the sheriff.

Runner Riggs arrived before our juice was served. He came in uniform, wearing a huge revolver. The adults in the place watched him with alarm, and the kids with glee. He looked like a rodeo star. He spotted us and came on back. He shook hands gingerly with Ballinger.

151

"You're some kind of federal?" he asked, after a flustered waitress had run to add his order to ours.

Ballinger handed him I.D. and Runner glanced down at it, nodded, and grew respectful.

"How can I help you?"

"Was there a bomb?"

"Oh yes, there was a bomb. It got the ATF expert all worked up and nervous, but he removed it okay. He wouldn't show it to us, but he talked about it." He looked at me. "Your Mustang's now parked in my lot at the jail. It's a little worse for wear, but I drove it to the lot myself and it runs okay."

"What kind of bomb was it?" Ballinger continued.

"ATF said it was plastic and set to go off if anyone did anything. If Jim had opened the hood, that might have set it off. If someone had started the car, that would have done it. Even if a door was opened hard or slammed, it could have set it off. About two pounds plus three different detonators. Complicated. I think the device was once more than a bomb. Some stuff attached to it had been removed."

"What kind of stuff?"

"They said it might have been nerve gas, but the canister was gone."

"How'd ATF get the bomb disarmed?"

"They removed part of the front grill on Jim's Mustang, cut some wires on the bomb through the opening, then undid and popped the hood with them half a block away and the neighborhood evacuated. They looked things over, removed the device, and took it away to study."

"Who came from the ATF?"

"A big guy named Griffin."

"Red-headed man?"

The sheriff smiled as our food approached. "Yeah. You know him?"

"We've met. Where is he now?"

"I don't know. You want me to use the radio or phone and find out?"

"I guess not. Griffin knows what he's doing and he doesn't

152

need me to get in the way. How much local stir did finding the bomb in the car make?''

''A bunch. Lots of people were watching. Some of them watched most of the night. The local newspaper came quick, and then some guys from Lexington television showed up. There's a bunch of newsies at my office wanting to talk to Jim here and wanting statements from ATF and me. If they knew about you, they'd want yours also. And my prosecutor keeps bleating and snarling, asking questions about what's happening.''

''You never heard of me,'' Ballinger said, smiling only a little. ''I was never in your town, Mr. Sheriff. Your guys should maybe push the story that it was probably locals mad at the courts and the probation department.''

''Whatever you say, Mr. Invisible. Are you with the fun people who keep coming around and checking on Jim here?''

''Yes. I plead guilty. Jim and I have made a separate peace on that.''

''Your various visitations have got my county politicals shook up. You ain't here for some kind of sting or some kind of druggie roundup or anything like that?''

''No. Passing through is all. Jim used to work for me. I've been keeping check on him hoping he'd work for me again, but he says he's got a job he likes and doesn't expect to change.''

Runner nodded. He said, without a smile: ''He's got a job good for maybe a year.'' *A Corner supporter.*

I drank my juice, ate my biscuits and gravy, and had two cups of black, strong coffee. Ballinger picked at his eggs, not as brave about gobbling them as he'd once seemed. The sheriff had a sausage omelette, biscuits and gravy, and a decanter of hot tea.

By eleven I was back in court, still unquestioned by the news media. I got into court by sneaking up back stairs and entered the courtroom without being intercepted.

Daggert gave me a tiny nod and an inquisitive look from on high. I suspected that Maude White had called him the night before. Whether she'd seen the police gathered for the excitement around my car I didn't know. I soon discovered he knew something had happened. Horace brought me a note scrawled from the bench.

"Are you okay?" it read.

I looked up and Daggert was watching me. I nodded.

I'd been told what to say to the news people. Ballinger had coached me. He'd also asked me to avoid them as long as I could.

I sat there. Much of my feeling was one of relief. I'd suspected someone was out there, someone from the past.

Now I knew it was so.

Ruth Thacker was just taking the witness stand. I guessed I'd missed the bridge ladies, who must have come and gone quickly, probably proving little, as Belle Trempen had predicted to me the night before.

The new witness took the oath and sat comfortably in the witness chair. She seemed more handsome to me than she had when I'd seen her before. She was corseted tightly inside a stylish blue dress. She looked around the courtroom serenely and, I soon decided, nearsightedly. A pair of glasses, cased in leather, protruded from her purse.

Vain.

Corner led her through preliminaries. I discovered she was thirty-one years old, that she had borne two children, now ages six and four, and that she was happily divorced. I also found that she'd graduated from Grimsley U. with a degree in education and a minor in Spanish (which I found interesting). Her only job, except for a few days of substitute teaching, had been working for Kentner Amusement Company.

Henry Lee sat with his client and listened to the testimony. Shirley watched her stepdaughter the way a rodent watches a hungry snake. I doubted than any affection had ever existed between the two women.

By now I'd figured out Corner's trial strategy: First, get rid of the junk stuff, prove the time and place and method of murder. Second, use up your less convincing witnesses. Then call your better witnesses and eventually pop your pictures of the dead man in front of the jury for shock value. Present the only witness who can tie Shirley Kentner to the murder plot. Let him tell his tale. Finish with a deposition from your doctor coroner.

"I want first to ask you about a minor point, Mrs. Thacker. Do you remember the clock with gold numbers in the room where your father's body was found?"

"Of course I remember it."

"Was it working, to the best of your knowledge, the last time you saw it before your father was killed?"

"Yes."

"And when would this last time you saw it have been?"

"The day my father was murdered."

"How did you happen to be in the house that day?"

"My father's child bride invited me. She called and asked me to stop by for coffee."

"I see. Were you and your stepmother friends?"

"No. Not at all. I was surprised when she called. I lost all surprise when I found out what it was she wanted to talk about."

"What did she talk about?"

"About my father. She said he was becoming more and more senile. She had decided, without outside medical advice, that it was Alzheimer's. She wanted me to talk to my brother about the three of us combining and getting him put away into some quiet, private nursing home until he died."

"Had you noticed any symptoms of Alzheimer's?"

"Pop could be forgetful and confused. But he did pretty well most of the time. He was a determined sort of man. He was sick, but he never let the sickness get in the way of what he wanted to do. Witness the marriage to his pretty baby bride."

"So you talked to Shirley. Was this discussion cordial?"

"Well, we didn't get into a fistfight. We talked clothes and Florida talk. Shirley likes Florida. Dad owned a condo on the beach at Siesta Key off Sarasota. Shirley likes the condo."

"Do you also like the condo?"

"Of course."

"Did you ever stay there?"

"I did before my father remarried. After that I didn't, because I wasn't invited to do so."

"Your father never invited you?"

"My stepmother never invited me. She ran things as far as the condo and Florida were concerned. I asked her several times, just trying to check things out. Each time she'd say it was rented or she had other plans for it at the time I wanted it. On the day Dad died she did give me some dates I could use it, which surprised me."

"All right. Did your father and his new wife ever argue in your presence?"

Lee sat silently, not objecting.

"Yes. They argued about cars, clothes, food, and drinking. They argued about his doctors and his treatment. She told him what to wear, eat, drink, say, and do."

"And so they argued and fought?"

"Bitterly. Like spoiled little kids. They argued even after he got to the place he couldn't walk far without her help."

"Did you ever hear your stepmother threaten your father?"

"Sure. She'd do that lots to get her way."

"What would she say to him?"

"She'd usually threaten to leave him. That would panic him. Once, when he was drinking, she told him she was going to put some medicine in his whiskey to stop his drinking. That was early in the marriage. Later Pop was too sick to drink."

"What was she going to put in his whiskey?"

"I don't know. She didn't come right out and say. She was a nurse. Poison, maybe."

Henry Lee said, "Objection."

"Yes," Daggert said. "That will go out." He admonished the jury not to consider the answer.

Corner frowned over at Shirley while this was happening, but she ignored him.

"Did you ever see your stepmother exhibit any sign of affection for your father?"

Ruth Kentner shook her head. "Never."

"Allegations have been made by the defense that your father may have been taking and secreting money from collections he made from locations where you have amusement machines installed. Did you ever witness anything like that?"

"No. We knew it was possible and we knew the tax people were watching him. But Dad *gave* us the business. We didn't have to buy it. He first put stock in the business corporation in my name and in my brother's name when we were younger, when he bought the business. We worked for him as we got older because it was where we could do best moneywise. He could have taken every cent he wanted and paid us whatever he decided was right. Even after he went into semi-retirement, he was still in charge. He did the route collections because we all knew it was his place to do them. He knew the business owners on our routes. My brother thought maybe Pop was shorting collections, but I was never sure of it. And my father could fix anything electrical."

"If he was hiding income from state and federal taxing authorities, then you understand that would have been a criminal offense."

"If he was hiding anything, he hid it for and with her," the witness said, looking hard at Shirley. "If that was what he wanted, then it was all right with us. I still believe she's got lots of money buried in Mason jars somewhere. He was sick at the end, sick enough so he'd have done anything she told him to do."

Lee stood up, sat down, and let it go.

"Let's go back to the clock one more time. You say it was working the day your father died. Do you recall if it was keeping proper time?"

"I thought it was." She nodded her head assuredly. "I'm a clock watcher. I like to know what time it is. If his gold clock was on the blink on the day he died, I believe I'd have noticed it."

"How did your father and Jose Garcia get along?"

"My stepmother liked to say they were *sympatico*. My father gave Jose money over and above his salary. He let him use the cars. And Jose did take good care of Pop. Right up to the time he killed him."

Henry Lee eventually cross-examined: "You've been divorced how long, Mrs. Thacker?"

157

"Less than a year. About ten months." She smiled. "You'd know as well as I know. You were my ex-husband's lawyer."

"That I was. But we settled it and had the hearing away from Grimsley County. I want the jury to know how long ago it was, not just keep it a dark secret between the two of us. Since the time you divorced your husband, how do you occupy your time?"

"There are the children. There's the business. I have many friends."

"Do you have custody of your children?"

"Joint custody."

"Where are the children now?"

"They stay with their father during the school year. He has family money. He sends them to a private school. They summer on the lake with me."

"So he keeps them eight or nine months a year?"

She frowned, then nodded.

"And where does your former husband live? I mean in what city?"

"In the Louisville suburbs. Anchorage. I go back and forth to visit my kids. I take them to shows and to the shopping malls in the city."

"And you also said you work in the business?"

"Yes. I work in the office. I'm no hand at fixing computer games. I oversee the office. I take trouble calls, write letters, and do general bookkeeping."

"And how long have you done that?"

"Five or six years."

"Let's talk about dollars then, Mrs. Thacker. How many dollars a month did the business bring in, on a rough estimate, in the six months prior to your father's death?"

"About a quarter of a million dollars a month, but it was increasing all the time."

"And since you and your brother and agents for the Internal Revenue Service began to do the collections, what's been the monthly average?"

"Not much more."

"How much more?"

"Well, maybe three hundred thousand some months."

I saw the jury was listening closely and doing their own computations.

"Then how much money do you estimate your father stole from *his* business a month when he was collecting?"

Lynn Corner jumped up. "Objection, Your Honor. This witness never—"

Daggert waved a hand, cutting Corner off. "I recall the subject of missing funds was part of direct. Therefore Mr. Lee may explore that area in any fashion he's so inclined. Objection overruled." He leaned forward, listening.

"Answer the question, Mrs. Thacker," Lee prompted.

"I told you already I don't think he stole anything. It was his money, so how could he steal it?"

"Do you now believe this sick, dying man was secreting money?"

"Yes. I think he was doing it for his wife and she, in turn, has hidden it someplace so that one day she can run with it."

"Ah! At last I see the explanation for the missing money. Your deceased father's wife has all this money, which may be hundreds of thousands of dollars. But he gave it to her so she could run off with her boyfriend, the Mexican handyman, who's serving a long term in prison. Is that it?"

"Yes. Or maybe she has someone else. I think there were others." She looked pointedly toward Daggert.

"Have you told the police and the prosecutor about this theory of yours?"

"Yes. I did tell them. I think she forced Pop to take money right up to the end."

"And did the police not, thereafter, make massive searches of your father's house, of lockboxes, of bank accounts, interview her friends, and dig into everything in sight and out of sight and not find these missing funds? Didn't they take big picture blowups of Shirley Kentner all over this state and adjoining states trying to find something?"

"She's smart."

"You say she's smart. But didn't you and your brother politick

159

with the commonwealth's attorney, hire his associates to settle a large, lucrative estate, and do everything you could do to get Shirley Kentner charged with conspiracy to murder your father? And wasn't this done long *before* Jose Ramon Garcia had ever pled guilty?''

Corner looked up, wounded. He shook his head, but remained silent.

''We knew what she'd done.''

''And hasn't this so-called smart woman spent more than a year behind bars in jail waiting for this trial?''

Ruth Thacker smiled widely and I thought the smile was the best thing that had happened to Shirley Kentner so far in her murder trial. The smile was full of both hate and satisfaction.

''Yes.''

''One more thing. Do you speak Spanish?''

''I speak it very well. I minored in it in college and I have visited both Mexico and Spain.''

Lee nodded, perhaps figuring he'd found a perfect time to stop. ''No more questions.''

Corner, perhaps wisely, had no redirect.

It was pushing noon on a Tuesday. Court recessed for lunch under the usual restrictions. I stolidly told some news people from the local paper, who'd already talked to the sheriff, that I didn't know why someone had put a bomb in my car and didn't know what kind of bomb it was. I managed to look blank and confused at each of their questions, and finally wore them out. The television people from Lexington had moved on, having gotten their story from someone else.

I was still full of breakfast biscuits and gravy, so I got a soft drink from the courthouse machine and walked to the sheriff's parking lot.

My Mustang had been reassembled. The parking lot was a high-traffic area, so I doubted that anyone had bothered it there. There was one deep scratch in the paint on the hood. I bravely popped the hood and looked inside. Everything seemed the same as I remembered it. When I closed the hood I looked around me. No one was watching. I found a twig and stuck it down into the well between hood and windshield, bent it, and left it sticking there, under pressure.

In the afternoon, there was major fighting about what photographs the jury would pass among themselves. State police detective Abraham Owens was the witness. He talked well and smiled well and made the citizens on the jury and the watchers in the courtroom feel like everything bad and evil was within the grasp and control of his capable hands.

Some of the photos were passed among the jurors. Some were not allowed into evidence. I thought both Lee and Corner were angry about what was in evidence and what wasn't allowed in.

A standoff.

And so the trial day ended.

I followed Daggert to his office.

"Tell me about these men accosting you and the bomb in your car."

"I went out to Dumont for lunch yesterday and two men followed me. Last night I went to the political meeting. When I came out, someone had gotten into the car and hooked up a bomb."

"Do you think either incident has any connection to this case?"

"I don't know. More likely it's out of my past."

He seemed excited. "If I put you under oath, could you say for sure that the men and that the bomb in your car have nothing to do with this case?"

"No."

He thought about it for a moment and then shook his head. "But, on the other hand, you couldn't say they did?"

"That's right."

He subsided. He looked out his window, losing me. When I cleared my throat, he waved me away.

CHAPTER ELEVEN

A white-haired man in Georgetown taught me about detecting liars. He admitted it was hit or miss, but said that it might one day help me. He talked to me about watching breathing changes, wavering eyes, and other body language.

When I asked him if Ballinger had studied with him, he said no, but I thought he lied.

JOSE RAMON GARCIA came over from the jail accompanied by four deputies, all of them bulky men. The armed deputies watched both him and the full courtroom.

Shirley Kentner sat with her own deputy, hers being the large lady deputy I'd seen working the radio at the jail.

Garcia wore leg chains and handcuffs and I could hear him clinking down the hall before he appeared in the courtroom door. He wore a white shirt and a bright figured tie under a cheap single-breasted suit. I knew about the suit and its source because one of the hot pre-trial arguments between prosecution and defense had concerned what clothes Garcia would wear during his appearance before the jury. The defense had wanted him to arrive in the courtroom clad in jail issues—loose sandals and an orange coverall with white *P*s—but the prosecution had prevailed. He would testify in the suit he'd appeared in for sentencing. Perhaps as a trade, Lee had been granted the right, over the state's objections during the preliminary hearing, to ask what apparel Garcia normally wore during both jail and prison time.

On seeing him up close, I wasn't overly impressed by Garcia. He was medium in size, only an inch or two taller than Shirley Kentner. He seemed, on inspection, thin, but I saw that his neck and arms were muscular and his movements deft and certain. He was the color of heavily creamed tea, three shades darker than my own color. His eyes were deep-set and so dark that you saw only black pools when the light wasn't directly on them. His features were snub, but clear. The suit was ill-fitting, but the man inside it appeared to be strong and fit. I wondered what life had been like for him in a maximum-security prison populated by many madmen, sociopaths, and sex-crazed deviants.

He had survived.

I knew for certain that I didn't remember him. Somehow, even after seeing and studying his pictures, I'd thought I might eventually recognize him as someone I'd met or known in past times.

Perhaps he'd been someone in the shadows, someone unseen? The Judge?

Garcia's guards took up positions near all the doors to the courtroom, their leather belts and gun holsters squeaking in the hush. The jurors witnessed all this, seeing it as part of the ongoing show. The courtroom was quiet enough so that all sound seemed magnified. Outside the courtroom windows, there were flurries of falling snow. In the halls, earlier, I'd seen armed state police and I knew that there was half a squad of them in and around the courthouse, guarding it. There were also deputies on the roof.

Ballinger had ordered that.

I had scanned the transcripts of Garcia's guilty plea and sentencing hearing. That guilty plea transcript was likely a preview of what was coming, but I wanted to listen carefully anyway, mostly because Daggert had said to do so.

Garcia's English was only slightly accented, and during his entire direct testimony, he uttered no words of Spanish. His voice was low and rich. I listened carefully.

Garcia sat uncomfortably on the witness stand, a hunter caged by chains. He wore, at most times, a semi-ingratiating smile. Once or twice I thought he insolently attempted to catch Shirley Kentner's eyes, but she never looked directly at him. She read her Bible and stared out the window during all his testimony. She exhibited neither hate for him nor interest in what he said.

Answering Corner's early direct examination questions, Garcia told the jury who he was and stated that he now was serving a ninety-year sentence.

"Where were you born?"

"In Mexico. In a small village just outside Mexico City. I lived my childhood there. I knew no father. Later my village was swallowed and became a part of the city. When I was twelve I moved north so as to find work."

"Did you find work?"

"A little. I had no formal education, but I hung about and learned to read and write at a mission school. That helped me."

"How old are you?"

Garcia looked at the floor. "I am now thirty."

I believed he was older.

"You came illegally into this country more than three years ago to seek work?"

"Yes. I came across the border with others. I could already speak some English, so it was easy for me to pass. Once into a city and away from the others who crossed in the night, no one questioned me."

"You wandered then as a migrant worker until you found work with and for Fiala Kentner?"

"I picked crops. I was cheated of my pay and abandoned north of Grimsley City when I became involved in forming a worker's union. Mr. Kentner gave me a job when I needed a job. It was a poor job, but one that I could do, much easier than following the harvests. There was, for me, plenty of food and a warm place to sleep. And Mr. Kentner was kind to me."

"You did mostly yardwork and gardening for him then?"

"Whatever was asked of me," Garcia answered. "I polished and drove his cars, weeded his gardens, washed his windows. I planted his flowers and cut his grass. I know some plumbing, and many things about household machines, but not as much as Mr. Kentner did. Still, I was useful to him and to her." His voice remained soft. I moved a little as I settled into the listening. His eyes caught my movement and he examined me, then passed on by. I believed that what was happening in the courtroom was of little interest to him. I believed also from his way of speaking and his smile that there was some amusement within him caused by the trial.

"Did you and Shirley Kentner become lovers while you were employed by the Kentners?"

"Yes. After a time." Now there was more subject interest.

"How did that come about?"

"One day she called to me to come to the fine house to help her remove curtains from the dining room windows. Her husband was at his office. She wore only a little clothing, an old shirt and shorts that I quickly found had nothing under them. She was beautiful. We kissed. I was dirty from working in the ground and I smelled, but we became lovers there on the dining room floor. I now believe she liked it that I smelled of the earth. She was accustomed to hot baths and the smell of her husband's medicines. I was different."

"And how long did this love affair last?"

"It continued at any and all times we could find for it until I shot and killed her husband for her."

"You admit you murdered her husband?"

"Yes. I killed him. I had to do it because she wanted me to kill him. I did not want to do it, because he had been kind to me."

"Did Shirley Kentner ask you to kill her husband?"

"Yes. Many times. She begged me to do it for her. She pleaded. We talked of it and planned it together. It was her dream and desire that he die. So much money."

"What was to be your reward for killing him?"

Garcia smiled. He looked at Shirley sitting in her chair staring out the courtroom window. "I was to take whatever I could find and then leave her house for Mexico, where I would conceal myself. I was first to take a car, but then buy or steal another, or steal new plates. She was to wait the necessary time to get his money and then find me. We had a meeting place arranged in Mexico City. She said it would take some time, perhaps a year, or even two years. But she swore to me that one day she would come. She was to be my reward."

"Did you believe her?"

"I believed her until I was caught by the police at a rest stop off the Interstate 24 south, below Nashville, Tennessee. I was not in

165

the car I had taken when I was caught. It was parked away from me, but the police arrested me. She was to tell the police that I had left on my vacation. I therefore could not be the one who had done Mr. Kentner's murder. When I found she had not told the police our story, I no longer believed.''

"Had you made the pretense of leaving on vacation the morning of the day you shot Fiala Kentner?"

"Yes. I believed it to be our plan. I walked early to the bus station. I bought a ticket to Cincinnati, where I had gone before. I talked to the ticket seller hoping he would remember me. I then got off at Churchill, the next town where the Cincinnati bus stopped. I walked back. It was fifteen miles.''

"So you walked fifteen miles back to Grimsley City?"

"Yes. By a back road. I was afraid to hitchhike. Someone might see and remember me.''

In the courtroom, as I watched and listened, I saw a middle-aged female spectator sigh. There were other females in the courtroom who watched Garcia with avid eyes, perhaps older women with either infatuations or death wishes.

"And then what did you do?"

"I hid in woods near the lake. After dark and after Shirley had returned her husband and gone to her bridge, I entered Mr. Kentner's big house. I found him there and we had our time together.''

"Did Mrs. Kentner tell you she would say to the ladies at her bridge party that you had left on a vacation that morning?"

"Yes. That was the plan.'' He shook his head ruefully. "I was her fool, just as Mr. Kentner was her fool.'' He smiled. "He was her fool many times.''

Corner led him on. Garcia described what had happened on the night of the murder. He coldly told of torturing Fiala Kentner to learn where money was secreted in the house.

"You burned him with a cigar butt and you cut him superficially many times with a razor blade?'' Corner repeated. "You glued his eyes shut.''

"His eyes watched me in reproach, so I closed them. The rest was necessary. I wanted his money first, then his life.''

"Hadn't Shirley told you where money was?"

"Some of the places. She believed there were many others where the old one had hidden things. She said he liked to hide things, to play games with her, to tease. She didn't like these games. She told me he would quickly tell me those hiding places because of the pain and his fear of the dark."

"And did Fiala Kentner tell you places where money was hidden?"

"Some places. He told me of one in the basement and of others in the bedroom."

"Was one of those places a big, gold-figured clock in the living room?"

"Yes."

"And did you damage the clock as you searched it?"

"Yes. I hurried too much. The clock stopped. That was near the end."

"Was that just before ten o'clock on the night you tortured and killed Fiala Kentner?"

"I believe so." If Garcia could hang his head and show sorrow, I believed I was watching such effort.

"Go on."

I saw Lee almost rise, then settle back down firmly in his counsel chair. *No objections.*

"I think the reason why the old one never told me all his hiding places was because when I burned him with one of his cigars to aid his memory, he became unconscious. Thereafter he was in and out of sleep. Perhaps it was the heart or cancer thing. He had become weak in the days before I killed him for her. He had many pains—chest, stomach, head. Time was running out, so when I, at last, could not wake him with cigar or knife, I shot him once and then, to make sure, another time. I knew where to shoot him to make sure. I read it in a book. Then I left. I took the vehicle. I took gloves to use while I drove it. I was to find another car, buy it or steal it, and abandon his car. But I did not find another car in time."

"How much money did you take from the Kentner home?"

"More than a thousand dollars, all that I could find. I also took his Rolex watch, believing it could be sold. I have since learned in the prison that selling such a watch would not have been easy."

"Did you open the drapes in the living room and place Mr. Kentner in a chair so that he could be seen from the street?"

"Yes."

"Why did you do that?"

"So that Shirley would know I had kept the oaths made in her embrace. So that she could be the one to raise an alarm concerning his death. So that she could say she didn't believe that his killer could be me, because I had left early that morning."

It seemed a possible answer to things I'd found puzzling. Stupid, but possible. Those who plot and commit murders aren't intellectuals.

I still didn't believe it.

I watched the jury. They were fascinated by Garcia and his story. As I listened and they listened I could make no determination of whether, in gross, Garcia spoke truth or lies. His testimony closely followed the transcript of his guilty plea. I thought that the jury believed most of what he said.

"So what you're telling this jury today is that you and Shirley Kentner together plotted the murder of her husband Fiala and that you killed him because she pleaded with you to murder him?"

Garcia looked down at the floor. "Yes. She loved me and I loved her. I wanted her and she wanted me. His death became necessary to both of us. He was old and sick, but he was alive and in our way."

Corner led him along while Lee continued to sit silently. Many lawyers make copious notes while witnesses for the other side are testifying. I had noticed that Lee made no notes concerning this witness. I had a moment of legal insight, in my watching, as to why he did not. He had heard and read the tale in the transcript of the guilty plea and read and re-read the confession and statements until he knew all documents intimately. He wanted to make no interruptions, he wanted no agonizing retellings. I believed he was waiting patiently for cross-examination time.

When defense lawyers have no statements to go to, then they

depose witnesses and ask questions. In this case I thought Lee had the advantage of reading what Garcia had said and need not disclose his own defense tactics until the moment of cross-examination.

Lee's time came just before noon. By then Corner had extracted every drop of blood from the death of Fiala Kenter. He had gotten Garcia to describe the temperature of the house (it was cold because Shirley purposely kept the heat turned low) and how it smelled (of cut roses bought by Fiala for Shirley) on the night of the murder. He'd had him describe, in intimate detail, the many liaisons between himself and Shirley Kentner, tell of how the affair had gone on hotly and secretly long after the time that son Alfred had caught the pair in bed.

I thought the jury was properly shell-shocked, and I believed, if they went to deliberations now, that they would quickly convict Shirley Kentner, who continued to either read her Bible or stare without expression out the courtroom window at the falling snow.

Lee stood for cross. He took a position near the jury so that the jury could watch Garcia's face.

"With the court's permission I will begin, but I expect to have to go into the afternoon," he said to the bench.

Daggert inclined his head. "I will recess soon."

Lee nodded and turned to the witness. "Mr. Garcia, do you know who I am?"

"You are her lawyer, sir," Garcia said, smiling. "They speak well of you in the jail. They say you are a good criminal lawyer."

"Thank them all for me," Lee said, sarcasm showing. "You understand, on Shirley Kentner's behalf, that I now must ask you many questions?"

"Of course, sir."

"Do you also understand that you are still under oath and must tell the truth?"

"Of course," Garcia said again. He crossed himself carefully, and a small alarm bell rang softly within me. I remembered that he'd claimed to have learned reading at a mission school, but also he had admitted to murdering a man. Maybe we can always forgive ourselves and wash our own sins away.

169

"Do you always tell the truth, sir?"

"I try," Garcia said, smiling.

"That suit you're wearing today in court, sir, is it *your* suit?"

"No. I was given it by the sheriff last year. I wore it before in this court when I received my sentence of ninety years."

"What do you normally wear in the Grimsley County jail?"

"I wear a bright orange overall. It has large white or black letter *P*s stamped here and there. I wear rubber sandals over heavy white socks."

"And so the sheriff took you out of those clothes and gave you the suit to wear to court?"

"Yes."

"This morning?"

"Yes. After my breakfast of fine scrambled eggs and fried doughnuts."

"All right," Lee said, satisfied. "Let's move to something else. During your time of working for the Kentners, was Mr. Kentner ill?"

"Yes. Sometimes he would stay all day in bed. Or I would help him and he would enter one of his cars and I would drive him wherever he wanted. He had cancer and he had heart sickness. But some days he was almost well."

"Could he walk?"

"Most times."

"And you would help him walk when he had problems?"

"Yes. I would assist him."

"Do you have a license to drive?"

"No. Mr. Kentner tried to get one for me. He got me a learner's permit instead. But I can drive."

"Did you drive him to various doctors' offices?"

Garcia nodded. "Yes. Perhaps a hundred times. He went to a heart doctor and a lung doctor. He had the cancer in his lungs and other places."

"And was there a walker?"

Garcia waited, not understanding the question.

"An aluminum walking aid," Lee asked impatiently. "Something that a person can stand between, holding to the arms, and use to aid walking.''

"Yes. I have seen that used, but not often. He believed he had no need of it on days when he was better. He would not use any cane, but he would lean on me when he was tired.''

"But he was quite ill, sometimes unsteady, sometimes short of breath, many times sick to his stomach?''

"On some days. At times he was better. We would wait for the days he felt better and would order me to deliver him to work.''

"We?''

"Shirley and I would wait. When he felt good, he would want to leave the house. I would drive him to the office, return quickly to the home, and there would be time shared. Shirley believed he didn't care that we made love. It was only that he wanted no one to know of it, particularly those of his family, because of his great pride. She said that secrecy was her bargain with him when they married.''

"Was it a written bargain?''

"I don't know.''

"Did Fiala Kentner ever ask you to follow Shirley and see if she was meeting *other* men?''

"Yes. He did that.''

"And did you follow her?''

"Yes.''

"Did she ever meet other men?''

"No. She loved me.''

"You and only you?''

"Yes.''

Something told me that Jose was lying. He did not like the questions, and his answers to them were terse and forced. I too found the questions bothersome. Why would Lee ask questions concerning other possible liaisons?

Lee moved on. "You speak our language quite well, don't you? I mean much better than you did when you entered a plea of guilty so that you could escape the death penalty?''

"I now have good English. I have studied hard in prison.''

171

"Did you speak English well before you went to prison?"

"Not well. I have learned from books and records there. I read many of your books and magazines. There is a library in the prison. And each day I try to learn new words from a dictionary."

"Do you like the part of the prison you inhabit better than you would death row?"

Corner was on his feet. "Objection."

Daggert nodded. "Yes. That will go out, although Mr. Lee may inquire into and about the plea bargain."

Lee smiled. "I will go to another point." He turned to the witness. "I want to ask you questions about what doctors you drove Mr. Kentner to visit," Lee said.

Garcia waited.

Judge Daggert sighed. He had been watching the clock. He lifted a hand. "I believe we will break for lunch now, ladies and gentlemen. Take Mr. Garcia back to jail first, then return for the defendant." He admonished the jurors, determined where they were being taken for lunch, and ordered lawyers and witnesses to refrain from eating there.

I waited until the courtroom cleared. Lee sat at his table, looking over papers from his briefcase.

"I will want to see Shirley soon, Mr. Lee," I said.

"Yes." He watched me. "How do you think the trial's going?"

I shrugged. "Might I ask something?"

"Yes."

"Why did you ask Garcia about Shirley and other men?"

"Because there were other men. The prosecution won't admit it, but she did see other men and Fiala likely knew it."

"What men?"

"She won't say and I'm forbidden by her to even ask names." He shook his head. "It wouldn't help anyway. If I could show her being out with other men, the jury would only believe she was easy or a tramp or sex-crazed. Nutty case. You ask her about it when you see her."

"I will."

172

I ate at a downtown lunch counter and returned early. Judge Daggert was in his chambers. He nodded at me coolly and lowered his eyes to paperwork piled high on his desk. I decided he didn't want to talk to me now.

I walked to my tiny office, looked over the sparse and useless mail, and then returned to the courthouse to wait for the jury and the trial cast of characters to return.

I sat in my chair and thought over possibilities. I remembered my father's funeral. I remembered having my eyes taped open. I remembered many things.

I now had an inner feeling, a hunch, about what had happened here in Grim City, but I still wanted to hear the rest of the testimony.

Eventually the jury returned.

We began again.

"Let's forget the list of doctors I'd asked about before," Lee began. "I will have others testify concerning Mr. Kentner's precarious medical condition. I will only ask you if there were many doctors and many visits to them?"

"Many, yes."

"Were some of those doctors in Cincinnati, Lexington, and Louisville?"

"Yes. I would drive him there and then I would help him to the offices. I am a very good driver of automobiles and I am strong. He would lean on me."

"Let's move on then. You say that you and Shirley were in bed every time you had the chance. Weren't there people who would drop by the house? Wouldn't Alfred Kentner and his sister come by? Wouldn't salesmen, postmen, delivery people, and the like come to the house? Wasn't Fiala watching you both closely?"

"Yes. But we were careful and quick after the time of Alfred. We would keep watch. We would double-lock the doors. Sometimes she would leave on almost all her clothes. And I would go out the back door as she went to answer at the front."

"And sometimes would she take off all her clothes?"

"Yes. When it was safe and she could. She liked to be without her clothes." He smiled at Shirley Kentner, who ignored him completely. "Many times."

"When she did this would you watch?"

Garcia took one quick glance at the prosecutor's table and, for the first time, he seemed unsure. My inner alarm bell rang again, this time more loudly.

"I would watch. It was a pleasure for me to watch."

"Did Mrs. Kentner, who you claim was *your* Shirley, have any scars or tattoos or moles or anything of an unusual nature on her often-seen body?"

"Not that I remember. Perhaps a mole. I would disregard that. It would mean nothing to me."

"Because you would see her with the eyes of love?" Lee asked sarcastically.

"Yes. That was the way of it."

"If I told you that Shirley Kentner has something or some things on her body and that those imperfections are obvious to the—if you'll pardon my use of the word—*naked* eye, would you believe me?"

"I don't remember any such things. She was beautiful always to me."

"Are there any imperfections you remember?"

"None."

"Are you sure?"

"Yes."

"Having established that, we will move on. Why did you take one of the Kentner vehicles?"

"Because that was her plan," Garcia answered.

"Wouldn't it have been wiser to purchase a vehicle, hide it, and use that for your escape?"

"Perhaps. But that wasn't her plan. I did as she directed."

"Didn't she tell you to get another vehicle?"

"Yes."

"And didn't she tell you to steal other license plates?"

"Yes."

174

"Did you do either of these things?"

"No. I thought there would be much time."

"After you had tortured and murdered Fiala Kentner, at what time did you leave the house?"

"After ten o'clock at night. Before eleven for certain."

"And when were you arrested, what day and what time was that?"

"It was the next day in the late afternoon south of Nashville in Tennessee."

"On Interstate 75?"

"No. On I-24. It leads to I-75."

"Why that route?"

"For deception." *I knew he was lying again.*

"You were caught not very far from where you began your trip. Perhaps two hundred miles. Why did you move so slowly?"

"I never believed anyone was after me. She swore to me she would throw them off. For a time I stopped at a roadside rest park. I was tired from the long walk, from Fiala, and so I slept sitting on a bench within sight of my car. I ate in a restaurant before that."

"How was Shirley to explain the missing vehicle?"

"She would say she believed it was in a garage being worked on."

"What day of the week was it when you were captured?"

"I believe it was a Tuesday."

"And where, in Kentner's house, did you kill him?"

"I tortured him both in the kitchen and in the bedroom. I shot him first also in one of those rooms, but the shot in the back of the head I did in his heart chair. That was after the knife and the cigar did not bring him back to wakefulness."

"What happened in Tennessee that made you sleep? You said there was a walk back of fifteen miles. But then you had to lie in wait for Fiala. Did you sleep then?"

"I think I dozed through the afternoon."

"Then it must have been all this work of searching Fiala Kentner's house and torturing and killing him that tired you out?"

"Yes." The witness had become wary.

"So, having killed Fiala Kentner and left his body to be quickly found and seen in his front window, you napped, dawdled, stole no new vehicle or license plate, and got caught?''

Garcia's eyes flickered. ''Yes.''

''Did you want to be caught?''

''No.'' Garcia shook his head vigorously.

''You've learned to read, but you never ever learned to run, is that it?''

''I believed that no one was after me.''

''Then why did you drive a deceptive route?''

''It was her plan.''

''Did you listen to the radio?''

''Yes. I like the music. I heard no news that concerned me.''

''Where is this vehicle you drove now?''

''I don't know.''

''Did you damage this vehicle in any way during your flight?''
''No.''

Lee went to his table and found a paper. He rustled it. Garcia watched both Lee and the paper.

''Here is a report of the Tennessee police. It says that the car had old bumper and brake-light damage. When did that happen?''

Garcia shrugged. ''I don't know. I remember nothing of that. Perhaps Mr. Kentner damaged it. Or Shirley.''

''Let us then discuss some more things about your claimed love affair more. Your education consists of what?''

''A little school. Mostly self-education. I struggled to learn reading and writing. Now, knowing them and your language, it's easier for me. I read many books and magazines.''

''And Mrs. Kentner: Did she ever tell you of her education?''

''I know she was a nurse.'' He smiled. ''We never discussed her education or my education.''

''To be a nurse is about sixteen years of school. What did you and Mrs. Kentner discuss when you were out of bed?''

Garcia smiled and I read malice in his eyes and voice. ''We talked mostly of her husband's death. I told her stories of my country, where a little money will buy many things. She told me stories about hate for her husband and love for me.''

176

"You had worked with union organizers before you came to Grimsley City. Do you know of written contracts?"

"I have seen them. I have never written one. It would have been beyond me then."

"You never wanted her to give you something in writing to protect you?"

"No. I believed. I loved her."

"Let's talk now about your plea bargain. Let's have you tell this jury about how you and the prosecutor made your deal."

Lee hammered away. We broke for an afternoon recess, returned, and he continued, not doing great good, not gaining much ground. Garcia's answers became shorter, more abrupt. I saw some of the jury yawn and look away. But they now knew that Garcia had avoided the death penalty by giving information about Shirley Kentner.

After four in the afternoon, Lee abruptly stopped. Corner asked a few rebuttal questions, and the court ordered Garcia returned to jail by his guards.

I thought the day had gone, by a wide margin, to the prosecutor.

Daggert smiled faintly after Garcia and company had exited the courtroom. He motioned the lawyers up to the bench and whispered with them. I couldn't hear what was transpiring.

After the conference at the bench, we adjourned for the day.

I followed Daggert to chambers.

"That's the state case," he said. "The rest will be defense. The state will rest first thing tomorrow after the coroner's deposition is read." He gave me a tired look. "Jim, Lee says you will talk to his client tonight before she testifies, if she does testify at all."

"She might not testify?" That gave me a sinking feeling.

"I don't know. I think she will, but it's Lee's case, not mine." He looked down at his desk and then back at me. "Could you walk over to the jail now and talk with Mrs. Kentner? Lee might be there, but he said you can have a free hand whether he's present or not."

"All right. Is there anything you particularly want me to ask?"

"No." He nodded tiredly. "You're on your own. I informed the prosecutor a few minutes ago that I was going to have you talk with the defendant before the trial was done, and he didn't like it." He smiled. "I then told him that this was my court and we'd follow my interpretation of the rules."

"He thinks we're both conspiring with Lee and his client," I offered. "He intimated that at the precinct meeting."

"I don't care what he thinks. I don't like his case." His eyes pierced me. "I also don't like Garcia. He's smart and dumb all at one time. But for the life of me, I can't figure things differently from how they look. Can you?"

"No. Not yet."

"The men who accosted you and the bomb in your car. I'll ask again if they could have something to do with this murder case."

"I see nothing yet to tie them to this case."

"Sure?"

I shrugged. "No, but a tie-in seems impossible."

"Go talk to Mrs. Kentner."

"Garcia said some things that didn't ring true."

"What things were those?"

"I thought he lied about his age and I did not believe his posturing, when he crossed himself. He's not a religious man. And I didn't believe him when he said that Mrs. Kentner met no other men."

"What do you know about her meeting other men?"

"Nothing. But he lied."

"Did you believe his story in chief?"

"It could be the way he tells it. It could be different." I shook my head. "I want also to talk to Garcia."

"Go see Shirley Kentner first," he ordered. "Then, if you must, you can talk to Garcia."

"Will you ask the sheriff not to return Garcia to prison until I talk to him?"

"Yes. If you want."

"I want. Can you call the sheriff and tell him that I'll speak to Garcia tomorrow?"

"All right, Jim."

I caught his eyes with my own. "Tell me anything you might know that I should know in questioning Shirley Kentner."

"I knew Fiala. As a result I also knew her. Nothing else." He looked darkly out the window and watched his town below. "I know that she's lovely. Perhaps I don't want to believe, or have this jury believe, that someone so lovely could have conspired to kill her husband."

I shook my head. "I think both of us see her and are enchanted by the way she looks. But the way she looks is not all of her."

He nodded.

CHAPTER TWELVE

The moving finger writes and having writ is subject only to appellate review.

THE CELL which housed Shirley Kentner was on the second floor of the jail. I'd been in the ill-smelling, crowded men's section of the jail on the floor below many times, but I'd never visited the women's quarters.

I arrived at the jail a few minutes before eight in the evening and stood for a time at the sheriff's receiving desk. I smelled the remains of what had been served for supper. Some of it had been made using onions. My own dinner had been canned Campbell's vegetable soup (my favorite, adding a little soy sauce and a pinch of ginger) mixed with only three-fourths of a can of water, peanut butter on crackers, and diet cola. I was economizing again. Almost two weeks to another pay.

I was nervous because I was seeing the woman. My hands were shaking and there was roaring in my ears, but I could hear well enough.

Shirley Kentner was waiting for me.

The heavy female deputy I'd first met as she'd operated the radio escorted me upstairs. I'd learned she was the jail matron and that her name was Adelaide—"Addie"—Taylor.

"How do you want to work this, Mr. Singer? You think you'll be safe alone in the cell with her or do you want me to step inside with you and hang out like a mouse in a corner or somethin'?" Addie asked.

"I'll have to talk to her privately," I said.

"Then I'll wait just outside," the matron said wisely. She eased her leather holster belt where it rubbed and smiled at me. "Could be she'll try screaming rape. It's desperation time. She was acting real sick and funny when we came back from court today. Usually she's okay, but today got to her. She's a bright lady. She watches the men on the jury a lot. She watches you a lot.''

"Thanks for your help."

Addie nodded. "That's my job. And the sheriff, he likes you okay even if he is Lynn Corner's man."

Shirley Kentner sat inside her ten-by-ten cell on one of two rickety chairs. I entered, took off my old coat, and laid it over the back and seat of the second chair and then sat on my coat. The only other place to sit would have been the bed or on the porcelain edge of a lidless, seatless toilet.

"You can put your coat on my bed if you want," she said tartly. "The bed won't bite and neither will I."

"It's okay. The coat's so old and decrepit I hate to put it where it can shed fuzz."

She shrugged coolly. "Up to you, Mr. Singer."

She was wearing a brown wool skirt which covered her knees, a bulky green sweater, and dark loafers. The clothes shrouded her figure, but also made her more mysterious to me. Her hair was pulled severely back into a blond bun. Her face, although lovely, seemed drawn and tense. I thought the trial had sapped her strength. I admitted to myself once again that I was intrigued and more than half in love with her.

"Thank you for coming to see me," she said. "My lawyer won't be here tonight."

"I can come back another time if you want," I answered. "I don't exactly know why I'm here tonight, but it was all right with Judge Daggert and your attorney, Mr. Lee," I said. "Some say it's best if people do have their lawyers present."

She shrugged. "Maybe, but not for me. We talked about it and Mr. Lee decided he'd not need to be here. Let's go ahead. Ask whatever you want to ask. I'll answer it."

I nodded and started out by going through the routine questions on the pre-sentence forms. Age, place of birth, education, and the like. She answered primly, watching and appraising me out of

181

soft, injured eyes that pierced me. She was both lovely and lost. I found my hands were still shaking as I wrote down her answers. And yet I quickly found she was normal, not too smart, not too educated. A woman who would not stand out except for her looks.

"When are we going to get to the part where you finally ask me how a nice girl got into a place like this?" she asked, when I paused in the routine.

"You said I could ask you anything I wanted to ask. Now I'll say to you that you can tell me whatever you want to tell me," I answered. "Interrupt me any time you want. Leave out anything you don't want to say. I'm here early because the judge and your lawyer directed me to come early, maybe to make the prosecutor angrier than he already is about how this case has procedurally gone. You've not been convicted and whatever you say to me will never become a part of any record if the jury finds you not guilty. I'll destroy the notes. Or I'll stop now and come back if you are convicted. In the company of your lawyer. Up to you."

"What's your best guess on conviction?"

"I don't know. This is the first jury trial I've watched all the way through. Other than Jose, the state hasn't shown me much. Your lawyer's a good one."

"Yes," she said. "Henry Lee's a good man." For the first time her face lightened.

"When he was alive, did your husband know Mr. Lee?"

"Yes. Fiala knew lots of people. He talked at times of making a new will and getting Mr. Lee to draw it up for him. Then he'd get peeved at me and not do it. I let it go. I didn't push him. I didn't want all his money, just the house and my share of it. We had an agreement."

I waited.

"I tell you, under any oath you want, and by all that's holy to me, that I never plotted to kill my husband," she said. "The first part of what Jose said on the stand was the truth, though. I did lead him on a bit and then get myself agreeably half-raped on the dining room floor tangled up in the curtains. And I guess I liked it. Jose was strong, rough, and demanding. He was more a hater than a lover. We stayed at it for a few weeks, hit and miss, until fatface Alfred sneaked into my house and caught us. That was the first and only time we ever took off all our clothes. Doing sex with Jose was like being on drugs. But when we got caught and Fi got mad at both of us, I broke the habit and I never let Jose in the house again except to do something inside that needed doing." She grinned. "Other than me. And when he came in, I went out. Even though things were different with Fi after I got caught, I still stayed away from Jose." She looked up at me. "I mean, I made me a bargain. Fi knew I'd broken it with Jose by fouling the nest and he watched me afterward. His kids know that was the way of it, but they're not going to admit it."

"How come Fiala didn't fire Jose?"

"I don't know. Sometimes I think he liked Jose a lot better than he liked me by that time. They'd cuss out people together. Jose hates everything and everyone. Fi would go out into the yard and talk to Jose or watch him working. He babied him. He let him drive the Sable wagon nights when Jose would go prowling around town."

"Did Jose ever follow you when you went out at night?"

"Yes. At times." She smiled. "When I didn't lose him as he tried to follow behind. He claims to be a good driver, but he's not."

"Did you see other men when you went out?"

"At times. Nothing bad. I'd see people. What Jose testified about concerning my arrangement with Fiala was true. I could do as I wanted as long as I didn't embarrass Fiala."

"And so you saw other men?"

"One or two men. Nothing serious."

"Who were they?"

"No names," she said coldly. "I'll give you no names. Besides, names wouldn't help. The prosecutor won't ask me about other names. He wants the jury to think I spent all my time with Jose. What a laugh."

"Why not use the names? If you called the men as witnesses the jurors would know that you weren't in love with Jose."

"It's not that easy. I'd be a tramp. And it wasn't that way, not ever that way. I thought it over. It wouldn't help. It would hurt. The men . . ."

"Yes?"

"One had a heart attack. He was old. He died. Another . . ."

"Go on."

"No. Nothing more. Not if I go to prison." Her voice had become agitated. "And I saw no men in the last few months of Fiala's life."

"All right," I said soothingly. "Did Jose ever wreck the Mercury?"

"Not that I know of. He was good with taking care of it, always washing it, working under it, tinkering with it."

"Did Jose have any friends?"

"No."

"Did he ever get mail or telephone calls?"

"He got some calls. I don't know who they were from."

"Local or long distance?"

"I don't know."

"Would Fiala help Jose with his work?"

"No. He was too sick. He'd just watch. He'd quit going to the office much, but he would still go collecting, and either Jose would drive him or I'd have to drive him."

"What day or days did he collect on?"

"There was no set routine other than the one in Fi's head. In some spots it was once a week. Some quieter places out in the county he'd go maybe once a month."

"Did you ever hear your husband and Jose talking?"

"Some. Usually they'd quiet down when I got close." She cocked her head. "Jose and Fi would talk about all the politicians who needed to be killed. They'd talk about poisons and guns and that kind of stuff. Intricate things, like calibers and makes of guns."

"Did you pick your husband up at his daughter's house on the night he was killed?"

"Yes. I delivered him there and brought him back later to our house. And I knew what he went to his daughter's to do and I didn't care. It was okay with me. It was one of the days when it was hard for Fi to walk, so I went to the door when I picked him up and helped him out to the car. I believed Jose was in Cincinnati on vacation. I was relaxed because of it. I didn't have to watch out for Jose. It was before bridge time, so I stopped with Fi at our house, helped him up to the door where he could find things to hold on to. I went to a drive-through restaurant, got a sandwich, and ate it, and then I drove back to play bridge.''

''How much help did your husband need?''

''Just someone or something to lean hard on. Once inside he could move along a wall or catch on to something. Or he'd use the walker if no one was around to see it. He had a horror of anyone knowing he wasn't mobile. But it didn't bother him to get other people to help him. He'd make a big joke of it, like he'd been drinking too much.''

''You didn't go inside your house?''

She shook her head. ''Maybe if I'd helped Fiala inside, Jose would have killed me also. I think about that sometimes in the middle of the night.''

''What makes you believe Jose might have killed you?''

''I'm not sure. It was crazy. Fi finds out about us and gets mad or acts mad. He's hateful to me, but he's still good to Jose.'' She shook her head. ''Then he has Jose follow me to see if I'm meeting anyone. Maybe there was a bargain and Jose was supposed to kill us both. Maybe Fi set it up. Do you think it could have been that way?''

''You mean he hired Jose?''

''Yes.''

''It's something you should talk to your lawyer about before you testify.''

''I already have.'' She smiled. ''You'd be surprised at all the crazy ideas and theories we've kicked around. You see, Henry Lee knows I'm innocent.''

''Why did you and your attorney have so much interest in the time when the gold clock stopped?''

"Because bridge normally lasts until after eleven or even midnight. Didn't you hear the ladies who played bridge testify this morning?"

"No. I had to be elsewhere. I didn't hear that testimony." Almost I told her that someone had put a bomb in my car, but it wasn't anything she needed to know and I wasn't certain it had to do with her case. Besides, she might already know about the bomb.

"The prosecutor tried to get my bridge friends to say I was watching out the window, but he didn't get far. If Jose opened the curtain so that I could see my dead husband, didn't he do it real early?"

"I see what you're driving at."

"Mr. Lee thought those were very important points." Her voice had taken on a frantic, lecturing tone. "I wish you'd heard it. You needed to hear it."

"What else do you want to tell me?"

"When I met Fi he was already, without a miraculous spontaneous remission, terminal. That's important. Remember it."

"Fiala was dying?"

"Yes. First time I saw him he was in the hospital for chemo. He was already sick then, but he was the kind who wouldn't let himself believe he was going to die. I knew he was sick, but the timing was hard to predict. He had an estimated six months to a year when I met him. He was still alive after three years. But he was much weaker near the end and it was hard for him to eat much. And like I said, he had problems walking. If I wanted him dead for his money so bad, why not just wait a tiny while longer? I'm a nurse. I've seen people die. I knew it was coming soon for him. What was my great need to have his money right then?" She waved a hand angrily. "I mean Jose tells that I had to have him. But look at Jose and look at me."

"Why did you marry Fiala at all?"

"It seemed a good idea at the time. He was hot after me with money and clothes and Florida. Florida was what got me. There's this really great condo he owned on the Gulf at Siesta Key. You can sit at a big window and see the ocean through the glass. You can smell the water. Anyway, he made me a proposition that included a wedding ring and I took it. I think chasing me and getting me to marry him was a thing he did to keep himself interested and alive. A project. And I've got a thing for older men, successful men.'' She smiled bitterly. ''And so we were wed and lived happily ever after.''

''How sick was he, how close to death?''

''There are doctors who'll testify to that,'' she said, looking away. ''Maybe I did get tired of waiting. That's what Corner keeps saying.''

''Did you?''

''No more than when I was ten days into the marriage.''

''Okay. I believe you.''

''Sure you do,'' she said mockingly. ''So it winds down to being my story against Jose's story. And Jose's this guy who comes right out and admits murdering my husband. That reduces my chances to slim and none. I see and know what's happening to me and I'm frustrated because I can't do anything about it. I can't figure a good reason why Jose keeps telling the story the way he's telling it. I try hard to theorize that one of my stepchildren, or maybe both of them, meaner and more needful than I am, hired Jose, but I don't believe that, except late at night. I guess they could have given Jose extra money he's already disposed of, and he's doing what he bargained to do for that money, but that's crazy. Mr. Lee checked. He hired a private detective. Jose never bought a money order in or around Grimsley City. We even tried Louisville and Cincinnati and Lexington and didn't find anything to hang a hat on. We gave our people Jose's picture, and sent them to every bank around. Nothing.''

I waited.

''I know I'm in a very small box. Someone's done a job on me.''

''You have no evidence at all that Jose made a bargain with Fiala's kids to kill Fiala and then implicate you?''

''No. We'll suggest the possibility. There's a pot of money and other stuff missing. It's possible the kids stole the missing stuff from Fi when he was in one of his black spells, mad at the world,

187

sulking for days. He or they then gave part of missing assets on to Jose. Fiala's kids wanted and needed him dead because of the money. They were uneasy about what he might do. If they waited until he died a natural death, they believed I might get him to Mr. Lee for a new will and take it all. I wouldn't have done that, but they know I could have. Maybe he also said something to the kids about Lee and a new will and scared them good. So he was better off dead for them.''

"Was your husband taking untaxed money from his collection boxes?''

"I knew he was doing it, but I never knew how much. I didn't often go with him. When I did, I'd sip a soft drink off to the side and Fi would do his business privately. Jose would drive him more than I did, but he wasn't allowed to even go into the spots, so he drove only on days when Fiala felt good and could walk. Fi would come home from collecting and sometimes he'd give me money, a thousand dollars, sometimes two thousand dollars, and tell me to buy myself something nice, use the money on anything except another hack at Jose. He'd laugh at me, but I knew he hated me for letting Jose jump me when he couldn't get it up.'' She shook her head. "For some reason he never hated Jose. He told me once that Jose was smarter than either of us or both of us together.''

"Were you affectionate and loving with Fiala?''

"At first I was.'' She smiled a tiny smile. "I got over it quickly. He was a mean man. He was arrogant. He wanted me to follow him around like a pet puppy, sniffing where he put down his pee-smell. I was supposed to look after him when he felt sick, which was most of the time. It was also my duty to jump his bones like a paid prostitute when he was up to that, which was almost never, after the first few months. I think he kept me around to make other men angry and jealous. I went to see a lawyer once about a divorce, but I didn't stick with it. Fiala was the one who asked me to go after we'd argued, but then that same Fiala talked me out of it. He gave me a new car, a woman to come in twice a week to clean, and a couple of new charge accounts. He knew where to reach Momma when I got stubborn.'' She sighed. "I am

188

what I am. And what I am is acquisitive. I've always wanted nice things and never had them until Fiala.''

''Silver filed a divorce for you?''

''We talked about it, but it never got filed. How did you know that?''

''I know Silver pretty well.''

''Silver,'' she mused. ''Silver's cute, but he's so damned young.'' Her eyes met mine and I thought she was thinking about Silver and times she'd thought about which now would never be. Her eyes misted over and I pulled my chair closer to hers to give comfort.

''Did Silver ever come to your house?''

''No. I went to his office just the one time. After that, I called him.''

''Silver thinks you're lovely,'' I said. ''He's on your side. He'll probably be the next prosecutor. That could help you if things go badly in the trial.''

''No. I'll die quick in women's prison. The people here at the jail are nice, but I pace this cell night after night thinking and hating Jose and Fi and Fi's two kids. I can't sleep and it's hard to eat. I've lost pounds and pounds. I'm padding my bras because it's gotten that bad. I hate being caged.'' I saw tears well in her blue eyes.

''How about the cleaning lady Fi let you hire?''

''I fired her first day. She was dirtier than the garbage pails.'' She grimaced. ''Flies followed her.''

''And so you will testify tomorrow?''

''Yes. We'll challenge them some. Me against the local mob. I called lots of people early and Mr. Lee talked to dozens, but no one could or would help me much, so it will be mostly me alone. We got along just fair in front of neighbors. Mr. Lee didn't call any for fear something would go wrong, like them saying something we'd not expect when they were on the stand. The prosecution didn't call neighbors because there was nothing. For my defense, there's a doctor who treated Fi at the hospital where I worked. There's his deposition and two others taken from other doctors about Fi's health problems. They'll read those to the jury.

189

Mostly they show Fi's deteriorating condition and that all I had to do was wait a little to have his money. Then I'll say my piece, and Mr. Lee will challenge the prosecutor to disprove my testimony and the medical testimony. I don't think the little bastard prosecutor or his horse-faced detective, who never believed a word I told him, can. I also don't think not disproving it will make much difference.''

"How's that?''

"I think I'm a loser. I've no faith in the system. I hate it like Fi and Jose used to hate.''

"Jurors are smarter than you think they are.''

"Mr. Lee's funny just like you,'' she said. "He's got what he calls a theory of the case. He says what we're doing will win for us. Or so he thinks.''

"Maybe it will. I'd vote not guilty.''

"Would you? Thank you for that.''

I shrugged. The "not guilty'' words were easy to say in her cell.

"Me and Jose,'' she mused coolly. "If he hustled me into bed again tonight, I'd wish for a sharp knife in my pocket. Why is he lying about what happened? What's his reason? He has to have some reason. Strange, cold bastard. Even when we made love he did it mean.''

"I don't know what his reasons are. Like you, I'm trying to figure them out. Haven't you anyone you can call as a witness who came to visit you in the house and saw that things were okay?'' I asked the question hoping she'd say more about the men she'd seen.

"No. We lived quiet at home. We'd go out to dinner most nights. I'd eat and drink and smile for people. That's what Fi told me to do and I did it. Fi would smile back at me and not eat much. He hurt a lot, more than he'd show. He'd never let on in public. Out there, we were the perfect couple, the millionaire and his blushing bride. So we'll go back to trial tomorrow with just me and the doctor's depositions. Mr. Lee says it has to be me against the angry mob, me against the fat children who'll inherit by the

190

law, plus by my blood, and my freedom. Me against the Mexican rape artist. Me alone.''

"I wish you luck.'' I didn't agree with the trial tactics, but Lee had been at jury trials longer than I had.

"You know I once offered to take a lie detector test and they wouldn't go for it.''

"You asked to take a lie detector?'' I'd not heard anything of that.

"Yes. The state wouldn't agree. The prosecutor said he didn't have any use for them, so he wouldn't cooperate in getting me one. My lawyer told me one I commissioned myself wouldn't help.''

"I don't know much about the admissability of lie detector tests,'' I admitted.

She looked down at the floor and then back up at me, her fine blue eyes catching and holding me. She had made me a part of her problems and I thought she sensed it.

"How's Judge Daggert taking it?'' she asked. "I knew him some, you know. Fi and he were close friends. Did you know that?''

"Yes. Did you and the judge become friends?''

She nodded. "In a way. Sometimes he'd come to our house to see Fiala. Other than Fi's kids, he was the only one who did visit more than once or twice. Fi and Daggert would sit around and talk politics and tell tall tales about the old days of golf and cards and drinking. They liked each other. My guess is it was mostly because they had no use for lots of the same local politicians.''

"Would they include you in these conversations?''

"Sure. I was their audience. The stories weren't any use to them without me listening and oohing and aahing.''

"Didn't Fiala finally become jealous of the judge?''

She nodded, admitting it. "The judge lost his wife and it hurt him deep. Fi said, at first, I was to be extra nice to him, and I was. Once, when Simon was there visiting, I could see he was down and real dark blue and we talked sweet. I told him there'd be another woman for him, but he said no. That seemed okay with Fi, but I guess it wasn't. A few days later, while Fi was out collecting and I was waiting for him to get home, the judge came and I let him inside and we talked some more. Fi came home and he didn't like it that I'd allowed Judge Daggert in to wait. That's the only time I ever saw Fi openly jealous of anyone. He was never that jealous of Jose. He knew or suspected there were other men I saw and called, but he sure hated me talking alone to Simon, even after him being the one who'd told me to be nice. He ordered me not to let Simon in the house again."

"Did he tell you why?"

"I asked, because it made me mad. Fi said that Simon was *his* friend and not mine. He got himself sick and crying talking about it." She shook her head. "God, he hated hard. When he was hating, he'd wish people death, disease, blindness, and paralysis. He was a first-class hater."

"But you and Judge Daggert were never more than friends?"

"No. No way. We talked. That's all. After Fiala blew up, I called Simon when Fi was out of the house and told him not to visit. And I called some other times afterward just to talk. But I never saw him outside the house." She looked up at the drab ceiling. "I wish that . . ."

"What do you wish?"

She shook her head and then went on: "Simon likes things I like. Having to hear my trial's hard on him. You tell him I said it was all right for him to do what he has to do. I won't blame him for it. You wait until I've said my piece on the witness stand and then you tell him that." I could almost feel her "willing" me to do her bidding, but I thought her words were false and that she hoped Daggert would help her.

"Did you know Simon before you met Fiala?"

"No. I knew who he was."

"I think you'll be all right."

She lowered her head and looked at the floor, forgetting me, closed in combat within herself on what had been and what would be. She was in a world where the answers were not yet seen, and it frightened her.

She looked up at me after a time: "There's one more thing I'll

192

testify to. I've got a great, big birthmark on the right side of my butt. If Jose kept seeing me nude, why didn't he remember that?'' She smiled. ''The one time we made nude love in bed, he never saw it, because it was just quick and missionary style. Do something for me. Turn your back.''

''You don't need to prove anything to me.''

''Turn your back,'' she ordered harshly.

I turned away.

''Okay,'' she said, in a moment. ''Turn back around.''

I did.

She'd raised her skirt and lowered the right side of her white panties. There was a dark purple birthmark in the middle of her white, right cheek, maybe three by four inches, almost oval in shape.

''I'm going to show it tomorrow,'' she said. She pulled herself back into shape and smiled. ''I'd like to drop my drawers and just show it, but Mr. Lee says it won't work that way.''

I watched her and mostly believed her story. I didn't believe she had been involved in the planning or actual killing of Fiala Kentner. I thought she was a beautiful woman, a woman who liked men, a woman who'd sold a part of her future for money, a woman as inconstant as the moon. A lot of woman.

So what? Who gave a damn what I thought?

I sat with her for a while longer, waiting until she was back in the world again. I had enough for my forms, for my pre-sentence report, when and if they needed to be filled out.

I got up and Shirley rose with me. She came close and kissed me softly on the lips and I kissed her back, feeling things rising within me. Somehow I'd known she was going to kiss me and so enlist me further in her army of defense.

''Addie's outside your door,'' I whispered.

''I know. I wanted to kiss you. Please help me if you can. I need someone so badly.'' Her eyes were full of desperation.

''Yes.''

''Men have chased after me since I was twelve. I like men, old men, young men, I like you. I know I'm not a good person, but I shouldn't have to go to prison for that.''

193

"Yes."

I tapped on the cell door for Addie. She came and smiled me down the steps. I thought she'd probably listened to us through the door, but I doubted she knew about the kiss.

That night, at my apartment and in bed, I dreamed dreams rather than nightmares. In my dreams a golden-haired woman whispered sweet promises to me. She came near and I sought to catch her and hold her, but she faded and only vaguely returned, so that she was always just out of my reach, but still close where I could see and want her. Other men also pursued her, and she smiled for all of us.

I awoke and I was ready for a woman, but that had happened before at nights and desire and ability had vanished by daylight.

I tried through the night to catch Shirley and hold her, but could not.

In the morning I awoke and was tired from the chase.

CHAPTER THIRTEEN

Conversation overheard between two reporters in the courtroom:
"These lawyers think they can change the world, but all they do is win or lose."
"Which is best?"
"In this case, who knows?"

IN THE MORNING a dyspeptic-appearing Judge Daggert started the trial at a few minutes after ten.

The lawyers, in "publishing" and thereafter reading the depositions of absent witnesses, had agreed that each would ask the questions he'd asked when the individual depositions had been taken and that they would collectively use Owen Smith, the long-time Grimsley County clerk, to read the answers each doctor gave in his deposition. It was agreed Owen "read well."

Owen came up from downstairs and read the doctor's parts in the three depositions, two for the defense, and one for the prosecution. The prosecution's deposed witness was the coroner, now on vacation in Florida.

I found out some new things: The Coroner, Dr. Stanley McCallen, early on in his deposition, seemed of the opinion that Fiala Kentner's death had been caused by the bullet in the back of his head, but, on cross-examination by Henry Lee, he also stated that Fiala Kentner had suffered a severe stroke, or cardiovascular accident, just prior to the time of death. He also verified that some of the tortures had occurred after Kentner was dead. To end it, his opinion was that Fiala's death had been caused by the bullet wound, but that he likely would have and could have died as a result of what he said was a trauma-induced stroke, which he described as a "massive CVA."

The jury listened intently. The first deposition had something good for everyone. It was as if Dr. McCallen was agreeably willing to say what each of the lawyers placed in front of him to say.

The two doctors deposed by the defense were Edward McCallen, Stanley's brother, and Robert Quenton Zahn. Neither of the two had examined the body of the deceased, nor had either been employed to do that, but both had treated him during the last months of his life. Both described him as a man in "the final stages of lung cancer complicated by both pulmonary emphysema and coronary artery disease." Both were cautious about how much time he had left to live, describing it as hours to a month or perhaps two.

County Clerk Owen Smith, fiftyish and finely dressed in a black chalk stripe suit, sat easily on the witness stand, an old hand at reading depositions for lawyers in need. He read his part well, stumbling only now and then over medical terms. If corrected, he would look over his rimless spectacles and smile at the lawyer correcting him.

"Yes. That's right of course. Sorry, Henry. Sorry, Lynn."

Both lawyers seemed to think that the depositions were important. Daggert read an agreed joint stipulation to the jurors about depositions, that they had been taken under oath, and that the jurors were to accept the depositions of the doctors as if each doctor had personally appeared and testified.

The jury listened.

The depositions proved, once and for all, that Fiala Kentner was dead. They also indicated his remaining life expectancy, before his murder, had been short.

Shirley Kentner walked to the witness stand when her time came. The courtroom had filled to watch her. She was dressed severely, but handsomely. Her hair was in a bun and she wore only a touch of makeup. She carried her Bible. Henry Lee asked her short, direct questions.

"Did you ever have sexual intercourse with Jose Ramon Garcia?"

"Yes."

"When did this begin?"

"One rainy summer afternoon soon after he was employed. My husband was ill and we had not been able to make love for a long time. I asked Jose to come help me with curtains while Fiala was at work. He did enter the house and then he forced me to have sex with him."

"But you admit you did not violently resist or report what happened to your husband or the authorities later?"

"No. At the time I wanted it to happen. I continued with Jose for a short period of time until my stepson, Alfred, caught us. I was confronted, and there was a family fight. Thereafter I promised my husband I'd end the affair. I did end it."

"After Alfred caught you, did you ever make love to Jose Garcia again?"

"I did not."

"Did your husband and his children watch you carefully to make certain you did not resume the affair after the time you were caught?"

"Yes. They would slip in and out of my house, at all hours, without warning."

"All right. Let's get to the meat of the prosecution's case. Did you ever ask Jose Garcia to murder your husband?"

"I did not. I never even hinted to Jose that I wanted Fiala dead. My husband was a terminally ill man. One reason he married me was because I was a nurse and he wanted my care." She wiped a tiny tear from her astonishing blue eyes. "I learned, in nurse's training, to *care* for sick people. I didn't learn to plot to kill them. I knew my husband was terminal, as the doctors have testified. Why would I kill him when I knew he was going to die soon? I'm not a fool. I did want some of his money, because it was promised to me when we married, but I had no need for money immediately. I don't gamble. I don't do drugs. I seldom drink. I didn't want all his money, but only enough to pay me for being a body servant to him, the money he promised me at marriage."

"You've heard Jose Garcia make his statements concerning you. Why do you think he is telling this jury you asked him to kill your husband?"

"I don't know. I'd like to blame it on my stepchildren, but I'm not certain enough it happened that way to do that. Maybe Jose now lies because he hates me."

I saw a male juror nod, liking the answer.

"Did you and your husband have a fight the day he died?"

"No. We did fight some, but that day was friendly. Jose left on a short vacation that morning, so Fi and I had a light lunch at home and watched television. I took him to his daughter's place in the late afternoon. Thereafter I picked him up. He wasn't feeling too badly, but he was having problems walking. He'd had dizzy troubles before and I wasn't unduly alarmed. I helped him to the door of our house and went to play bridge. The police came and I was called home after Alfred arrived there."

"And you were shocked?"

"Yes. When they told me a vehicle was missing, I remembered it was Jose's favorite, so I told the police they should perhaps look for Jose."

I remembered that Lee had gotten a number of police officers to testify that Shirley had said to "look for Jose."

"There was a clock that was stopped."

"Yes. At shortly before ten. The clock was all right earlier."

"And you heard Mr. Garcia admit he broke that clock?"

"Yes. Sometimes Fi kept money hidden in the clock's works. He liked to hide money here and there around the house."

"What time did you normally come home from bridge?"

"Usually after eleven and sometimes after twelve."

"So if Mr. Garcia executed your husband around ten o'clock and opened the drapes so the body could be seen by you, there was at least an hour's time that the body was in view before you could have seen it?"

"Yes."

"Have you offered to do certain acts to prove your innocence?"

Corner stood up. "Your Honor, may we have a conference at the bench?"

Daggert nodded. "Come up."

198

I was near enough to hear part of the low conversation. Henry Lee strongly wanted to bring in the offer of the defendant to submit to a lie detector test. Corner wanted it kept out. He seemed very confident in his low-voiced arguments.

Daggert listened to both of them. He sent the jury out as the lawyers argued bitterly and more loudly.

"I'm going to let it in," Daggert said finally. "I'll only let in the fact that she offered to take the test and that the state refused the offer. This defendant is charged with murder. The results of a lie detector test might not be available to the jury unless there was a pre-agreement between the parties that they would be. But an offer to take a lie detector test, made in writing, and refused by the state, should be a part of the evidence in this case."

Corner shook his head, seemingly shocked. "Show my continuing objection to any testimony of this nature. And we may want to take it up," he finished gravely.

"Take up to the appellate court whatever you please, Mr. Corner," Daggert said coldly.

Lee smiled at both Daggert and Corner, satisfied at winning this major skirmish. Thereafter a letter from his office, signed by both himself and Shirley Kentner, offering for Shirley to take a lie detector test, was marked and admitted into evidence, then shown to the jury.

The jury read it with interest.

Lee then asked: "On or around the time you were supposed to have plotted with Jose to run to Mexico, or at any time, did you ever buy any traveler's checks, withdraw any money from any bank account, obtain a passport, or do anything that would indicate you were planning a trip?"

"No. I did nothing. Nor was I planning anything."

"Were you completely surprised when Jose accused you of plotting with him concerning your husband's death?"

"Yes. Sometimes I think he did it because I broke off with him. Sometimes I also believe if I'd helped Fi past the door that Jose would have killed me also."

Corner rose, shook his head, and sat back down.

Lee's voice was careful: "Jose has testified that he followed you sometimes at night when you went out alone. Did he do that?"

"Yes."

"On more than one occasion?"

"Yes. Several times."

"Why did he follow you?"

"I'm not sure. I believed it was for my husband."

Lee asked a few more routine questions. He asked about money. Shirley described Fiala's generosity. She said she kept no accounts in her own name except those she'd had before marriage and that they had been unused for a long time. She said she believed that Fiala was secreting untaxed money, but didn't know what had happened to the money or what had happened to whatever he purchased with it. She professed no knowledge of diamonds or other hidden jewels, but she did testify that, when able, Fiala liked to visit big flea markets.

She then testified about her birthmark. She offered to go into a private room with a female deputy and have that female deputy examine the mark. Instead, the prosecutor agreed to stipulate she did have such a birthmark, its size and location, color and texture.

Shirley seemed, to me, serene and confident.

Corner cross-examined her ferociously.

"Are you telling this jury that you quit having sex with Jose just because your husband found out about it?"

"Yes."

"Why didn't you just refrain from having sex with him originally? You've told us you let him into your house to help you with something. Wasn't that *something* your longing for Jose Garcia coupled with your hate for your husband?"

"No."

"Where's the money, Mrs. Kentner?"

Shirley smiled nicely. "Ask your legal associate's clients. Ask Jose."

"I'm asking *you*. You were in almost constant attendance upon your husband Fiala. You helped him collect. You helped him get around. He wouldn't use a cane, so *you* became his cane. If there

200

was money or a cache of jewels hidden away, then *you* would be the one who knows what happened to it. You stole it. You smelled it out and stole it.''

''No. When I went with him on collections, I did no counting, no score keeping. I took what money he gave me and I bought things for the house, *our* house. I've no money of my own. You know that because you and your people have looked and looked. You dug big holes in my backyard in your search. You contacted all my old friends and you sent your police to every bank within two hundred miles.''

''Your Honor,'' Corner said, ''that ought to go out.''

Daggert shrugged.

I thought, when both sides were done, that the issue was in doubt.

In mid-afternoon, with the trial testimony done, the lawyers conferred with Judge Daggert on instructions and discussed how much time would be necessary and would be allowed for final arguments.

When that was finished, and while the lawyers were working on verdict forms and instructions, Judge Daggert beckoned me in.

''It'll be over soon now,'' he said softly, staring out his window at the winter-grey Grim City world below.

''Yes, I know. I still want to interview Jose.''

He shrugged. I knew somehow he was displeased with me. ''Talking to him means nothing now. All that's left are final instructions and final arguments made by the lawyers, both of whom badly want to win this case.''

''Would it be all right if I went to the jail now to see Jose?''

''Do you have anything you're not telling me, Jim?''

I sighed. ''No. A few crazy ideas.''

''Why bother then?''

I shrugged.

* * *

I took precautions with the help of the sheriff and a willing, watchful Ballinger.

I met with Garcia inside the jail, but not in the cell area. Instead, I sat behind an absent chief deputy's table in a tiny office near the booking desk. Two of the deputy sheriffs, both of whom had accompanied Garcia to court, brought the prisoner to me, escorting him to my borrowed room. He was manacled and wore leg irons.

Garcia spoke to me in the semi-uneducated Spanish of the mountains and valleys from the door into the room. *"Hueno.* Can some of these irons be removed for my interview with you?''

''Can the manacles and leg irons be removed while I talk with Señor Garcia?'' I asked the deputies in English.

Both deputies shook their heads in unison. ''No. We got strict rules, Mr. Singer,'' the larger one said.

They sat Jose in a chair across from me and retreated to the door, waiting there, listening and watching.

''Close and lock the door behind you when you go outside it,'' I said. ''I have rules I must follow also.''

''He could attack you, Mr. Singer,'' the large deputy said. ''He's strong and moves right quick even inside them irons.''

''Please wait outside the door after locking it behind you,'' I answered crossly. ''I will talk to Mr. Garcia alone.''

The two deputy sheriffs looked at each other uncomfortably and finally nodded.

''Call out if there's trouble,'' the older deputy said anxiously.

''I'll do just that.''

Garcia waited impassively until they were gone and the heavy door was closed behind them. He said in coarse, colloquial Spanish, ''I thank you for your courtesy in requesting them to remove the chains and irons.''

''It was nothing. I'm sorry they wouldn't oblige us. Do you know who I am?''

''You were pointed out to me after I testified in court.'' He smiled. ''I do not believe you hold great favor with the attorney for the state.''

"True. Mr. Corner didn't want me to talk to you, but Judge Daggert has ordered it. They will be returning you to prison later today or in the morning, so I needed to speak to you before that time."

He waited patiently, a man who had waited that way before.

"I've watched the trial from its beginning. Some things puzzle me. The jury could soon return its verdict. But I also must be satisfied for there to be a final verdict," I lied.

He eyed me politely, his eyes unconvinced. "I do not understand what you mean."

I leaned toward him. "Could you explain to me again why you opened the curtain after dumping Mr. Kentner into his reclining chair in front of that window?"

He thought on my question for a moment. We were still speaking Spanish. "It was, as I said, a signal. It was not a good one, for many have commented on it. There are things I should have done, better plans I should have made and followed. Another day uncaught, a faster journey, and I might have escaped. But I was told by my lawyer that the police were, within hours, looking for me. I would have gotten caught even had I stolen another car or found different license plates."

"If you crossed the border, would you have been safe?"

"Yes," he said. "Once into the mountains, I would never have been caught, not even by the *soldao.*" Once again, he used the uneducated word rather than the correct *"soldado."*

"Go on with this plan."

"The plan was to leave Mr. Kentner in plain view in front of his window so that my Shirley would and could see his body before she entered the home. If no one saw him before she found him, then she could have driven to the house of a neighbor and reported something bad had happened at her house, have requested the police to come, and then thrown suspicion away from both of us, as she promised to do."

"Why did you kill him so early in the evening? Why not more at the time when Shirley normally returned home?"

He shrugged. "I sought his hiding places. He died in the looking."

"He died before ten o'clock at night?"

"Sometime around that time." His eyes evaded mine. "After I had sealed his eyes and searched through most of the house."

"The coroner says that some of the torture was done on a dead man's unfeeling body."

"I didn't know that then. When I did torture him, he would, now and then, come awake and tell me new hiding places."

"So at about ten you gave it up and shot him in the back of the head?"

"That would likely be about the time."

"Or perhaps earlier than that?"

He smiled and said nothing.

"You must have known that the police would have a good description of the Sable wagon and its license tag."

"I suppose I knew, but I did nothing about it. So I was caught."

"How about the other car that came during the time from after six to before ten?"

"What car was that?" he asked.

I smiled and looked over at the wall of the office. The sheriff's chief deputy, his wife, and two small children stared back at me from a posed picture. Next to it a clock with a loud motor made audible sounds. Even in this distant office, I could smell the odor from the cages inside the jail.

"I don't understand your part in this," Garcia said to me crossly. "Another man talked to me after I had been to court for my guilty plea. Where is he? Why do I now see you?"

"The man you saw before is gone. You know how things are here in this damnable Yankee country. They change at the whims of crazed politicians. Do you like this country?"

"No. I do not like it."

"Yes, I agree. The man before me retired. I'm now the officer of the circuit court system, the probation officer. I make recommendations to the court about what should happen to those found guilty of breaking laws."

"You then will soon make a recommendation concerning Shirley Kentner?"

"Yes. I will do that." I smiled. "If she's convicted." I looked at the loud wall clock. "The jury will do its work. They will argue about the truth of what you said and the truth of what she said. Who is one to believe when there are two different stories?"

He shrugged. "They should believe me, for I have told the truth. Will you also discuss my own case with your judge? The length of my sentence is now on appeal."

"Perhaps. It is possible."

"Then let us proceed quickly with your remaining questions."

"There was an aluminum contraption in the room where the body was found. Why was it there?"

"The walker," he said. "I made him use it to walk after I had used fire and razor on him. He was weak and couldn't support himself much of the time. I would not help him. He disliked his walker, but he used it often that night."

"Could he support himself early that night?"

"Yes. At first. And thereafter there was the walker."

"No cane?"

"Never a cane. He was always too vain to use a cane."

"The walker was checked by fingerprint experts," I lied again, remembering there'd been no fingerprint evidence. "There were none of Mr. Kentner's prints on it. There were some of yours."

"I remember I carried it into the room from the kitchen and placed it beside him. Perhaps my prints were from that time. I don't know why his prints wouldn't be on the walker, unless it was because he was sweaty and ill."

"Perhaps your memory is wrong that he used it that night?"

He shrugged.

"What other purpose could such an instrument have had? Do you know of any?"

He shook his head solemnly. There was now a tic by his right eye. I had found him to be quick with answers, intelligent—but not surprisingly intelligent. The question was whether he was what he seemed to be, a Mexican laborer who'd seen rough places, or more than that.

"Did you ever do time in jail before the Kentner murder?"

"Yes. Several times in Mexico. Three times in this country for drinking or fighting."

"When was the second and final time you shot Mr. Kentner?"

"Maybe near ten. He would only tell me where a tiny amount of money was each time I asked questions. Sometimes money would not be there. I would then punish him for his lies. I shot him for the second time with a killing shot when he no longer answered me, despite my prodding."

"How long did you stay at it with him?"

"A long time. It started before seven. I consulted no watch after that." I could see him calculating. "More than three hours."

"That's a long time for a man to live who is terminally ill and being cruelly tortured."

He nodded. "He was a strong man in many ways."

"All you got from him for hours of effort were the watch, a little more than a thousand dollars, and one of his cars."

"The one I drove most and liked best," he said. "It has many glass windows and a driver can see well. My patron and I both thought it was the best of his cars on the road." He smiled. "It goes where it's aimed. A station wagon."

"A fine vehicle?"

"Yes."

"Did you wreck it?"

"No. Perhaps a bump once or twice. I am a good driver, but I like to drive with much speed."

"You and Fiala became friends, didn't you?"

"He was good to me. He paid me little, but there was food, fine drinks, and a place for sleep. He hated many things. He hated well. And there was the woman." He sighed.

"Yes, the woman. After you were caught with her, did you and Fiala ever speak of that time?"

"Some. He never seemed angry with me. A few times I thought he wanted to hear how it had been between us."

"And did you tell him?"

"No."

He smiled as he said it and I thought he had.

"She is a beautiful woman," I said.

He nodded, reading me. "She has conquered you also. What a woman she is!"

"Did Fiala ask you to follow her when she left the house at nights?"

"Sometimes. Sometimes he did not seem to care. I followed her to know there were no other men than me. It made him happy, and she was not bothered by it."

I went on: "If you needed extra money, would Fiala give that to you also?"

"Yes. He was generous with me."

I nodded agreement and considered him again.

He yawned widely. "I tire and want to go back to my cell. You have been most courteous to me, but I am very sleepy. Tomorrow I will be returned to my prison."

"For how long?"

He watched me, his eyes suddenly grown unsure. "Who knows? Perhaps my appeal of the sentence will save me some years."

"One or two more questions and I will call the deputies to return you." I leaned forward and captured his eyes with mine. "Tell me of the diamonds and other things you removed from the Kentner house. *Tell me* to whom you delivered those precious things, for I don't believe you acted alone."

He shook his head, eyes downcast at the accusation. "I know of no diamonds or other jewels. Or, let us say, I knew nothing that night. I was told later by federal people, who questioned me in prison, that such things might have been stolen from the house. Federal tax officers promised me special treatment if I would help them. My answer to them and to you is that Shirley must have such things hidden. I admit that had I found jewels I would have taken them also and they would have been found with me. But the old one told me nothing of diamonds or other jewels. I asked and searched only for money."

"I see. I find another thing of interest. We speak all our words in Spanish. When you were first brought to me here in this office, you spoke to me in that language. How did you know I spoke it?"

"I knew." He laughed a little. "One of the deputies called you the *'spic P.O.'* I notice such things. There is now much time for me to notice."

"Yet now you work very hard at learning English. Why?"

"It is a thing to do. In the prison, English is spoken, not Spanish. If I live out my term, I might try to stay in this country."

"I thought you didn't like this country."

He smiled. "It is easier to live here than in Mexico. In Mexico, many poor people starve."

"I am certain about the jewels," I said softly, staring at him. "You're not deceiving me on them. I believe I know where they went and for what purpose. I know who you delivered them to. And I know that Shirley Kentner saw other men when she left her house."

"You know nothing. You are some kind of petty court officer, a minor functionary, a nothing." His eyes dismissed me. "You seek to entrap me in things of which I have no knowledge. You are a fool who believes I am also a fool."

"Perhaps." I smiled at him. "The question to me is are you a special man, a leader, a judge? Perhaps you are what you now say. But you lie about the jewels and you also lie about the woman."

"No!"

I spoke a name and his eyes flickered.

When I exited the jail, I could see that Ballinger had placed extra men nearby as guards. There were men on the courthouse roof and men walking the streets and watching out office windows.

Armed and ready.

The two deputies I'd been falsely cross with smilingly followed me outside. I pointed up toward the guards on the roof and smiled.

"I believe all's safe. I doubt that anyone will come for Garcia. My instincts tell me he's not a man waiting impatiently for armed rescue from jail. Not yet, anyway." I shook my head. "He may be a leader in follower's clothes. Tell Ballinger I said that. Tell him I'm going on to look around another place or two. Tell him I have this hunch."

"Do you want to return the equipment?"

"No. Because I have this other place to go, I will keep it yet a while."

*   *   *

From the sheriff's I returned to the courtroom area. I unlocked my office and sat for a time thinking about the woman and her single, small kiss.

It was dark and empty in the halls. Horace slept outside the jury room. I could hear vague sounds as the jury argued inside their closed room.

Horace awoke and saw me. He smiled and beckoned.

"They're hung up good in there. I can hear them fighting and calling names."

I nodded.

I went back downstairs. I checked over and then unlocked the Mustang and drove down to the river. I parked for a time in the lot where my father had been killed. On this cold, moonless night there were no boats in the lot, no parked cars, no drug buyers or sellers, no racing cars or wine drinkers. The river below was calm and without night traffic. The local newspaper had reported there was a ice at Cincinnati and that a lot of the big boats had tied in both above and below it.

I sat there and watched the moving, muddy water and thought again about all that had happened, going over it all. I found once more a wild explanation for both Kentner's death and other matters.

It seemed I had to be wrong. Even if I was right, it was unlikely I'd ever convince anyone.

I was and had been a watcher. I reported what I saw and let others make decisions, others be convinced.

But not this time?

A new notion came. If I went where I wasn't expected and asked rude questions, something might happen.

The ballpoint pen Ballinger had given me before my talk with Jose remained in my pocket. I got it out and looked it over. It looked about like any other ballpoint pen.

The gas tank was half full. I started the Mustang's motor and drove around, coming nearer and nearer to the place I sought, thinking, working up courage, keeping anger and fear banked.

Eventually I stopped.

I parked and walked up to the door. I could see the lake water. The house was dark inside, but I rang the bell anyway.

No one came to the door. I rang three times. When I turned at last to go back to my car, the two men from the courtroom and the Dumont restaurant came out of the darkness that shrouded the sides of the house. They were on me swiftly, competent at their business, larger and stronger than I was. I thought I recognized them.

I tried first to run, then to fight. I caught the younger one with a decent elbow and kicked at the older. I heard the older one curse me and something hard came rushing at me out of the darkness.

There was pain, and bursts of light exploded fearfully behind both my bad and good eyes.

When I awoke, my arms had been tied in back of me. My feet were tied together. I hurt. My eyes were covered with something, but at the very top of the covering I could see a little light and I was buoyed by it.

I heard noises and I knew that people were near me.

A whisper came: "This time we'll blind you the first time you lie. You must tell us the exact truth."

"Yes," I said.

"You know that I ache and yearn to do this thing?"

"Yes. I know it."

"All right. Who knows you are here?"

"No one. I came to ask questions."

"What questions?"

"About bombs. About missing diamonds."

"Be careful now. I am holding a razor-sharp knife in my right hand. I can whisk away your blindfold and take your eyes so quickly that all you'll ever see is a flash of light and quick, wet dark." He was silent for a moment. "You fear for your eyes and I see that the threat makes you sweat."

"Yes," I said. "I'm sorry. Ask what you will."

"What were *you* going to ask about diamonds?"

210

"About where they are now. I figured they were once packed and hidden inside Fiala's walker on the night he was killed. It's light and hollow, made of aluminum. It came to me that Kentner, a man who was good with his hands, could have taken off the rubber tip from a leg and so made an opening into the tubular frame. He might then have poured jewels inside and used cotton to make things secure enough so there'd be no rattling. A theory. Is that how it was?"

"You are not without cleverness. And bombs?"

"You saw me smelling about and I was a nuisance, and so needed to be dealt with. Ballinger and his people were already all over the area, so it seemed little would be lost if I died. So you made a calculated decision. You sent your men to frighten me or perhaps dispose of me. When that failed, a bomb was placed in my car."

"Why? You knew nothing."

"You weren't afraid of what I knew. You were afraid of what I'd find."

"You were sentenced to death years ago. You escaped. In partial payment for that escape, Jose ran down and killed your father."

"There was another reason for that also."

"Perhaps."

"I guessed when in the trial there was testimony about damage to the Sable station wagon. But you did not give the order on my father."

"True."

I waited.

The voice sounded sorrowful. "I became your friend. I almost died of fear that first day I saw you at law school. I decided that you were a child of luck and should live. I would, one time only, grant mercy, ignore my own solemn judgment and spare you. But you kept asking questions and snooping. You had the ear of the judge and the continuing attentions of the bastard known by us as 'Butcher Ballinger.' Do you swear that you never knew I was involved until tonight?"

"I swear. Until now I was unsure. But someone had to be

211

writing the script for the play I saw in court. I became a devil's advocate for a doubting judge. Daggert didn't believe Shirley guilty, for many reasons. He was suspicious. He infected me with his disbelief. If it wasn't Shirley who had her husband killed, then someone must have. Kentner was dead. Someone stole from him, profiting from his murder. That had to be whoever knew what was in the walker and what else was to be found in his house. It would need to be someone who could promise a devout follower, like Jose, that one day he would be free, that one day he would stand rewarded. It had to be a someone who figured that the missing estate assets would be ignored by Fiala's children if it helped their claim to get all that remained. A smart killer. A skilled man. Someone who understood the situation. Perhaps a lawyer."

"Why not one or both of Fiala's children? I believed you would seek that way."

"I did. The daughter speaks Spanish. She could have done a deal with Jose. She didn't like me coming around her father's house. Her brother needed his share of the money badly. I could see them jointly hiring Jose to both do the job and implicate Fiala's wife. But both knew that their father was soon to die, and because they met with him daily, including the day of his death, they were certain he'd not yet cut them out of his will. Why have him sign an agreement giving them more of the profits if they were going to have him killed that same night? Besides, there was nothing they could promise Jose to make him dally about, wishing and waiting to be caught."

"But perhaps your own Judge Daggert? He could promise Jose the moon. Surely you realize he's in love with Shirley?"

"Yes. He is that. But he speaks no Spanish and has no need for money."

I did believe Daggert and Shirley likely had committed the sin of jointly dreaming of Fiala's death.

"Why not a planned murder-suicide paid for by Fiala? I thought long about making it appear more that way. Fiala was sick and in constant pain. Maybe he could have hired Jose to end him and even given Jose some of his hidden money to include Shirley's death."

"Fiala was a bully of a man who wanted to stay alive as long as he could. He was still in control. Suicide was not for him. Besides, his suicide would have had everyone looking for the jewels."

"How then did you arrive at me? My involvement in the whole matter was tiny."

"You speak the language, Silver, but then other people in this may speak it better. I now believe you are more fluent than you've allowed me to know. But I never believed it could be you until the smart bomb was placed in my car. Someone had to order that. Someone who knew of and could control such things. Could it be the 'Judge' from my sun hell? If so, that Judge could not be the dead Fiala. Could it be Fiala's son and daughter? Or Judge Daggert? If there was one person in Grimsley City who I believed, in my fancies, could ever be a secret leader of an insurrection group below the border, you had to be that man. You are single. You have a doting mother. You go off on long vacations alone. When Shirley consulted you on divorce, my guess is you learned that Fiala was hiding assets, if Jose had not told you before. You wanted the diamonds for yourself . . ."

"Not only for me, but for my cause," Silver said. "I found my cause years ago. Someday, when I rise to a position of much power, I will help that cause become more than dreams. I speak good Spanish. I was a god to those people, something reborn out of their old legends."

"Your cause is a crazy nightmare."

His voice lowered. "You speak like a man on top of things, a man with a future. You have none. Your time ends soon."

"Best hold on a bit."

"I dislike your tone, but I will listen to a why."

"Ballinger is a clever man, Silver. I told him of the men who followed me to Dumont and the complicated bomb in my car. He realized, as did I, that someone from my past stalked me. He therefore equipped me with a magic pen before I talked to Jose earlier tonight. You should closely examine that pen. I believe it remains in my shirt pocket."

I felt a hand at my pocket.

213

I heard other noises. I heard a door splinter, loud shouts, a gun-shot, then two more.

Silver whispered softly into my ear: "We will tell them what we said was a great joke, ace. We will tell them I knew you were wired all along. You will support me, for I now give you your eyes."

I waited, deathly afraid of his knife.

I wanted the blindfold off my eyes.

Soon, it was.

CHAPTER FOURTEEN

"Probation officers shall serve at the pleasure of the appointing judge."

IN APRIL, Shirley appeared one rainy night, smiling up at me when I opened my apartment door. I smelled her perfume and worried about what she was wearing and not wearing under her shiny raincoat.

"I owe you," she said simply. "I pay my debts."

"You owe me nothing."

"Not true. I'm alive again because of what you did." She waited confidently for me to invite her inside.

"Did you know my father?"

She nodded. "I met him and he was lonely. We were friends." She smiled again, tantalizing me. "One day we might have been more than that."

"Could Jose have followed behind you for Fiala or himself and seen you meet my father?"

"I'm not sure. I never believed it because I was careful. When your father was killed, I thought it was as the newspapers reported it."

The longer she was there, the more I wanted her. I thought that if I took her inside, maybe things would work out physically. But I didn't invite her in. Mostly because I desired more than what was offered, more than a single night.

So I took nothing other than a kiss and a few whispered words.

After that night, I saw Shirley only at a distance for a time. Maybe she avoided me. I know I didn't avoid her. I kept remembering the words she had whispered after that single kiss and wondering about them, exploring their meaning endlessly.

* * *

A month after Shirley's visit, there was a primary victory party in Daggert's aristocratic home. That was in late May, the evening of primary election day, after the votes had been swiftly tabulated.

I walked alone to the party from my apartment. I now had a "kind of" girl, but not a date for this night.

A deputy clerk I'd been late dating wanted nothing to do with me publicly, but still liked what was happening enough to continue our secret relationship. She had some hopes of repairing her failed marriage. I was a back-door, late-night man until all was settled. I'd heard the reason her marriage had gone bad originally was because I wasn't the first late-night man she'd had a run with. But she was a warm and pretty lady, liked me a lot, and was willing to put up with my good and bad nights.

She'd lately admitted she'd called me several times late at night. She told it to me softly, saying she liked the sound of my voice and so she'd called to listen.

She'd been my anonymous caller.

The starry, starry night that surrounded me smelled of blossoming flowers. It was late Kentucky spring complete with calling birds, kids in convertibles, and recent memories of the Derby. It was the best of what life had to offer in the commonwealth and it had been a good day for the downtrodden.

Judge Daggert had beaten Lynn Corner by a margin of over a thousand votes, more than enough to withstand any election recount tricks. Branch Lester Baker, whom I'd known as a mediocre point guard for Grimsley U., first son of a wealthy Grimsley County family, would be the new commonwealth's attorney after the first of the year, assuming no one ran for the opposition party. No one had for a long time.

Silver was lost in federal custody. His mother had mortgaged her home for lawyers and possible bail, but Silver remained in jail. The two men who'd assisted him and accosted me had also vanished into complicated federal jungles.

Lame-duck Corner was dallying and hadn't yet filed any of several possible state charges against the trio, but Baker had already promised filings after the first of the year.

"How about your father?" he'd asked me anxiously the day he was approved by the party machinery.

"Up to you, Branch. I've no burning desire for added revenge. And it'd be a tough case to prove. I guess all there is are his bloodstains on Fiala's station wagon. Maybe a DNA test on his blood and the stains would be good evidence, but there's not much else."

"Thanks, Jim," he said, patting my shoulder. "I appreciate that, but I'll go after someone if you want."

My father was at peace. I believed he'd sought death by alcohol poisoning down the years after my mother died. Death had eluded him for a long time until a flirtation with Shirley Kentner had cost him his life, either on Kentner's order or Jose's bloody whim. *Someone jealous about Shirley.*

I arrived late. I was tired. Since six in the A.M. I'd worked at my precinct passing out DAGGERT FOR JUDGE cards.

Daggert stood near the stern portrait of his father and accepted congratulations. I gave him my hand. There was a group pressing behind me.

"Howdy," I said.

He smiled. "Howdy yourself, P. I. P. O." Meaning his private eye probation officer.

We were friends and he was pleased with me.

I moved on.

Two tables of snacks were in the dining room. I considered them and marked them for wait and see. I was no longer always hungry for goodies.

A bar operated in the kitchen. A short white man and a large black lady I remembered from the country club tended things jovially. They were serving good stuff, Maker's Mark, Dewars, Stoli, plus beer by the bottle or on tap to a crowd of black and white people, party workers, party voters.

I had a diet cola.

I thought Daggert looked fit. He was a careful man these days, who might refuse even a social drink. He was fifteen pounds lighter than he'd been in January.

217

He was happy, and I knew a reason for his newly found happiness.

I danced early with Anne Melville. Other guests drank, ate, and talked loud politics, but there were a few dancers. Everyone, it seemed, had voted for Daggert. Some of those present in the house were liars, mending fences unseen.

Anne whispered, "Smile, Jim-boyo. We've saved our jobs and you're a local hero. The bar might even run you for president."

"Tell me what you hear?"

She nestled a little closer. "Simon would have won by even more if it weren't for the rumors. Nasty people claim his car and hers were seen parked last week at a motel in Lexington. I've also heard they were spotted betting horses at Churchill and at a night-club in Cincinnati." She shook her head. "Lord knows if any of it's true."

"People asked me about them at the polling place. Most of them seemed friendly about it."

"Yes. An older man and a younger woman, a familiar story. Now smile for me. Can't you smile? It's said you smiled when you did a dandy dirty to District Judge Rainbolt."

I did smile for her, but only a little. "That wasn't me. It was Silver. He did it to Rainbolt and then got people to believe it was me."

She shook her head, not believing me. No one did. Judge Rainbolt was up for election in two years, and not very many liked him. So the story about his false ascension to appellate heights had surfaced again with me as the hero/villain.

"I wish I was thirty again, Jim," she said wistfully. "I'd look for someone like you. You look neat. You've put on weight and you're calmer."

"Thank you, Miss Annie." We danced a little more and then parted, uncomfortable with each other for the moment and afraid to voice what we felt about Daggert's behavior.

I was *better*. I now usually awoke without my good eye being covered by a protecting hand. I'd practiced in front of my shaving mirror until I could hold both eyes full open. I no longer looked perpetually tired.

It was a brisk party. People came in, had a drink or three, shook hands, patted or kissed each other, cheered for Daggert, and went back into the night. I saw Sheriff Runner Riggs and most of the party hierarchy. Making amends.

Late at night it wound down to just a few of Daggert's close friends in the kitchen, bartenders long gone.

Horace Donaho was wide awake on a kitchen chair. I was now his sworn pal and a good *spic* for all seasons. He had already confided to me that he'd had a long nap before the party.

"It was because someone put the bomb in your car, wasn't it?" he asked me. "Someone local here might have stolen some tree-stump or coal-mine dynamite and wired you up," he added wisely. "But no pro stuff. So you figured it out from that?"

"But why didn't Silver and his Mexican pals just ignore Jim and his car?" Anne asked Horace.

"I ain't for sure," Horace admitted, unable to think of a quick answer. "What was it, Jim? Was it that the trial was still in doubt, and here you was nosin' right up at Silver's front door?"

"Something like that. It likely seemed a good chance for them."

"They was afraid because you was gettin' close," he said, deciding. "And you was gettin' close that way because of info I fed you."

"Sure," I said.

"The judge here, he told me I was to help you."

I nodded at both of them. Help me, but not tell me all. I believed, deep inside, that Horace had known the names of men, including my father, Shirley had been friendly with or visited near the time of Fiala's murder. Someone had told him not to reveal those names to me because such might blunt and sidetrack my investigation. And that someone, obviously, was Daggert. Knowing names might have confused me and lessened Shirley's value to me.

We sat in the kitchen. We were down to Daggert, Anne Melville, Horace, me, and two newcomers who'd waited until the party was over and then come carefully through Daggert's back

219

door for a drink and congratulations to the winner without being seen by the political crowd.

Henry Lee and Shirley Kentner stood silently away from the four of us. Shirley's eyes were luminous, watching, and waiting, bright enough to draw night moths.

Daggert took control of the conversation and situation. "It was lucky for all of us that I hired Jim as P.O. and the court's P.I. I could figure the legal situation, but I couldn't do much about it. I hoped maybe the jury would find for Shirley here. If it hadn't, then I'd have had to make a tough call."

"Granted Mr. Lee's motion for a directed verdict?" I asked.

He inclined his head. "Judges have that power even after a verdict. But it doesn't happen often."

"Would you have done it?"

He smiled. "I never had to make a decision. If I'd granted such a motion, the fence gossips in this county would have had a field day, and my father in our ancestral hall out there would have been disgraced along with his bumbling son. Early on, knowing it might get that way, I called a friend for advice."

"Ballinger?" I asked, knowing.

"We went to law school together," Daggert said. "He told me things about you and encouraged me to hire you. He said you were lost and injured and might be useless or you might figure things out. It wound up the best way. You made things happen. You wandered around and looked confused. Even when you found something I could use, like the men who were after you at the restaurant in Dumont and the car bomb, you wouldn't say what I wanted, even after I put the words in your mouth."

I was amused by the fact that Ballinger was a lawyer. He hated lawyers. Or so he'd said.

"So I got hired?"

"Sure. And you passed the state test last month. I'm proud of you."

I smiled. The test had not been hard.

"I never believed the prosecution's case from the beginning," Daggert continued.

"You mean because you knew the principals?"

"Partly."

"All right. You further mean because you also had only the testimony of a confessed killer doing ninety years and using prison time learning English," I added. "Jose told me he hated this country, but still he was studying English in prison. We both recognized that was because he hoped to get out of prison, not die there of old age. If he harbored such a hope, who could inspire it in him?"

Daggert smiled at the room, liking questions and answers. "Silver. The rising, young political star of Grimsley County. The next commonwealth's attorney. The man who Ballinger claims looks like an Aztec god."

Lee nodded and took a hand. "There's all the missing stuff, but let's all please admit for the sake of IRS accuracy that it could have been taken before that night or on that night. If someone outside the family stole it, then it's not taxable until its return. There's no way of knowing when it was acquired by Fiala. Maybe it was *all* acquired in the taxable year that Fiala died."

Daggert nodded. "Great idea to use in your dealing with the federal estate people. I assume that's why you're running it up as a trial balloon here."

Lee smiled happily. "All please salute it. The federals partially have. Helps my client here and her stepchildren."

I'd heard in the clerk's office that a deal had been proposed and the government's tax case was close to settlement. Shirley would keep the fine house and lots of money. Fiala's kids would get less than they'd hoped for, but still a lot of dollars.

Horace said, "People around town say Silver's talking his head off in custody. He says he knew where jewels and cash were hidden from Jose. A guy I know at the federal courthouse in Lexington told me that the feds found lots of diamonds plus guns and explosives under the floor at Silver's mother's home."

I heard Daggert's phone ring. Daggert ignored it for a moment, but then walked to the kitchen wall phone.

We waited for him to return, but instead he beckoned me.

"Call for you, Jim. You'll want to take it elsewhere."

Who knew I was here?

"Okay," I said, figuring who was on the line.

He pointed me down the hall to a phone on a table under his father's proud picture.

"How you, Carlos?" Ballinger's voice said in my ear. "I figured when you wasn't home that Simon Daggert had won and you were there."

"He won big time."

"I talked to your old pal Silver today. For various reasons he wants you to believe he'd never have hurt you a second time. I promised to pass the message, but he would have. He'd have sliced your eyes out if my boys hadn't broke in."

"You thought during the trial that Jose's people were coming to break him out?"

"So did you, Carlos."

"I guess that's part right. Where's Silver now?"

"I won't tell you. His mother might ask you under oath. She's busy damning us all and giving the federal system hell and hot water," he said jovially. "What you don't know can't hurt you."

"And how's Silver taking his reversal of fortune?"

"He loves intrigue. Now he's doing it with me because I'm all there is. He doesn't like being caged."

I remembered how Silver hated the idea of aging. He was a man who needed freedom and women. There would be none of that.

Ballinger continued: "I think Silver made some election promises to Jose that now he can't pay off. Jose's still mostly silent except when he says bestowing death on Fiala was a thing of mercy. Silver talks lots. Anyway, Silver don't want any more enemies that he already has. He's a smart-enough lawyer not to want you mad when you testify against him. He's told me things and so, to repay, I told him I'd pass on his message." He was silent for a long moment. "You were lucky again. We gave you a wire to speak to Jose in jail and you kept it for your talk with Silver. You avoid a car bomb and a confrontation with Silver's pals. I could use your luck working for me."

"No interest. I do have an interest in things I'm hearing about stuff you found in Silver's mother's house."

"Someone's leaking. I best not find out who it is. I'll admit to you we did find a lot of good and bad stuff." His voice was confident. "Tell me one more thing, Carlos. What would have happened the night I had my men at the jail if, in your later wanderings, Silver had ignored you?"

"I'd have pushed some. I was, for example, going to confide to him that the authorities were checking the voiceprint of the Fiala murder report caller against his voice. And I was going to tell him you were in town investigating him."

"I believe you'd really have done that," he said respectfully. "You call me if you change your mind on a job, and you wish Simon my best."

"Okay, but no more pictures of the blinded."

"Okay. I guess they was coming from my folks. You think about my job, hey? I'll get back to you."

"No job," I said to a buzzing phone. I hung it up and wondered if Ballinger and I were done.

I walked back to the kitchen. The crowd was the same. Henry Lee and his client still stood as a lonesome twosome.

I watched Shirley. She was dressed cunningly in a blue dress that matched her eyes. Her hair was no longer in a bun, but loose, falling in a deadly shade of stunning gold to her shoulders. Her lips were sultry red.

Henry Lee said to me, "You made the difference in the case, Jim. When His Honor here brought a hung jury back into the courtroom and reopened the case for you to testify, over Corner's screaming objections, you made it easy for the jury."

"Sure, but some of the jurors already thought Shirley was innocent."

"Not guilty" had been a popular verdict. ACCUSED BEAUTY FOUND NOT GUILTY—CONSPIRACY TO KILL BY OTHERS. I'd been written up and hailed as an enterprising probation officer turned private investigator. At the same time television and newspapers had whittled Lynn Corner down to a bumbling prosecutor. Media had made Shirley into a national heroine. Newspapers and magazines were still writing about her, sneaking pictures. People, mostly men, waited outside her lake house for an appearance. Daggert said she'd had dozens of mailed and phoned marriage proposals.

I said: "I thought early that Fiala Kentner might have hired his own death from Jose plus bought a deal to blame Shirley. Fiala suffered badly from one of the oldest of human maladies: jealousy. I discarded Fiala's children's testimony because their words reeked with greed. Both were willing to deny their father was a dying man to improve their fortunes. I'm now sure they'd read Jose's confession and courtroom statement in Lynn Corner's offices and were carefully tying their testimony to Jose's. I believed my jealousy theory right up to finding the car bomb."

Daggert nodded. "I saw that Jose had picked a poor escape route, and Jim realized it also. I-24 leads to I-75, and that goes to Florida. At Nashville you'd likely take another route to truly make a run to Mexico. Jose was dawdling along, wanting and waiting to be caught, carrying out his deal with Silver. Get caught for the cause, and I'll get you out."

I nodded at Daggert approvingly. He saw it and his voice got stronger: "I talked to Ballinger yesterday, Jim. Was that him on the phone? It sounded like him."

"Yes. He called to congratulate you and to tell me things were going well," I said.

"Okay. Ballinger said yesterday that Silver told him he first met Jose south of the border. Silver used vacations to visit there, sometimes saying he visited elsewhere to keep up a smokescreen. Silver's full of charisma. He hungers for power. Somehow, Ballinger believes by chance, he met and became of importance to a ragtag group of terrorists. He was handsome as a god, amoral, gregarious, and he could likely speak the language a lot better than he let on to Jim. Silver's new pals asked questions and he gave the right answers. In the world of the terrorists his word became law."

Shirley asked softly, "How did Jim get into it?"

"Silver's people captured Jim. He was observing them for Ballinger. Silver soon made his annual visit to play god. It was a lark for him, but also dead serious. Jim escaped. Silver must have about died when Jim showed up at U.K. law school. But, when that went okay, he talked Jim into coming to Grimsley County. More fun for Silver, and a chance to complete the ordained punishment."

"All done now," Horace said.

"Mostly done," I said, facing Daggert. "Anne Melville told me that you started to recover after your wife died and before Fiala died. That would have been before Shirley was indicted and jailed. Then state and defense left you in the case, and you worried. I think you resolved then that if Shirley convinced you she was innocent, she'd never go to prison. So you started thinking directed verdict, a defense automatic motion, one almost never granted."

"Stop it, Jim," Shirley said coldly.

Daggert ordered: "Go on."

"Simon was attentive to you, Shirley. And Fiala became jealous. To Fiala, you were his property. He saw you and Simon were alike."

She smiled at me bravely. "We never did a thing about it. We talked. We were friendly. Once, no more than just one time, we thought out loud on what might have been."

"On the phone?"

"Yes. I called Simon to warn him not to visit our house again. I thought maybe Fiala was plotting against him."

"Did Fiala tell Jose?"

"Yes. He told him not to allow Simon inside the house."

"Perhaps Jose later heard you call on the telephone? Perhaps Fiala heard?"

"I'm sorry if that's what set things off," she said coolly. "We had no intention of hurting anyone."

Maybe yes, maybe no.

"How'd the judge know of your birthmark?" I asked her.

"How do you know I did know of it?" Daggert asked, his voice rough.

"You told me early on that Shirley would present physical evidence of her innocence. The only physical evidence offered in trial was the birthmark."

"Henry Lee told me about the mark." Daggert smiled without warmth. "I'm offended that you believe Shirley and I were secret lovers of some kind. We never were."

"I did inform Simon about the birthmark," Lee said.

I held up my hands. "I'm not accusing anyone of anything. I'm curious and so I'm satisfying my curiosity. But, Judge, will you admit that you hoped I'd find something that would allow you to use your legal powers without huge problems?"

Daggert stood silently.

Lee said confidently: "We'd have eventually won."

"Perhaps. It's said the jury was hung. Who hired you as defense counsel, Mr. Lee?"

"Shirley did."

"You knew that the judge was troubled about the case?"

"I sensed it. We talked after I accepted the case. It became apparent."

"Did there come a time when you were confident your client would never be convicted?"

"I believed her story." His voice was smoke and silk.

I nodded. "You and the judge became trial allies. I read some law, gentlemen. You can't mention lie detector tests without both sides, prosecution and defense, agreeing to it."

Daggert smiled cagily, infecting Lee, who grinned.

"Is that the law?" Lee asked.

"Not in my courtroom," Daggert said, still smiling.

"Judges are people, Jim," Lee said. "In all jury trials, judges act also as thirteenth jurors. Read better lawbooks. A judge takes sides if he or she sees such will bring about justice. In this case, no one can ever argue that it didn't."

"Hoorah," Horace said, not liking the feeling of tension in the room.

I looked at Horace and smiled. "The pair of you did another thing to keep up my interest, old pal Horace. You opened my office door early one trial morning. I'd been making waves about the open curtains in the Kentner house. I never understood those curtains until I decided Jose was likely ordered to open them after Silver and the loot were clear of the house. It would harm nothing

226

and make no difference if Jose was arrested before he left the house or afterwards, because he was supposed to be arrested. But you both wanted me to keep going hard. So you, or maybe the judge here, opened my office door and made a burglary mystery of it."

"We'll 'fess up, Jim," Daggert said lightly. "We did it. And I took you past the Kentner home twice with evil intent. I pushed you every way I could think of. I urged you to sneak, to snoop, to conjecture. You did that. You never forgot anything you saw or heard. You were intent and dogged. So, as a result, Shirley's free and bad people are not. That's as it should be."

"I give up," I said, smiling only a little.

"No need for that," Daggert said. "I want all of you to know—including Shirley, who may hate me for saying it—that I was never sure what I'd do. I'm not certain I'd have had the judicial guts to have granted a naked directed verdict for a defendant. I likely would have finked and fallen."

Shirley shook her head, not believing him, but I thought what he was saying might well be true.

Anne Melville watched Daggert and Shirley. I thought an old dream was dying inside her.

I said: "Is there something you wanted to ask, Anne?"

"Maybe," she said, recovering. "Why did you go from the jail to Silver's mother's house, Jim. You had nothing, although I know you said on the stand that Jose reacted a little to Silver's name. What sent you, with your ballpoint pen wire, to his mother's house?"

"Silver himself. He was late to the political meeting and so could have overseen the bomb in my car. A deadly part of that bomb had been removed. Silver wanted only me dead, not his political pals. But more than that, it was a small thing Silver said when we first talked about the trial. He said something that everyone else disagreed with."

Everyone listened.

"He combined Fiala with a cane. Fiala never used a cane because he was too vain. But Silver remembered he did use one. I asked myself why. I thought Silver might have believed it because

227

he was in the house on the night of Fiala's murder. He saw the walker. He extracted the cache of jewels from that walker. Because Fiala had a walker full of jewels, Silver assumed Fiala used a cane to get around. Or that was my screwball figuring.''

Shirley nodded and then shrugged.

''Another thing, Judge,'' I said. ''I intend to resign end of next month.''

''The job's yours as long as you want, Jim. It won't take that much of your time now that the murder trial's over.''

''Mr. Lee's made me an offer.''

Lee smiled. ''I can use him, Simon.''

Daggert nodded. ''You're an old thief, Henry.'' He looked at me, eyes approving. ''You'll do well with Henry, Jim.''

''What'll happen to Lynn Corner?'' I asked all.

Horace said: ''He still secretly runs the party, for now. He'll be named attorney for various county boards come January. He'll lose lawyer friends who now have those jobs.'' He shrugged, then smiled. ''Eventually, someone else will take over the party.''

Everyone smiled.

I watched Shirley, hiding my longing as Anne Melville hid hers.

In earlier times, I thought, Shirley might have been a famous courtesan. She was the eternal temptress, a woman who'd love many men down all her years, a woman drawn to older, successful men. If someone big from Glittertown West had seen her in her teens, she might have found a hundred million lovers, some of them offscreen.

A chance for that, with all the news ink she'd gotten since the verdict, might still exist. I wasn't sure she'd not take such a chance.

I wondered if Daggert would be enough for her if she remained in Grim City. Would any man?

I remembered what she'd whispered softly to me in my hall: ''There'll be a time for us, whether tonight or later.'' Her blue eyes had been dead sure. ''I promise.''

I again had faint, jumpy doubts about all of my solutions to her case. Men who'd loved Shirley had suffered and been murdered and gone to prison.

She was smart, strong, and exceedingly beautiful.

Was it possible that portions of what Jose had related in court were the truth?

Her eyes found mine once more, and I was blinded by the light. Her eyes calculated me, made me promises, and told me believable lies.

I shivered and went to the kitchen table and poured myself a seldom-wanted scotch. I drank it down in a single gulp, pleaded tiredness, shook hands, patted, and went out into the night. I asked the rest of my questions only of myself as I lay in my dark bed.

In the morning I found I'd covered and protected my good eye once more.

AFTERWORD

Anyone with legal knowledge of the Commonwealth of Kentucky will recognize what's depicted in this book is not a fully correct recounting of the actual system used there.

What I did was overlay my Indiana system with what I wanted from Kentucky. I changed what I wanted and, at times, made up my own law. Here and there I married the laws of the two states, and here and there I divorced them and added my own fictional versions.

There is no Grimsley County or City.

J. L. H.
April 1994